Dave Zeltserman recently left software development to write crime fiction and study Kung Fu. He lives in the Boston area with his wife, Judy, a homeopathy practitioner. *Small Crimes* is his third novel.

Small Crimes

—Dave Zeltserman—

A complete catalogue record for this book can
be obtained from the British Library on request

First published in 2008 by Serpent's Tail,
an imprint of Profile Books Ltd
3A Exmouth House
Pine Street
London EC1R OJH
website: www.serpentstail.com

ISBN 978 1 85242 971 3

Designed and typeset at Neuadd Bwll, Llanwrtyd Wells

Printed in the UK by CPI Bookmarque, Croydon, Surrey, CRO 4TD

10 9 8 7 6 5 4 3 2 1

To Alan Luedeking

Chapter 1

This was going to be our last game of checkers. Usually we played in my cell; this last game, though, we were playing in Morris's office. Over the last seven years we had played tens of thousands of games. Every fourth or fifth game I'd win, the rest I'd let him beat me.

Morris Smith ran the county jail here in Bradley. He was a large round man in his early sixties, with soft rubbery features and small wisps of hair framing his mostly bald head. I liked Morris – at least as much as I liked anyone. He could have made my life difficult the past seven years; instead he treated me about as well as he could've.

I spent a few seconds studying the board and saw that I could force a checker advantage and a sure win, but I could also set myself up to be triple-jumped. I pretended to be deep in thought for a couple of minutes and then made the move to let him force the triple jump.

Morris sat silently, his small eyes darting over all the possible moves. I saw a momentary glint in his eyes when he recognized the combination leading to the triple jump, and watched with some amusement as he tried to suppress a smile. He pushed his checker in place with a large, thick hand that shook.

'I think you made a mistake there, young fellow,' he said, his voice coming out in a low croak.

I sat there for a long moment and then cursed to show that I realized how I had screwed up. Letting loose one last profanity, I made the move I was forced to make and watched as Morris pounced on the board, making his triple jump and picking up my checkers.

'That should be about it,' he said.

We played out the rest of the moves. I knew Morris took great satisfaction in removing the last checker from the board. When the game was over, he gave a slight smile and offered me his hand in a conciliatory shake.

'You gave me a good game,' he said, 'except for that one mistake.'

'What can I say? You've been kicking my ass for seven years now. I just got to admit I've met my match.'

Morris chuckled, obviously pleased with himself. He glanced at his watch. 'Your paperwork is all done. You're a free man. But if you'd like, I could order us some lunch and we could play one more game.'

'I'd like to, but it's been a long seven years. I've been craving a cheeseburger and a few beers for some time now.'

'I could have that brought here.'

'Well, yeah,' I said, hesitating, 'but you could get in trouble doing that, Morris. And, besides, it wouldn't taste the same in here. No offense.'

He nodded, some disappointment showing on his round face. 'Joe, I've grown to like you over the last few years. I didn't think I would after what you did to get yourself in here. Can I give you some friendly advice?'

'Sure.'

'Why don't you start fresh someplace else? Maybe Florida?

Myself, soon as I retire in three years, I'm moving to Sarasota. You can keep these lousy New England winters.'

'That's not bad advice, but one of the conditions of my parole is to stay in Bradley—'

'You could petition for a change of address.'

'Well, yeah, I guess I could, but my parents are getting up there in age, and I'd like to make up for lost time.'

He shrugged. 'I hope you at least think about it. I don't think Bradley's a good place for you anymore.'

'I appreciate the advice. But I don't have much choice in the matter. At least not right now.'

We stood up and shook hands. I turned away to pick up my duffel bag and Morris asked whether I wanted to call my parents for a ride. I told him I'd get a cab. I made a quick phone call, signed whatever paperwork I had to, and was led out of the building by Morris. A cab was waiting for me, but there was a man bent over, talking to the driver. The cab pulled away, and as the man stood up I recognized him instantly. I'd have to with the way his face was carved up and the thick piece of flesh that was missing from his nose. At one time, he had been a good-looking man, but that was before he had been stabbed thirteen times in the face.

Morris looked a bit uncomfortable. 'Well, uh,' he said, 'it was a pleasure having you as my guest, young fellow. If you ever want to stop by for a lesson on the theory of checkers, feel free.' Then, seriously, 'Try to stay out of trouble.'

He gave me a pat on the back and waved to the other man before disappearing back into the building. The other man stood grinning, but it didn't extend to his eyes. Looking at him was like staring at an open-mouthed rattlesnake.

I nodded to him. 'I don't want any trouble, Phil,' I said.

Phil Coakley just stood grinning with eyes that were hard glass. Phil was the district attorney in our county. I knew he'd been stabbed thirteen times in the face because that's how many times they told me I'd stabbed him. That was a good part of the reason I'd spent the last seven years in county jail.

'I'm sorry for what happened,' I said, keeping my distance.

Phil waved me over, his grin intact, but still nothing in his eyes. 'I don't want any trouble either, Joe,' he said. 'As far as I'm concerned you've paid your debt to society, and what's done is done. I just want to clear the air, make sure there are no hard feelings. Come on over here. Let's talk for a minute.'

I didn't like it, but I didn't feel as if I had any choice. When I moved closer to him, I could see the scarring along his face more plainly, and it was all I could do to keep from looking away. The damage was far worse up close. He looked almost as if someone had played tic-tac-toe on his face. As if he were some grotesque caricature from a Dick Tracy comic strip. Parts of his face were uneven with other parts, and that chunk of flesh missing from his nose, Jesus Christ. As tough as doing so was, I kept my eyes straight on him.

'I hope you don't mind, Joe,' he said, 'but I asked your taxi to come back so we could talk for a few minutes.'

'Sure, that's fine.'

'I've been waiting out here almost an hour. Your parole was supposed to be completed by noon.'

'You know how Morris is. He takes his time with things.'

Phil gave a slow nod. 'Look at you,' he said, 'Joe, I think jail agrees with you. Your beer gut's gone. Damn, you look better now than you've looked in years. But I guess you can't say the same about me.'

'If there was any way I could go back and change what I did—'

'Yeah, I know, don't worry about it. What's done is done.' He paused for a moment, his grin hardening again. 'I often wondered how you were able to serve out your time in a county jail. Arson, attempted murder, maiming a district attorney, and you end up in a county jail. I've been trying for the last seven years to have you moved to a maximum security prison, but I guess you were born under a lucky star. Even drawing Craig Simpson as your parole officer.'

I didn't say anything. He gave a careless shrug, still grinning. 'But that's all in the past,' he said. 'You paid your debt, even though seven years doesn't quite seem long enough. What was your original sentence? Twenty-four years?'

'Sixteen to twenty-four,' I said.

'Sixteen to twenty-four years.' Phil let out a short whistle. 'It seems to me like a hell of a short sentence for what you did. And you only had to serve out seven years of it in county jail, all the time being waited on hand and foot by old Morris Smith.'

'It hasn't been all that easy. My wife divorced me—'

'Yeah, I know. My wife divorced me, too.' He paused. 'I guess she had a difficult time looking me straight in the face.'

He had lost his grin. I just stared at him, stared at the mass of scar tissue that I was responsible for. After a while, I asked him what he wanted.

'I just wanted to clear the air,' he said. 'Make sure there are no hard feelings between the two of us. Also, I want to talk a little police business with you. After all, you were a police officer in this town for twelve years. You hear that Manny Vassey's dying of cancer?'

'I heard something about it.'

Phil forced his grin back and shook his head slightly. 'The man's only fifty-six and he's dying of stomach cancer. Manny always was a tough bird. Normally I wouldn't have a chance of cracking him, but, when a man's dying, sometimes he needs to unburden himself. You know, at one point I think every drug, gambling, and prostitution dollar that flowed through Vermont went into his hands. You remember Billy Ferguson? I think you investigated his murder.'

'I remember.'

'I guess you would,' he said. 'It's not as if we have a lot of murders here, and I don't think we ever had one as brutal as that one. How many years ago was that?'

'I don't know. Maybe ten.'

Phil thought about it and shook his head. 'I think it was less than eight and a half years ago. Only a few months before you maimed me. I'll tell you, Joe, that was one hell of a brutal murder. I don't think I ever saw anyone beaten as badly as Ferguson was.'

He waited for me to say something, but I just stood there and stared back at him. After a while he gave up and continued.

'Billy Ferguson was in way over his head with gambling debts,' he said. 'As far as I could tell, he owed Manny thirty thousand dollars. I suspect Manny sent one of his thugs over to collect and the situation got out of hand. Do you remember anything from your investigation?'

'That was a long time ago. But as I remember, we hit a brick wall. No fingerprints, no witnesses, nothing.'

'Well, I'm not giving up on it. I'm making it a point to visit Manny religiously.' Phil laughed, but his grin was long gone. 'I'm spending time each day reading him the Bible. I think he's beginning to see the light. With a little bit of luck I'll get a confession any day now and clear up Ferguson's murder along with a few other crimes that have always bugged me.'

I didn't bother saying anything. He was wasting his time, but he'd find that out for himself. Manny Vassey was joined at the hip with the Devil, and there wasn't a chance in hell he'd ever find God or confess to anything. My cab pulled back up to us. Before I could say a word, Phil grabbed my duffel bag from me and swung it into the cab's trunk. 'Be seeing you around, Joe,' he said as he walked off.

Chapter 2

I sat back in the cab and took out of my pocket a worn and creased photo of my two daughters. The picture was taken at Courtney's first birthday. Melissa at the time was only a little over three, and the two girls were standing side by side, Melissa holding Courtney's hand to keep her standing upright. They wore matching yellow dresses, both with pink ribbons in their long blonde hair. Both girls looking a bit chubby, Courtney more so than Melissa. I felt a tug at my heart seeing the shy little smile breaking out over Melissa's face and the look of total confusion on Courtney's. I remembered the rest of that day. The way Courtney's face had ended up covered in chocolate ice cream, and Melissa later hugging Courtney like she was some sort of doll. And both girls jumping onto my lap, both giggling like crazy. I had few other memories of my girls, at least ones that I cared to remember.

After a while I carefully slid the photo into my wallet. Then I closed my eyes and thought about how I had ended up the way I did.

Nine years ago I was up to my eyeballs in gambling debts. I was in deep, a lot deeper than Billy Ferguson ever was. Back then I was out of control. It wasn't that I was a coke fiend, but I did too much of it, and I did too much drinking and too much gambling. Way too much gambling. Especially on football games. I would've been better off flipping a coin than the way I picked them. There were weeks I was shut out completely. But that's the thing with degenerate gamblers – you always think you have an edge, that you'll make it all back with one big bet. Of course I never did. All I ever accomplished was getting myself in deeper.

I owed Manny a lot of money. I was paying him back as much as I could, but it was never enough and he kept putting the pressure on. When he threatened to hurt my wife and children, I knew I had no choice. I agreed to do jobs for him to work down the balance. At first the jobs were small, fairly inconsequential, but over time Manny kept upping the ante. Somehow I had to get out from under him. I started taking bigger chances with what I stole from the police evidence room. The sheriff of Bradley County, Dan Pleasant, who was maybe the most corrupt law enforcement officer I'd ever met, found out that Phil had discovered some of my forged documents and was building a criminal conspiracy case against me. I thanked Dan for the information and told him I'd take care of things.

I was pretty coked up the night I broke into Phil's office. I found the documents implicating me. I was pouring gasoline around his office when he showed up. It was past midnight and he had no right showing up when he did, but there he was. We just kind of looked at each other. He knew what I was up to, and he should have left and called the police. Instead he tried to stop me. Now Phil's a big guy. He was a star linebacker in high school and even played in college, but I was fighting for my life. I guess I was also kind of crazed from the coke and the adrenalin.

Somehow I got him on his back and grabbed a letter opener from the desk. I guess I was stabbing him with it. To be honest, that part is nothing more than a blur in my mind. I really don't remember too much of it. What I do remember is at some point Phil had stopped moving. I got off him, lit a match, and waited for the fire to spread before leaving.

The funny thing was I had always liked Phil. I always thought of him as a solid person, a good family man, just an overall decent human being. If I'd had a real knife, like a fishing or hunting knife, I would've killed him that night. The letter opener wasn't sharp enough. I did damage – Jesus, did I do damage – but I didn't kill him.

About the time I was setting the fire he must've pulled a silent fire alarm. I didn't see him but he must've done it then. The police and the fire trucks showed while I was leaving the building. I just about walked into them. My dad was working as a fireman then, and he was with them. Hell, I think I was still holding onto that bloody letter opener.

I was arrested that night. I could see the disappointment in some of my fellow officers' faces, but I could also see some anxiety. Several of them would go to prison if I talked. Harold Grayson, probably one of the better lawyers we have around here, was hired for me by the police union. He wanted me to plead innocent, claiming I suffered diminished capacity due to my excessive cocaine use. I refused and pled guilty instead. It seemed time to take my medicine. And I kept quiet about everything else I knew. I also worked out a deal with Manny – I'd keep quiet about him, too, in exchange for wiping my slate clean. No one else was implicated.

During the last seven years, when I wasn't playing Morris at checkers, I spent my time trying to understand how I had taken the turn that I did. It shouldn't have been that way. There was nothing in my background to suggest I'd end up a crooked cop, a cocaine user and a degenerate gambler. I'd had a normal childhood. I was born in Bradley, spent my whole life there, played quarterback for my high school team, and ended up marrying my childhood sweetheart. I'd only been out of Bradley County a few times in my life and never more than a four-hour drive away. Hell, I'd lived the perfect Norman Rockwell existence.

As a kid, I watched *Adam-12* and *Dragnet* and can only remember wanting to be a cop when I grew up. After I graduated from high school I joined the Bradley Police Department. I never looked to make any money on the side, but the bribes were there waiting for me and I took them. Some of the local bars would offer me fifty bucks to look the other way on Friday and Saturday nights about their customers maybe driving home drunk. And then I started getting my weekly stipend for ignoring what was going on at a local strip club named Kelley's. And there were other things. Like us splitting up money that disappeared from the evidence room and helping ourselves to what we could take off the occasional drunk. It started out small, little crimes, nothing big, but that's what got me into gambling and cocaine. The payoffs and thefts made me feel dirty and made me want to unload the money as quickly as I got it. I'm pretty sure that's what got me started.

The big crimes began one summer night about twelve years ago. It was three in the morning, and I was having trouble sleeping. I had gotten into my cruiser and was driving around town when I noticed the front door of a jewelry store jimmied open. As usual, I had my service revolver with me, and when I went to investigate I found Dan Pleasant and several of his boys ransacking the place. So I had a choice; bust our county sheriff and several of his officers or go in for a split. I guess I felt uneasy busting a fellow officer, especially feeling as dirty as I did, so I took my cut. Dan worked with a fence in upstate New York, and my share was fifteen grand – which I pissed away as quickly as I got it. After that robbery I joined Dan on others and got hooked up with Manny.

When I thought about all the things I did, none of it seemed possible, but all I have to do is look Phil Coakley in the face to prove to myself it all happened. So now I was an ex-police officer, a felon, and a divorced husband. I hadn't seen or heard from my ex-wife or kids since the day I was arrested. Other than Morris I hadn't had any visitors or company for seven years, not even my parents. When I thought about all that I'd lost for money I didn't even want, I could barely believe it.

Chapter 3

Bradley County is made up of half a dozen towns and sits in a valley on the edge of the Green Mountains. Back when I was a cop, the population of Bradley County, not including the eight thousand students who attended two liberal arts colleges in Eastfield, was around seventy-two thousand. Bradley is the largest town in Bradley County and its population alone is twenty-four thousand.

When I was a kid, once you got five miles away from the town center all you saw was farmland, cow pastures, and woods. About twenty-five years ago, a defense contractor moved in, bought two hundred acres of farmland, and built manufacturing plants on it. By the time I got arrested, more and more cow pasture and farmland was paved over for strip malls and shopping centers.

Even with the loss of farmland, jobs in Bradley County were evenly split between farming, dairy, manufacturing, and tourism, with tourists being either leaf peepers or parents visiting their kids at college.

For most people life in Bradley was uneventful. Just the typical middle-class, bucolic New England town. For most people, anyway.

The cab let me out in front of my parents' house. They had a small three-bedroom ranch on Maple Street, less than a mile from downtown. My dad had bought it forty-five years ago for six thousand dollars. Even though it had less than twelve hundred square feet of interior space, the house was probably worth two hundred grand now. Joe Sr, my dad, had grown up in Bradley, just like his dad before him. Dentons had been living in Bradley for almost a hundred years. Morris had told me that my dad had retired from the fire department a few months after I was arrested, although my dad never said anything to me about it during the half-dozen phone conversations we had while I was in jail.

I looked over the front yard. The grass was freshly mowed and the flower beds were neatly arranged. Paint was beginning to peel in a few spots, but other than that the house seemed to be in good shape, at least from the outside. I carried my duffel bag to the front door and rang the bell.

When I had found out three weeks ago that my parole had been approved, I called my parents to tell them I'd be staying with them until I could get back on my feet. It shouldn't have been any surprise that I was coming, but it took a while before my dad opened the door. He had an odd look on his face as he stood staring at me. I watched the slow transformation while he manufactured a pained smile.

'Joey, I almost didn't recognize you,' he said. 'Come on in, I'll make you something to eat.'

He led me back into the house. He turned once and gave me a quick nervous glance before chattering on about whether I'd like eggs or hotdogs and beans. I told him I planned to go out and get something to eat.

'Nonsense. Tell me what you want and I'll cook it up for you.'

I saw arguing was useless. 'Okay. You got any salami?'

'I got some. I'll make you a sandwich on Wonder Bread with a little mayonnaise. How's that sound?'

'Sounds fine.'

I followed him into the kitchen. He seemed ill at ease as he made me my sandwich. He also seemed to have aged quite a bit more than the seven years since I'd seen him last. He slouched as he stood, his shoulders more stooped than I remembered and his jowls heavier. When I had last seen him, his hair was mostly black with a little gray mixed in. Now there was a lot less of it, and what was left was white. He was only sixty-five, but he looked closer to eighty.

'Where's Mom?'

'She's volunteering today at the library.'

'I thought she'd want to be home to greet me.'

He gave me an uneasy smile. 'Friday's her day to volunteer at the library. She'll be home later.' He cut the sandwich in half, put it on a plate, and handed it to me. 'I'll make you some coffee,' he said.

'How have the two of you been? You never really said much during our phone calls.'

'We've been fine, Joey. My blood pressure's high, and they've got me on some medication, but other than that and some arthritis I'm in good health. Your mom spends a lot of her time volunteering now.' He paused for a moment. 'I don't know if you've heard, but I retired from the department.'

'I heard something about it.'

I looked out a kitchen window and watched two squirrels chase each other around the backyard. After they chased each other out of sight, I asked if he had heard from my ex-wife.

He shook his head. 'No, son, we haven't heard from her. Not since you went to jail.'

'What?'

'That's right, son.'

'You haven't heard from Elaine once in seven years?'

'No.'

'Not even to let you talk to your grandchildren?'

He shook his head.

'Or send you pictures of them?'

He gave me a sad, uneasy smile. 'She has full custody of the girls. She doesn't have to contact us. I guess she decided to make a clean break. Joey, you know she moved shortly after your sentencing. But we never got her new address. We don't know where she moved to.'

I couldn't help feeling angry thinking of my parents being cut off from my kids. 'I'm surprised,' I said. 'Elaine always liked you and Mom. I would've thought she'd want to keep in touch with you. And I would've thought she'd want my kids to know their grandparents.'

He shrugged. 'I don't know, son.'

I took a bite of my sandwich and chewed it slowly, buying myself time to process what he was telling me. 'It's not right,' I said after a while. 'Now that I'm out, I'll see a lawyer about changing this.'

'Well, I don't know. You can think about it, Joey, but going to court can be expensive, and your mom and I don't have the money to help you with it.'

I stared at him until he looked away. I didn't believe him. The two of them were nuts about my two kids, and I knew they'd do anything to reestablish contact with them. Of course, he knew I was broke. My house was gone and Elaine had taken whatever savings were left. The only thing I had was two hundred dollars that were in my pocket the night I was arrested and my car. At least, I hoped I still had my car. My dad had agreed to take care of it for me while I was gone.

'I forgot to tell you,' my dad said, trying to smile. 'You got a phone call. I wrote down a message for you.'

He took a piece of paper out of his pocket and handed it to me. Dan Pleasant had called and wanted me to call him back.

'Dad, is my car in the garage?'

He shook his head. 'Ron Hardacher up the street let me keep the car in his garage. It got too difficult moving your car and my car all the time. I drove it every two weeks like I promised and got the oil changed every six months. Here, let me get you the keys.'

He went over to the desk in the kitchen and fumbled around in the top drawer until he came up with a set of keys. I asked him if he could give me a key to the house also.

'You don't need one,' he said. 'You know we never lock the doors. Joey, it's not that we don't want you staying with us, but this is only temporary, right?'

'Sure, only until I find a job and get myself set up. Thanks for taking care of my car and thanks for letting me stay here.'

The coffee had finished brewing, and he poured me a cup. As he handed it to me he looked like he wanted to ask me something. He hesitated for a long while, his mouth forming a small round circle. Then he muttered something about feeling tired. He turned from me and started toward his bedroom.

I took the rest of my sandwich and the coffee to the phone. I ate the sandwich slowly. After I was done, I gave Dan Pleasant a call. He wasn't in, but I left a message and sat and waited for him to call back. I only had to wait five minutes before the phone rang. I picked it up and heard Dan's voice.

'You there, Joe?' he asked.

'Hello, Dan.'

I heard a soft laughing noise. 'How you doing, Joe?' he said. 'Christ, it's been a long time.'

'It didn't have to be. I'd been sitting in your jail for seven years. You could've stopped by anytime.'

'I didn't think that would be a smart thing to do. But we do need to talk. Why don't you drive out to the Mills Farm Road out in Chesterville. I'll meet you there in a half-hour.'

'I don't know, Dan, I'd feel more comfortable if we talked somewhere more public. How about Zeke's Tavern?'

There was more soft laughing. 'That wouldn't be very smart, Joe. No, I don't think we want publicity. I also don't think it would be very smart to show your face at Zeke's. I'll meet you out in Chesterville in a half-hour.' There was a click as he hung up.

I walked two doors over to Ron Hardacher's house and got my Mustang convertible out of his garage. I knew Dan would prefer it if I were dead, but I wasn't worried about meeting him on an isolated road in the country. If he thought he could get away with killing me he would've done it years ago.

I put the top down and headed toward Chesterville. As I got about five miles past downtown Bradley, I could see that the strip malls and shopping centers had expanded into what used to be open space. Eventually I got past them and all the traffic lights. The road became quieter and more scenic, with rolling hills and cows grazing lazily along them. It was a warmish fall day and I felt good having the wind in my face. At times I'd open it up to a hundred before slowing the car down. As I drove I felt a sense of peace that I hadn't felt in years. It startled me to realize how long it had been since I'd felt that way.

I turned onto Mills Farm Road and drove down the dirt road until I spotted Dan leaning against his pickup truck. He looked pretty much the same as he did the last time I saw him. A tall, lanky man with a large head and a big mop of brownish hair. His last name, Pleasant, fit him well; he always seemed to have a warm, pleasant smile on his face. I pulled up behind his truck and got out to meet him.

His eyes dulled for a second as he glanced at my Mustang convertible, and then his warm, pleasant smile was back in place. Dan was never happy that I'd bought the car. He always held a tight rein on his deputies, demanding they use the extra money made as a retirement fund. No big-ticket purchases. No fancy cars, no boats, nothing that would bring them any attention. The car was the only thing I'd ever bought. All the other money I made I pissed away. Still, after all these years, I could tell Dan still resented me for buying it.

He took a step to meet me and gave me a warm handshake, then placed a hand on my shoulder. 'It's good to see you, Joe,' he said. And if I didn't know him better I would've sworn he meant it.

'How you're still sheriff I'll never know,' I said.

He laughed. 'I'll keep running as long as they keep voting for me. How long has it been since you've had a beer?'

'I think you know the answer to that.'

'It was a rhetorical question, Joe. But I think I got a good solution.' He opened the door to his truck and took a couple of bottles out of a cooler. He handed me one of them.

'You're looking good, Joe. Morris treat you okay?'

'No complaints.'

'I had to work my ass off to keep you there. Our DA friend fought like hell to have you moved to a maximum-security prison.'

'I know. He told me.'

'He did, did he?' Dan showed a thin smile. 'Did he tell you he was using every favor he had to get you shipped out of state to Danamora? It almost happened, and I'll tell you, you wouldn't have had much fun there, my friend. I had to pull a lot of strings to keep you in Bradley.'

'That was the deal.'

Dan laughed and shook his head. 'I went way beyond our deal for you. It cost me quite a bit of coin to get you that early parole, especially after Coakley's heartfelt victim's statement to the parole board. Shit, he even had me moved to tears. Even with the greasing, I don't think you'd be out now if you hadn't taken responsibility and pled guilty in the first place. That move worked out for you in the long run, Joe.'

'That wasn't why I did it.'

'Yeah, I know. I always figured you didn't want to risk taking the stand. A smart move. God knows what other business our DA friend would have dragged in.'

'That wasn't my reason.'

Dan waited for me to explain, but I wasn't going to. He wouldn't have understood even if I had. It wasn't in his makeup to understand something as simple as that I didn't feel making Phil go through a trial after what I did to him would be right. It's funny, though, it seemed as if Phil resented my pleading guilty. As if I'd robbed him of his day in court. If I had realized that at the time, I would've given him his day and let Grayson argue his bullshit diminished capacity case.

After a while Dan realized I wasn't going to explain any further. He took a long drink of his beer and started laughing. 'Still the same old Joe, huh?' he said, his eyes crinkling pleasantly. 'I got presents for you anyways.'

He took two envelopes from his inside jacket pocket and handed them to me. The first one was stuffed with hundred dollar bills. I counted sixty-five hundred dollars. The second envelope had some forms. As I was reading them Dan explained they were for my pension.

'Just sign and date them and it's all set,' he said.

'You're kidding.'

'No sir. It's all taken care of. For the record you're retiring after twenty years on the force. You'll collect thirty-four sixty a month. Plus full medical and dental.'

'How'd you swing this?'

He gave me a little smile. 'A piece of cake, Joe. And, after all, you did join the force twenty years ago. If somebody forgot to check that you spent the last seven years serving time for arson and attempted murder, hey, what the hell.

'Now, Joe,' Dan went on, his eyes hardening a bit, 'as far as

I'm concerned this makes us even. Me and my boys appreciated your keeping us out of the matter, but you were damned stupid to leave that building with Coakley still alive. It hasn't been the same since.'

'What do you mean?'

Dan finished his beer before answering me, a glint of spite in his eyes. 'There's been more attention on us thanks to you. Times are a lot leaner now, a lot less money to be made. Most weeks I'm just living off my salary. But the real problem is Coakley. You changed him.'

Dan flung his empty bottle into the grass meadow we were standing by and got himself another beer. After he had a healthy swallow of it, he shook his head sadly.

'Our DA friend was always a straight arrow. There was never a chance in the world you could cut him in on a deal, but he was always a decent man, businesslike, and never out to screw anyone. You've turned him into a vengeful sonofabitch. The guy's out for blood, Joe. Anything he can nail you with he will, and I'm afraid he might drag me and my boys down with you. You know Manny's dying of cancer?'

'I heard about it.'

'Did you know that Coakley is working on him every goddam day? He visits Manny on his deathbed and reads him the Bible. He's trying to work the fear of God into him, and I'm afraid he might be succeeding.'

'That's not going to happen,' I said. 'Manny is about as hard a nut as you're going to find. No way is he going to be cracked. Phil's wasting his time.'

'Don't be so sure of that.' Dan shook his head gravely. 'Manny's not the same man he was seven years ago. He's changed. I visited him a few weeks ago and was not happy with what I saw. He's scared, Joe, I could see it in his eyes. He's wavering, and if he confesses we'll all go away, but you're the one who'll go away for murder. And for first-degree murder you won't be sitting out your days in county jail.'

'I don't know what you're talking about.'

'Come on. Don't kid a kidder.'

'I still don't know what you're talking about.'

'Play dumb all you want. It doesn't change anything.' Dan let out a soft sigh. 'Remember Billy Ferguson? I know you were doing collections for Manny back then, and I think Coakley suspects that also. What both Coakley and I know, however, is that Ferguson emptied thirty grand out of his retirement account the day he was beaten to death. What I alone know is that you bet thirty grand the next week with a bookie out of South Boston. And as usual you lost every bet.'

'Whoever told you that was bullshitting you.'

'Come on, Joe. As I said before, don't kid a kidder.'

'No, Dan, I'm not kidding you. I had nothing to do with Ferguson. If a bookie told you that then he was paid off.'

Dan smiled genially as he considered what I said. 'Maybe. It doesn't matter. If Manny gives a deathbed confession that you killed Ferguson then you'll go down for his murder. And even if he doesn't, knowing what I know about what you used to do for Manny, there's still enough to send you away for a long time. So as you can see, we've got a serious problem. One that's got to be taken care of right away. Manny or Coakley, your choice.'

'I don't know what you're talking about.'

Dan lost his smile, his large face growing deadly stern. 'Look, Joe, you're the cause of this mess and you're going to take care of it. Plan A is for you to get rid of one of them. I don't care which. If Manny's gone, Coakley can piss all he wants but it's not going to get him anywhere. And if Coakley goes, Manny won't have anyone pressuring him and he can just die quietly in the night.'

'Forget it. I'm not doing that.'

'Not doing what, Joe?'

'I'm not killing anyone.'

'You won't, huh? Don't play all high and mighty with me. Manny's dying of cancer, for Chrissakes, snuffing him out at this point would be a blessing.'

'How am I supposed to get to Manny while he's in the hospital?'

'You're a smart man. Figure it out. And if you can't, then finish the job you started on our DA friend. After what you did to his face you'd be doing him a favor. One or the other, Joe. I don't care which.' Dan paused to scratch behind his ear. 'I'm giving you a couple of days. Three at the most. And if it's not done, I'm moving on to Plan B. I got to tell you, Joe, I don't like Plan B nearly as much as Plan A, and I guarantee you wouldn't like it at all.'

He finished what was left of his beer and tossed his bottle away. When he faced me again, a pleasant smile had melted back onto his face.

'Just get the job done and we'll have no problems. We can all live happily ever after.'

'What would you be doing now if I hadn't been paroled?'

'I would have had no choice, I would've moved on to Plan B. By the way, Joe, when this is done it might be a good idea for you to get out of Bradley. You might want to think about moving to Albany and being closer to your two girls.'

My heart skipped a beat. 'How do you know Elaine's in Albany?' I asked, trying to keep my voice composed.

'I know things, Joe. And your ex, she changed her name. My guess, she didn't want you finding her. Her new name is Elise Mathews.'

'Did she remarry?'

'I don't think so, at least she hadn't last I checked.'

'Any idea how my girls have been?'

He made a face as if to say how the fuck would he know that.

We stood staring at each other for a long moment. Dan finally broke the silence, telling me I had three days tops. 'Try and finish this mess earlier if you can, Joe. But get it done. I really don't want to go to Plan B.'

He offered me his hand and then nodded so long, a big friendly smile playing on his face. I watched as he turned his pickup truck around and drove off.

As I drove back to my parents' house I thought about the situation. I was pretty sure Dan was overreacting to things. The Manny Vassey I knew would just as soon spit in Phil's face as say a word to him. It didn't seem possible that he could have changed that much. Still, it was troubling thinking of Manny accepting daily visits from Phil and sitting still so he could listen to the Bible being read to him. More likely Manny was playing some con on Phil, maybe just having fun playing with his head.

I didn't bother asking Dan about Plan B because I knew what it had to be. Dan was guessing that if I were to end up dead Phil would lose interest in Manny and let him and his secrets die in peace. Years ago I hid a tape recorder in my coat pocket and recorded a conversation Dan and I'd had about a coin shop we had broken into. The exchange was kind of a heated one in which I pretended to be unhappy with my cut, and Dan, trying to soothe the situation, went into great detail about what was taken and how much his fence in upstate New York was able to get for us. I'd placed that tape and a journal I made of the crimes we committed together in a safety deposit box and arranged for the contents to be delivered to Vermont's attorney general on my death. Later I told Dan about my safety deposit box. He wasn't happy about it, but I could tell he respected me for it. For him to consider Plan B meant he either thought there was a chance I was bluffing or maybe that he had a shot of excluding my evidence due to hearsay. Or it could be that Manny had worse on him than

I had. He was deluding himself, though. If that tape and journal ever came out he'd do a hard twenty years.

I pulled up in front of my parents' house and sat quietly and thought the matter over. I wasn't going to murder either Phil or Manny. I had already done enough damage for one lifetime. Instead, I'd visit Manny, figure out what game he was playing, and then talk sense into Dan.

Chapter 4

I found my mom in the kitchen preparing dinner. When she saw me she gave me a nervous, anxious smile and wavered for a moment before coming over to peck me on the cheek. Like my dad, she seemed to have aged excessively during the last seven years. She had shrunk somewhat, and her hair, which used to be mostly blonde with only touches of gray, was now completely white. She stood in front of me trying to smile, her eyes tiny in her now raisin-like face.

'You look tired, Joey,' she said, and then she moved back to the stove and her sauce-stirring.

I started laughing, I couldn't help it. 'After seven years that's the first thing you have to say to me?' I asked. 'Oh, and by the way, I missed you, too.'

'Of course I missed you,' she said, her voice faltering a bit. 'But you do look tired. Have you been eating enough?'

'I've been eating fine. Mom, the county jail is only a twenty-minute drive. You and dad could have visited me once.'

'We didn't feel comfortable doing that,' she said half under her breath. She started to say something else, but it died in her throat.

I watched for a minute as she stirred the sauce, her body tense, her eyes and mouth rigid. I asked her where Dad was.

'He wasn't feeling well so he's taking a nap.' She hesitated. 'Let me see if he's up.'

I watched as she made a beeline towards their bedroom. She closed the door behind her. They tried to keep their voices low, but the walls were thin and I could hear most of what was said.

'*Your son is home. He's in the kitchen right now.*'

'*Can you keep your voice down? Joey's going to hear you.*'

'*The door's closed. He's not going to hear me. I want you out there with me.*'

'*I'm tired. Let me rest for a few more minutes.*'

'*Oh no you don't. You come out there with me!*'

'*Jesus, Irma, he's your son. He's not going to bite you.*'

'*I want you out there with me. You're the one who insisted that he stay here!*'

'*Alright, alright.*'

I heard him get off the bed. The door opened and my mom came out first with my dad tailing behind her. He gave me a weak smile as he passed by and then walked over to the kitchen sink to fill up a teapot. My mom went back to stirring her sauce. After a minute of that I told them I was going out.

'You're not going to join us for dinner?' she asked, actually surprised.

'I don't think so. I'll be back later.'

'Why don't you join us? I'm making ziti and meatballs.'

'I'd rather not, especially if the two of you are going to be so damn ashamed of me.'

'Don't be like that,' she snapped back at me. 'How do you expect us to feel after what you did?' My dad looked up from his teapot but didn't say anything.

I had to get out of there – I could feel my hands trembling. As I turned to leave I heard her call my name.

'Stay for dinner,' she said. 'Joey, you shouldn't go out tonight. The town paper printed a story today about you being released and what happened. They put your picture on the front page. It would be better if you didn't go into town.'

I stared at both of them for a long moment, barely able to recognize either of them. Then I turned and got out of there as fast as I could.

More than just my hands were trembling by the time I got to my car. I had to take a dozen or so deep breaths before I could calm myself down. It's funny, but after all I had lost, I'd hung on to the thought that I wasn't completely isolated. That I could somehow reestablish my relationship with my parents and use that as a starting point to rebuild my life. I used to lie on my cot and idealize the way it would be when I got out. That they'd forgive me in their hearts and mean it when they said they'd help me get back on my feet. But I had just been kidding myself. It had never been like that with the two of them, and now they were nothing but two old people who were willing to let me live in their house for a few weeks.

The hell with it.

I sat in my car for a long moment before I felt I could move. And then I drove to Zeke's.

Zeke's Tavern is a few blocks from downtown Bradley. It's been around since the early nineteen hundreds and is a hangout for cops and locals. A dark cavernous place that always smelled heavily of cigarettes and stale beer. Inside were a couple of pool tables, a dartboard, a jukebox, a few beat-up tables, and a long chipped and stained mahogany bar. Zeke's had a kitchen in the back where they'd cook up burgers and other standard bar food.

I spotted Bill Wright and Tony Flauria sitting at the bar. They were joking about something but stopped when they saw me. I nodded at them and got back only blank stares in return. I moved to the opposite end of the bar, waved the bartender over, and ordered a cheeseburger and a pint of a local brewed ale.

About the time the bartender was placing the pint in front of me, Flauria had gotten off his bar stool and was heading towards me. Bill Wright looked somewhat queasy around the eyes as he tagged along. They were both cops. Flauria, as far as I knew, had always been clean.

Flauria stopped about a foot from me and gave me the evil eye.

'How you doing, Tony?' I said.

He sniffed a couple of times in the air. 'I thought I smelled a pile of shit coming from over here.'

'I'm doing great,' I said. 'Thanks for asking.'

Flauria just stood glaring at me. Then through wire-tight lips, 'You disfigure anyone lately, you pile of shit?'

'Not yet, but the night's young.'

'You dirty piece of shit,' he stated, his beefy face flushed with malice.

'Joe, what the fuck are you doing here?' Bill Wright asked. 'You should just get the hell out of Bradley and consider yourself the luckiest fuck alive.'

'Big words coming from you, Bill. I thought you'd be buying me a beer right now for keeping my mouth shut all these years.'

'I don't know what the fuck you're talking about,' he said, but he didn't look too good, his skin color dropping a shade. Flauria, though, was still simmering with violence.

'Why don't the two of us step outside?' he offered.

'I don't think so, Tony. I got nothing against you and see no reason to hurt you.'

'You got no reason to hurt me?' he asked, flabbergasted. 'After what you did you think you have the right to walk in here and act as if you belong here?'

I could sense his thick body tensing. I sat quietly and drank my beer, my eyes focused straight ahead. Bill said something to Flauria about it not being worth it. In the bar mirror I could see him forcibly restraining Flauria, and Flauria was just barely smart enough to let himself be restrained.

'Let's get out of here,' Flauria spat. 'This place smells too much like an outhouse.' As he and Bill left Zeke's, he pointed a thick finger at me and warned me not to come back. 'You're not welcome here.'

The bar was mostly empty but the few people that were around were staring at me. A blonde, about twenty-five, came over and sat down next to me. She had come into the bar about the time Flauria was being forcibly restrained.

'Wow, that was something,' she said.

I didn't say anything. I really couldn't.

She made a loud sniffing noise. 'I don't know. You smell pretty good to me.'

I turned to see her grinning. She was thin, maybe a little too thin, but nice to look at. She had on dark granny-type sunglasses, which was a funny thing to wear in a place like Zeke's – making me think that she was a druggie. Her grin melted into a soft smile. 'You look pretty good too. Anybody ever tell you you look a lot like Bruce Willis, at least when he had hair?'

'Thanks, I guess.'

'People have told me I look like a young Meg Ryan. What do you think?'

It was hard to tell who she looked like with the dark glasses she was wearing, but she was blonde and thin, and I guess I could see the resemblance around her mouth.

'I'd take you over her any day of the week,' I said.

'In that case, why don't you buy me a drink?' she asked. 'How about a Cosmo?'

'I have no idea what that is,' I said, 'but if you want it, I'll buy it.' I waved over the bartender, who had taken a more sullen attitude towards me, and ordered a 'Cosmo'. I watched as he poured vodka, Triple Sec, and cranberry juice into a cocktail shaker and wondered why anyone would want to drink that. She let me take a sip of it after it had been poured into a Martini glass. It was too sweet for my taste.

'Come on, what was going on here before?'

I turned to face her. With her long straight blonde hair and shit-eating grin, she reminded me a little of Elaine, at least before Elaine had turned sour. As I looked at her I noticed her body was more athletic than thin. Her arms and face were nicely tanned. It took an effort to look away from her.

'Old business,' I said. 'Nothing I'd like to talk about.'

I could feel her staring at me. It did something to me to feel her staring at me.

'Come on,' she said after a while, 'you tell me your secret and I'll tell you mine.'

'I'm sorry. I'm not in the mood for this.'

'Okay, I'll tell you mine anyway.' She reached over and whispered in my ear, 'I haven't had a good lay in months.'

I looked over and saw her shit-eating grin. Her eyes were blackened by the sunglasses but she was grinning her big grin. Like only she knew the joke.

'Buy me another drink,' she said. I bought her another one. After my burger was brought out, I bought her one also. When we were done eating she told me she wanted to go for a ride. 'Come on,' she said as she took my hand, and I let her lead me out of the bar.

When we got to the parking lot she told me that we'd take her car. She breathed lightly in my ear, 'I know a place where nobody will bother us. And I'm going to do things to you tonight you'll never forget.'

She had a later-model green Taurus. 'I'll drive,' she said. It had gotten dark. I got in the passenger side and sat quietly and watched the shadows as we went by. Within minutes we were out of downtown Bradley and heading towards Eastfield. I guess neither of us was in the mood for small talk. As we drove, I could at times make out her face in the moonlight and could see the intensity burning in it.

It took a while before we got to where she was going. We first had to turn down several narrow country roads to get to what was nothing more than a dirt path. Then we drove on that dirt path for miles. Eventually she stopped the car.

She moved herself around so she was sitting sideways and leaning against the driver's side door. I could see her plainly in the moonlight. Her skin looked as if it were smoldering. I moved towards her. She put out an arm to keep me away.

'Wait,' she said. 'I want to hear your secret first.'

My head was buzzing. It had been almost eight years since I'd been with a woman. I could barely talk. 'I did something pretty bad a long time ago,' I said.

'Come on, you have to tell me.' She started to lift up her shirt, teasing somewhat, showing off a slightly rounded belly and the bottom area of her breasts.

'Let's just leave it at that. I did something bad.'

'Come on,' she pleaded. 'You're not playing fair. I told you my secret.' She rolled her shirt up farther to fully expose her small breasts for a few seconds before lowering the shirt to just barely cover them.

I shook my head. I figured she was a wack job who got off on bad boys and violence, but I wasn't going to play her game. Even though it had been eight long years since my arrest, I wasn't going to play her game. I wanted her badly – at that moment I would've wanted anyone badly – but I was still going to tell her that it wasn't working out when she exclaimed, 'Oh my God!

'You were in the paper today!' she went on. 'That's why you looked familiar. You're the guy who stabbed that DA! Holy shit!'

I just stared at her, stared as she gave me back a crazy smile.

'What was it like to stab someone like that?'

'Why would you want to know?'

'Come on, it must have been a rush.'

'No,' I said, 'it wasn't any rush. I'd give anything not to have done it.'

She seemed taken aback by that, at least for a few seconds. Then her crazy smile flashed back on. Her shirt had a little rip near the top and she took hold of that and ripped it the rest of the way. Her small round breasts were fully exposed. I could see her chest heaving wildly. The whole thing was crazy, she was crazy. 'Tear my pants off,' she moaned as she writhed in front of me.

When I reached for her, she whispered, 'You don't even know my name. It's Clara.'

Something clicked in my mind. I usually observe everything around me. Even if I'm not fully aware of it, I'm noticing things and filing them away. In my mind's eye I could see her green Ford Taurus idling a few doors from my parents' house. I could see it pulling away from the curb when I left earlier to drive to Zeke's. I reached up quickly and knocked her dark sunglasses off and saw pure hatred boiling in her eyes. She still had her crazy smile plastered on her face, but her eyes were nothing but black holes of venom and hate. I could see the resemblance then. I should've seen it earlier, but it's hard for me to remember the way Phil used to look. I did remember that Phil had a daughter named Clara.

She started screaming rape then. She was screaming at the top of her lungs, screaming so loud that I thought something inside her was going to rupture. It's funny what goes through your mind at a time like that. For a split second I just found it kind of interesting how wrong I had been. How what I thought was lust heating her up was in fact a completely different and more violent emotion. Then I realized I had to get out of there.

As I turned towards the door, she was on me. One hand was clawing at my face, her other arm wrapped tight around my chest. All the time she was screaming rape. I saw them off in the distance then. Two guys running towards the car.

I tried to push her off but she kept clawing and screaming. I had no other choice so I used my elbow. I swung it behind me and felt it hit something hard. She made a short moaning noise and her grip loosened enough for me to get away from her. I was out of the car and watching as those two guys ran towards me.

They were less than thirty yards away. They were both big boys, probably played offensive line on their high school football teams. The guy leading the charge was holding a tire iron. What I did next surprised them. I raced right at them.

The guy with the tire iron was caught off guard – he just wasn't expecting it. He was off balance somewhat as he tried to hit me with the tire iron and only glanced it off my arm. The blow hurt but didn't do too much damage. I was right on target with my punch, though. I put my whole body into it and caught him flush in the jaw. His mouth exploded into a pink spray and he was out before he hit the ground.

I turned to face his partner. He had stopped in his tracks. I could see he was scared – I was more than he had bargained for. I guess they thought their job would be nothing more than pulling me out of the car and beating me senseless. He took a cautious step towards me and looked like he was going to throw a haymaker at my head. I feigned left and then hit him hard with a right jab to his stomach, and then followed that with a quick rabbit punch to the side of his head. My last punch knocked him off balance, and before he could regain it, I kicked his feet out from under him. As he lay on the ground, I grabbed his arm, swung it behind him and broke it by kicking down hard with my foot. He screamed and then I think he passed out. In any case, he stopped moving or making any noise.

I could make out a jeep parked off in the distance. The guy on the ground in front of me couldn't have been more than twenty-two. I regretted what I did to his arm – he'd never be able to use it quite the same again – but I wanted to put him out of action as quickly as possible. It was a tough lesson to have to learn. I searched his pockets but couldn't find any car keys.

I went over to the other boy, the one with the busted jaw. He was still out cold. Like his friend, he was also only in his early twenties. I searched his pockets and found a key for the jeep. As I was standing up, I was pushed hard from behind and almost knocked to the ground. Clara had jumped on my back and was screaming every vulgar obscenity I'd ever heard in my ear. She was also scratching up my face and trying to get to my eyes. I threw myself backwards and landed with a thud. The blow knocked the wind out of her. She looked a little woozy, but she was still conscious. I got to my feet and started running towards the jeep.

When I got in it I looked in the mirror and saw that she had scratched me pretty good under my cheekbone and had missed my eye by only an inch. I put my hand to my cheek and felt a warm stickiness. Blood was beginning to trickle down my face. I put the jeep in Drive, turned it around, and started back down the dirt path. The headlights momentarily caught Clara and her two accomplices. Clara was sitting with her face in her hands, her thin shoulders convulsing as she sobbed. The two boys were still lying on the ground as if they were dead. Even though they had tried to frame me for rape, and possibly had even planned to beat me to death, I couldn't help feeling sick to my stomach about what happened to all three of them.

I could understand the hatred that must have been burning inside her to push her into such a crazy plan. And it was crazy and juvenile and poorly thought out. I don't know how in the world she thought she was going to explain what her two friends were doing on that dirt road so they could just happen to come across me while I was 'raping' her. But I could understand the hatred that drove her to try framing me. I could imagine her looking at her father's face every day for eight years and hating me just a little bit more each day. I could imagine how her rage must've boiled over when she heard that I was being paroled after only seven years. She probably had convinced herself that she was only correcting a gross miscarriage of justice – that it would be only right for me to end up serving another twenty years, and in a harder place than county jail. I was lucky she hadn't gotten herself a gun and walked into Zeke's and started blasting away. And I wouldn't have blamed her if she had.

I made up my mind then to leave Bradley. I'd only been kidding myself for a long time. There are some crimes that just can't be forgiven.

Chapter 5

I drove to the Bradley police station and told my story to the desk sergeant, Frank Schilling. Frank and I went way back. He was a year older than I was, and as kids we used to play football and baseball together. At one time we used to be friends and we were both ushers at each other's weddings. Now, though, he didn't seem too happy to see me and he sure as hell didn't believe my story.

'I got to tell you, Denton,' he said, 'that doesn't sound like the Clara I know. When she was younger she used to babysit my kids. She's a good kid. I don't believe she'd pull a stunt like that. It sounds like bullshit to me.'

'Frank, I swear, that's what happened.'

He made a face when I called him 'Frank', sort of like he was smelling bad cheese. 'Why don't you call me Sergeant Schilling,' he said.

'You got to be kidding.'

He gave me a cold stare. 'You been drinking tonight, Denton?' he asked after a while.

'I had two beers at Zeke's.'

'I'll send someone over to check that out. You doing any drugs?'

I shook my head. 'I've only been out eight hours now. Where would I have had time to get drugs?'

'You've had plenty of time to get into this ugly mess.'

I started to say something, but forced my mouth shut.

He let out a long, pained sigh before asking if I was willing to submit to a drug test. I told him I had no problem with that.

He looked over his notes. 'And you don't know who those two boys were that you worked over?'

'No, they didn't look familiar. But then again, I've been gone for a while. The jeep I took off them is out front. You could check to see if the registration is in the car.'

'You just beat the hell out of those two boys and left them in the middle of nowhere,' he said with some disgust.

'I told you they were trying to frame me for a rape—'

'Yeah, that's your story,' he said. 'I'm going to sit you in the interrogation room until we sort this out.'

The Bradley police station has a single interrogation room that is almost never used. During my twelve years on the force, I had never used it. The first time I ever sat in that room was the night I was arrested for arson and attempted murder. Frank brought me back there and had me sit and wait. Two hours later the door opened and Phil walked in. His skin had a sickly pallor, making it look as if his face had been dipped in wax.

He sat down across from me and told me to tell him my story.

'Your daughter followed me from my parents' house to Zeke's. She picked me up at the bar, drove me down a dirt path off Cumberland Road in Eastfield, and tried to frame me with a rape charge. She had two friends waiting there, one with a tire iron. Maybe they were planning to beat me to death.'

He sat expressionless for several minutes as he stared at me. As difficult as it was, I stared back. I tried not to look at the road map of scars that had been left on his face. Finally he asked about Clara following me from my parents' house.

'You're an intelligent man, Joe,' he said. 'If you knew my daughter had been stalking you, why would you get in a car with her?'

'It wasn't something I was consciously aware of at the time.' I hesitated. 'I had just left my parents' house. I was upset. But at some level I remembered her car. It wasn't until it was too late that things clicked.'

'And you didn't recognize my daughter?'

'No. I hadn't seen her for a long time, not since she was a kid. And she was wearing dark granny-style sunglasses to hide her eyes.'

He leaned back in his chair and continued with his staring contest. Neither of us moved, neither of us said a word. After about five minutes of it he broke it off and told me that the two boys were in the hospital.

'The one you punched in the face suffered severe damage to his jaw. He won't be talking for months. You shattered the other boy's arm in three places. The surgeon had to use several rods to reattach the bone. He'll have to undergo intensive rehabilitation and probably will never have full use of his arm again. I know both of them and they're from good families. Are you proud of yourself, Joe?'

'I had no choice. What would you have done?'

'Not what you did, Joe.'

'I did what I had to.' I hesitated before asking him how his daughter was.

His eyes showed some life for the first time. For a moment I thought he was going to take a swing at me. 'She's in shock,' he said softly. 'Her shirt was torn off and she's got a black eye and bruises all over her body. How'd her shirt get torn off?'

'She did that herself,' I said.

'And her bruises? She did that herself?'

'I was trying to get free of her after I realized what was

happening. When I saw her friends running to greet me, I tried a little harder. I didn't try to hurt her, though.'

'That was awful thoughtful of you, Joe. Those scratches on your face look more like the defensive wounds a rape victim might cause. Just as my daughter's injuries look consistent with a rape.'

'Phil, you don't want to do this. Not to yourself and not to your daughter.'

'I'm just going by the evidence, Joe.'

'No, you're not. I have no interest in pressing charges against your daughter and her friends. I came here to clear this up and make sure they leave me alone from this point on.'

'That's awful generous of you, Joe.'

'Look,' I said, 'this won't make it past a grand jury. It would only end up embarrassing you and making things difficult for your daughter. How in the world can you explain her two friends being out in the middle of nowhere to conveniently save her?'

'First of all, I am past embarrassment. You made sure of that, Joe. As far as those two boys being out on that dirt path, my guess is it was just a coincidence. Nothing more, nothing less. I'm sure Clara and her friends hang out there occasionally. Those two boys were probably there to drink or hunt.'

'There were no guns or alcohol in their jeep.'

'Maybe they were going to meet friends. They'll tell us when they're able.'

I just started laughing. The whole thing was just too laughable. 'Phil,' I said when I could. 'How are you going to explain her stalking me and picking me up at Zeke's?'

'You don't even remember fully my daughter being outside your parents' house. As you told me, it's only some subconscious impression of yours. And about Clara picking you up…'

He seemed momentarily lost. He opened and closed his mouth. Then he got up and left the room.

As I sat there I couldn't help feeling anxious. I wasn't worried about having sexual assault and battery charges brought against me. As much as Phil would love to send me to prison, I couldn't see him using a frame. He'd wait until he had a real crime. Besides, this whole thing would collapse on him if he tried bringing charges. I guess what I was anxious about was the level of hostility I was seeing. I had every reason in the world to expect it from Phil and his daughter, but from Frank Schilling and Tony Flauria? And from my own parents? With them it was more passive, but it was there all the same. You have dirty cops who get busted all the time and the world moves on. I wasn't the first and I'm certainly not going to be the last. Hell, Dan Pleasant was dirtier than I ever was and he had more blood on his hands. There've been a few people over the years who've died in his custody. They were lowlifes and nobody ever cared much about it, but in one way or another, I knew their deaths were convenient to Dan. Still, people smile and wave back to him on the street and vote him back into office every election.

It's funny, it wouldn't be this way now if Phil had died that night. The memory of what I did would've faded and the hard feelings would've worn away. The problem is Phil is there to face them every day. Every day they have to be repulsed once again by my crime. Because of me they have to feel awkward and self-conscious around him and try to pretend he's not some sideshow freak. There's just no forgiveness for that.

Phil didn't return to the interrogation room until after two in the morning. He looked more somber as he sat down across from me and could barely meet my eyes.

'Your friend Dan Pleasant was here,' he said. 'He looked over my report and remembered that one of his deputies had been assigned to check your parents' house periodically to make sure there were no problems. No surprise that his deputy claims to have seen Clara's Taurus parked near their house.' He hesitated for a long moment. 'I talked to my daughter also,' he added, 'and she admitted to me what she did. If you want to press charges against her and the two boys you put in the hospital, let me know.'

'I told you before, I have no interest in pressing charges. I just want to be left alone. And I don't blame your daughter.'

He met my eyes then. 'I don't blame her, either,' he said. 'The only person I blame for this is you, Joe. Why don't you get out of here.'

I got up and left the room and didn't bother to look back.

Chapter 6

I didn't get to bed until three in the morning and I had a restless night of it. At times my mind would race with images from the past – things that I had thought I had long forgotten; other times I was closer to hallucinations. I wasn't quite awake, but I wasn't quite asleep either.

The stuff that went through my mind – Jesus; they were memories that should have stayed buried. At first it was only small stuff, small crimes, but still they were things I didn't want dredged up.

When my older daughter Melissa was three and a half – only a couple of months after Courtney's first birthday – she had cut herself on a broken glass. It was mostly a superficial cut, I think she needed a few stitches, but there was blood everywhere. Elaine was hysterical, and at the time I was out of my mind on coke and trying to place a bet with my bookie. You see, I had a chance to take Miami plus two and a half over Buffalo in a playoff game. The Dolphins had shut out San Diego the week before and how was I supposed to know Dan Marino would shit the bed and lose that game by nineteen points? So now I'm back there and Melissa's screeching like a banshee and Elaine's hysterical about us needing to drive right away to the emergency room, and I can barely hear my bookie over the phone. Remember, at this point

I'm coked up to the gills. So I unholster my gun and point it at them, telling them to let me make my fucking bet in peace. There wasn't a chance in the world I would have used my gun. I just needed them to shut up so I could make one more loser bet.

Other memories raced through my mind. They were things that I'm pretty sure happened, but I couldn't swear my life on it. I might have been mixing up different events, merging them into a single memory. Or I might've been making it up entirely. All I know is they seemed real.

One night I had broken into a hardware store with Dan and his boys. They had a safe that Dan thought he could break open, but he had trouble with it so we ended up carrying the safe out of the store and loading it on the back of his pickup truck. Now I'm riding with Dan and I guess we didn't secure the safe properly and the damn thing ends up tumbling off the back of the pickup and onto the road. It took five of us to pick it up in the first place, and now it's just Dan and me. He radios his boys who were in on the heist and the two of us are standing in the middle of the road next to the safe waiting for help to arrive. Dan's as calm as can be, making small talk about this and that, and I'm going out of my head with worry. I want us to drive away and leave the safe where it fell, but Dan insists on waiting. His boys show up and help us get it back onto the pickup, but I'm sweating bullets through the whole goddam thing, my heart beating like it's going to bust out of my chest.

And then there was another time a drifter stuck his nose into a liquor store that we were breaking into. Dan and his boys ended up taking the guy into one of their cars. I never found out what happened to that drifter. Dan had made a few jokes about the hole the guy had dug himself into, but that was all I ever heard.

Other memories snaked in and out of my consciousness. I had a doozy of a hallucination right before I woke up. I was back with Clara in her car. I had just knocked her sunglasses off and realized what was up. She was grabbing onto me like before, but I couldn't break free of her. I elbowed her and punched her until her face was a raw mess, but she wouldn't loosen her grip. I had no choice. I grabbed the car key from the ignition and started stabbing her with it. Stabbing her over and over again in the face. I must have stabbed her over thirty times, but she still wouldn't let go. And I noticed a chunk of her nose was missing, and how I could play tic-tac-toe on what was left of her face, and how much she now looked like her father...

I bolted up in bed and realized I was drenched in sweat. My bed sheets were soaked through. It was six thirty in the morning. I felt a dull throbbing around my temples and got up and made my way to the bathroom. I looked like hell; worse than if I was suffering from a bad hangover. My eyes had a hollowed-out look and my skin was sickly pale. The flesh along my cheekbone where I had been scratched had swollen and was looking pretty bad. I took some aspirin and then splashed cold water on my face until I felt better. Then I went back to my room, got dressed, and shuffled towards the kitchen.

My parents were both up. My mom was at the stove making eggs, and my dad was sitting at the kitchen table reading his newspaper and drinking coffee. My mom didn't bother to turn around. She greeted me with an unconvincing 'good morning' as she worked on her scrambled eggs. I could see my dad's eyes grow sick as he noticed the scratches along my cheek.

'You got in late last night,' he said.

'Sorry if I woke you.'

'I heard your car pull in around two thirty.'

'I'm sorry. Something happened last night. I couldn't help it.'

My mom had turned around. Her raisin-like face seemed to shrink as she stared at me.

'I told you not to go into town but you wouldn't listen,' she complained, a shrillness edging into her voice. 'What happened?'

I poured myself some coffee and sat down at the table across from my dad. 'I'd rather not go into this now,' I said. 'Could I have some breakfast?'

'I'll get you some scrambled eggs. You can make your own toast.'

'Who scratched you?' my dad asked.

He was looking as sick as can be. I sighed and told him it was Clara Coakley.

'Oh, Jesus,' he moaned, and for a moment I thought he was about to start bawling. 'What in the world were you doing with her?'

My mom made a bitter face as if she had something to spit out. 'Didn't I tell you not to go into town?' she muttered half under her breath. 'You have to act as if you know it all. Sometimes I know what I'm talking about.'

'Look,' I said. 'I didn't do a damn thing. That girl came up with some crackpot scheme to either have me thrown in prison for rape or to have me beaten to death. I'm not sure which. Any case, it's over.'

Both my parents looked horrified. My dad, flustered, asked if I had gone to the police.

'Yes, I went to the police.'

'They believed you?'

'They had to believe me,' I said. 'It's what happened.'

'Did, uh,' my dad hesitated for a moment as he rubbed his jaw, 'did you file charges against Clara?'

I shook my head. They were quiet after that. Nobody said a word as my mother finished with the eggs and then spooned them onto three plates. We ate mostly in silence. I could tell there was something on my mom's mind. She couldn't hold it in any longer and made a remark about my dad mentioning that I had asked about Elaine and my two girls.

'I find it hard to believe that she cut you and Dad off completely from my kids,' I said.

'We can't blame her for that,' she said.

'Don't you want to see your grandchildren?'

'Of course I do,' my mom said. 'But I also want what's best for those girls. Elaine couldn't stay in Bradley after what you did, not with the abuse Melissa and Courtney were taking from the neighborhood kids. I'm sure Elaine has had a difficult time having to move to a new area and start over on her own. And she has had to support herself and those two girls for the last seven years without any help.'

'How do you know she hasn't had any help?'

'You're right, I don't know,' my mom said, her tone somewhat uneasy. 'Maybe she has had help. Maybe she's remarried. And Joey, that's all the more reason to leave her alone.'

'Don't you miss my girls?'

'Yes, I miss my granddaughters, but I understand why Elaine has done what she's done. And Joey, you should respect her wishes.'

'I don't know what you're talking about,' I said. I could feel a hot anger flushing my face. 'You don't think I love my girls? I'm thinking of seeing a lawyer about changing the custody order.'

'Why would you want to do that?' my mom asked.

'What the hell do you mean?'

'Don't swear at your mother!' my dad snapped.

'I want to know what she means. She doesn't think I care about my girls?'

'Be honest with yourself,' my mom said. 'You haven't seen them in over seven years, probably closer to eight. And Joey, you never had much to do with them before that. It would be best for the girls if you left them alone.'

I just sat there and stared at the two of them. Sat there and felt a hotness burning my face. I wanted to tell them to screw themselves, that I knew where Elaine was and they could go cry themselves a fucking river for all I cared.

'Joey,' my dad started to say, 'think what's best for Melissa and Courtney—'

I didn't hear the rest. I was too busy getting out of there.

Bradley to Albany, New York, was a three-hour drive. I decided what the hell, I'd find Elaine when I got there, and I headed off. It was Saturday and there was a good chance I'd find her and the girls at home. I'd still get back in time to visit Manny and satisfy myself that Dan was worrying about nothing.

As troubling as my sleep had been, my three-hour drive to Albany was the exact opposite. My mind just seemed to clear itself of all worry as I drove along and watched the countryside. After a half-hour I pulled over and put the top down. One of my few times outside of Bradley County had been a weekend trip to Albany with Elaine. It was several months before we had gotten married. I didn't really care much for the city, but I remembered Elaine liking the restaurants.

The three-hour drive went by fast. I had to change radio stations a few times along the way, but was able to find a decent classic rock station each time. I just sat back, listened to tunes, and enjoyed the ride. By the time I got there I was about as relaxed as I'd been in years.

It wasn't hard finding Elaine. I stopped off at the central police station, bringing a couple of cups of black coffee, and identified myself as a retired cop. I chewed the fat for a while with the desk sergeant, and by the time I got around to asking for an address for Elise Mathews he was feeling friendly enough towards me to drop everything to find it. He didn't even bother asking what I wanted it for. We shook hands and I was feeling pretty good by the time I left.

Elaine was living in half of a two-family house. The neighborhood looked kind of shabby and I got some curious glances from a few of the kids playing in the street. The house itself needed work. The wood flooring on the front porch was rotted – if I stomped down hard enough my foot would've gone through the boards. The house also needed to be repainted and some of the shutters were hanging half off. I tested the handrail and found that it was loose. I didn't like the fact that my kids were living in a dump like this. I should've felt angry about it, but as I stood there all I could feel was nervous, like butterflies were fluttering around in my stomach. I rang the buzzer and as I waited those damn butterflies flapped around like crazy, just about driving my heart into my throat. I have to admit, as much as I wanted to see my daughters I felt somewhat terrified at the thought of them being there. After several minutes Elaine opened the door. She stared at me blankly for a long ten count before she recognized me, or at least before she was willing to recognize me. From her expression I knew Melissa and Courtney weren't home.

'They let you out early, Joe.'

'Yeah, they did,' I admitted. 'The state of Vermont considers me reformed and ready to be a useful member of society again. You know what they say about fooling some of the people some of time.'

Elaine had dyed her hair a brownish red, and like me had lost the extra weight she had been carrying around her middle. Her body looked closer to what it was in high school. She didn't have any makeup on and she seemed tired, especially around the eyes, but she still looked better than she had in years. She seemed to be making up her mind about something.

'Everything's still a joke to you,' she said at last.

'Give me a break. I was only trying to break the ice. It's been a long time, Elaine.'

'How'd you find me?'

I made a face. 'It's not important. Come on, why don't you let me in?'

'No.' She was shaking her head. There was nothing in her eyes, though. No hate, no love, no feelings of any kind. Just blank and empty. 'The girls aren't home now. They're playing with friends. But I don't want you in my house, Joe.'

'You're going to make me stand out here? I drove three hours to see you. Why don't we talk over a cup of coffee?'

'You're not coming into my house. If you try to I'll call the police and have you arrested.'

I could tell she was serious. I took a deep breath and held it in while I counted to three. 'How about I buy you a cup of coffee somewhere,' I suggested.

She gave me a long look before nodding her head. 'Only for fifteen minutes,' she said. 'I'll go grab my coat.'

'Could you bring some pictures of the girls?'

She disappeared back inside and when she came out again she was wearing a cheap threadbare cloth coat, something not even a Salvation Army store would sell. Other than her directing me to a coffee shop a few blocks away, neither of us said a word. When we got there we took a booth. I ordered a turkey club and a piece of apple pie and she stuck with only a cup of coffee.

'How have you and the girls been?' I asked.

'We've been fine. I've been working as a receptionist and going to school nights to become a paralegal. It's been a struggle, but we're all fine.'

'I'm sorry,' I said. 'There was nothing I could do to help you. But at least I was able to leave you the house and our savings.'

She started laughing. It wasn't a malicious laugh, just something she couldn't control.

'What's so funny?'

'You didn't leave me anything, Joe. There was only twelve thousand in savings and I cleared less than six thousand when I sold the house. Afterwards a business associate of yours came by. His name was Manny something. He made me give him what I had. He promised me he'd hurt Melissa and Courtney if I didn't, and I believed him.'

For a long time I couldn't move. Just sat there frozen. 'That dirty sonofabitch,' I swore. 'I made a deal with him. He wasn't supposed to go near you. I'm so sorry about that.'

'It was only par for the course.'

'Come on, Elaine, that's not fair.'

'Why isn't it? You abandoned us throughout our marriage. When you weren't throwing away our money on drugs you were burying us with your gambling debts.'

'I'm so sorry for that also, but I haven't touched cocaine or made any bets in almost eight years. And I'm never going to again.'

She didn't say anything. She took a sip of coffee and looked away.

'Look, Elaine—'

'My name's Elise now.'

'Why'd you pick Elise?'

'Is that any of your business?'

'Forget it. I'm sorry. Elise. It's a beautiful name.' I took a deep breath before going on. 'During the seven years I was in jail I kept thinking about the damage I did to you and the girls. I want a chance to fix things. I want a chance to have a relationship with my daughters. And maybe it's not too late for us. I'm going to be getting a monthly pension of thirty-four sixty and that could help—'

'You're going to receive a pension?'

I showed her a little smile. 'Well, yeah, it's been arranged. I'm on the books for twenty years of service.'

Elaine started laughing, kind of a sad laugh. It went on for a while. 'That's the problem in a nutshell, Joe,' she said after her laugh had died out. 'If you had come here today and told me you were planning to go to a trade school or college so you could work towards a new career, then maybe I could've believed things had somehow changed, that you had somehow grown in jail. But nothing has changed, Joe. You still want to take the easy way out. Regardless of whether it's right or wrong. You haven't changed at all. You're still missing that same moral center you've been missing your whole life. And look at your face. How long have you been out of jail? And you've already gotten your face scratched up?'

'These scratches are nothing,' I said. 'Trust me, they mean absolutely nothing.' I started to feel a little hot under the collar. 'And what do you want me to do? You want me to throw away thirty-four sixty a month?'

'I don't care what you do. It doesn't affect me one way or another.'

'I'm not throwing away that money,' I said.

'I wouldn't expect you to.'

'Damn it. If I have to throw away that kind of money to make you happy, then fine, I'll do it.'

'Forget it, Joe. It doesn't matter. It wouldn't change anything.'

'Give me a break, for Chrissakes!'

'Joe, I've given you thousands of breaks. More breaks than you'll ever realize. All I ask is that you give me and Courtney and Melissa one break and stay out of our lives. That's all I'll ever ask of you.'

I felt helpless as I watched her drink her coffee, as I watched the utter indifference in her eyes.

'When I was in jail I realized that for a long time I've only been drifting along,' I said. 'There's nothing of any meaning in my life now, at least nothing positive. I need to change that—'

'You can change that, Joe. You can do something positive by leaving Courtney and Melissa alone.'

'You're acting as if I'm some kind of monster. Elaine, I mean Elise, I made one mistake—'

'One mistake? You stole eighty thousand dollars and tried to hide the fact by setting Phil's office on fire. When he caught you in the act, you tried to kill him and ended up maiming him horribly. That's your one mistake? But you've done more than that. You've spent far more money on drugs and gambling than you possibly could've earned in a lifetime as a police officer. I don't know how you made all that money, but I know it wasn't legal. It wasn't that you made only one mistake, Joe. Let's be honest. You were only caught once, but you've been making mistakes for almost as long as we were married.'

'Everything's so damn black and white with you, huh, Elaine? And you're as pure as the driven snow?'

'Joe, I didn't come here to fight with you.'

'Fuck you. Let's see if you can be so damn honest with yourself. When I was drowning in cocaine and gambling, what were you doing? Did you try once to help me?'

'I was afraid of you!'

'Come on, you want us both to be honest now. I never hit you or the girls. I almost never even raised my voice. You were the one who was yelling most of the time. Who are you kidding that you were afraid of me?'

'You pulled a gun on me. On me and Melissa!'

'That's right,' I said, lowering my voice. 'I did that once. And it makes me sick to think about it. But you know that as coked up as I was, I never would have hurt either of you. So Elaine, you want to know the real reason you never tried to help me?'

'You would never have let me help you.'

'Yeah, right, keep telling yourself that. Back then I was begging for help, but you just watched and let me drown. And you know why? Because you were so damn embarrassed about what our neighbors and your coffee club and your precious playgroups would think if word got out that your husband was a coke addict and a degenerate gambler.'

The waitress came with my club sandwich and apple pie, but I had lost my appetite. I just sat and watched Elaine as she tried to regain her composure. I could see some doubt flickering in her eyes. She knew there was more than a grain of truth in what I said, just as I knew there was in what she had said.

I tried to change the subject. 'How about those pictures?' I asked. 'I've been dying to see pictures of Melissa and Courtney.'

'I didn't bring any.'

'What?'

'I'm sorry, Joe,' she said, 'it wouldn't do any good to show you pictures. I'm not letting you back into our lives. For everyone's sake, please just forget about us.'

'Goddam you, Elaine. You couldn't even let me see pictures of my girls? And what the hell are you doing cutting off my parents? Not even letting them see their grandkids?'

'Perfect note for me to leave on,' she said. 'I'll walk. Don't bother getting up.'

At this point I was simmering. Probably hot enough to fry an egg on. In as calm a tone as I could possibly muster, I told her, 'Don't kid yourself that you're holding all the cards. Custody orders can be changed.'

She had started to get up, but she sat back down.

'You couldn't handle a custody hearing, Joe.'

'And why's that?'

She showed me a smug little smile. 'For the same reason you pled guilty after you were arrested. I know you've probably convinced yourself it was so you could spare Phil the trauma of having to sit through a trial. But as you've been saying, let's be honest with ourselves. You pled guilty because it was the easy way out. If you'd had a trial, you would've had to sit and listen to all the evidence piled against you. You couldn't do that, just like you couldn't sit through a custody hearing and listen to all the crappy things you've done over the years. It's not something you're capable of.'

'I might surprise you.'

She nodded. 'You might, Joe. But I don't think so.'

I sat and stared at her as she sat smug and believing she had a clue what I was all about. I took a deep breath and tried to get myself under control. This wasn't what I had wanted.

'Elaine,' I said. 'I'm sorry, Elise, I came here to try to reconcile with you, and to let you know that I plan on making up to Melissa and Courtney for being such a rotten father and for all this lost time. I wish you felt differently towards me. I don't want to fight you, but I am going to be part of my daughters' lives.'

'Joe, I know in your head all of this makes sense to you. I know you think you can magically become this good person and dad to our daughters, but trust me, it won't work out that way. It could never work out that way with you. You'll end up hurting them. And I'm not going to let that happen.'

'I guess I'll see you in court, then,' I said.

She stood up. I could see her trembling slightly. She started to walk away, but she stopped and faced me. 'Joe,' she said, 'I am going to hope that you have grown somewhat. Maybe you'll realize you can give your life meaning by giving our daughters a chance. I wish you the best.'

'Godammit!' I had the money Dan had given me in my pants pocket, the bills rolled up and held in place with an elastic band. I slipped a hundred dollar bill from it, wrapped the bills back up with the band, and tossed the roll to Elaine. 'That's over six thousand dollars,' I told her. 'Use it for our daughters.'

Her eyes narrowed as she stared at me. 'How'd you get this money, Joe?'

'What difference does it make?'

'Some things never change, do they?' She dropped the roll of bills onto the floor. 'I'm not touching your dirty money.'

'Jesus Christ, Elaine, don't be so fucking dramatic. I'll just mail it to you, then.'

'You do and I'll burn it.'

She walked out of the coffee shop. I sat frozen as I stared at the roll of bills that she had dropped. Other people in the coffee shop were doing the same. A heavyset man with long greasy hair got up and started to bend down to pick up the money. I told him if he touched it, I'd bust his head.

'Hey, it don't bother me how dirty it is,' he said, still reaching for the roll. 'If you guys don't want it…'

I repeated myself about busting his head. He backed away and sat back down.

I got up and picked up the money. Then I settled the bill and headed back to Bradley.

Chapter 7

On my drive back to Bradley, I thought about Elaine and knew I shouldn't have expected anything different from her. She had closed herself off to me a long time ago – as she had every reason in the world to. I had abandoned my family when I'd drifted into cocaine and gambling, and maybe even before that. Most evenings I was out of the house until past midnight and most mornings I snuck out without saying a word to anyone. I guess I was hiding from them. I felt dirty and had gotten paranoid that my little girls would see how dirty I had become. I couldn't deal with that, so I hid from them.

Melissa and Courtney were six and four when I was arrested. Now they were fourteen and twelve and I had almost no memories of them. I couldn't even imagine what they looked like now – I could barely even remember what they looked like back then. Just about the only good memories I had were of Courtney's first birthday.

I had no chance of ever reconciling with Elaine. Thinking otherwise was a pipe dream, and thinking that I could get back into my girls' lives was an even bigger pipe dream. Elaine was right. I blew whatever chance I had with my girls and in no way did I deserve another, not after all the things I'd done. Not with all the baggage and bodies and damage dragging behind me.

Melissa and Courtney didn't deserve that. I guess at some level I had known that for a long time.

It was funny, but my reason for driving up was to give Elaine the six grand and to talk her into letting my parents see my kids. I screwed up on both fronts. Seeing her, I just started kidding myself, and then once she just started pushing my buttons, I guess I had to start pushing hers also. That was the thing with the two of us, we knew how to push each other's buttons.

Elaine and I had known each other since we were in grade school; she was my first and only girlfriend and we were married at nineteen, and now we were nothing more than strangers. It made me sick inside to realize how tightly her heart had closed to me. I hadn't seen her for almost eight years, but as soon as I did I realized I still had feelings for her. I knew how tough things had to have been making it on her own these past eight years. She had no other family, no one but the girls. An older brother had died in Vietnam and her dad never quite got over that and died of either a broken heart or a heart attack (take your pick) when she was in high school. Her mom got sick after that and lingered long enough to see us get married. She had some uncles and aunts in other states, but I knew she wasn't close to any of them. I wish she had stayed close to my parents, but I wasn't going to cause her any more grief, especially after everything I'd put her through.

When she started walking out of the coffee shop I realized how I needed to give my life meaning. I know this will sound corny, but it became so clear to me – I had to live in a way that Melissa and Courtney could be proud of. Also, just as importantly, I needed to support my girls and Elaine. Whatever I could do financially I was going to do. I made up my mind then. I would throw away the pension papers. Whatever money I was going to make, I would make honestly. And I would send Elaine and my girls whatever I could. In my heart I made a promise to my girls that that was what I was going to do.

I still badly wanted to see Melissa and Courtney; even if it was only for five minutes. If for no other reason than so I could tell them how sorry I was. How they deserved so much better. But again, what good would it do them? Probably just screw them up.

Fuck it.

It was three in the afternoon by the time I arrived at Bradley Memorial Hospital. I checked at the front desk and got Manny's room number. He had a private room and I could see him – or at least what had to have been him – lying on a bed. Manny used to be a thick, heavy man with skin like hard rubber. What was lying on that bed was a third of what Manny had once been. It was almost like a balloon that had been mostly deflated. And that thick rug of black hair he had was gone. But it was his eyes that got me. They weren't the same hard ruthless eyes that I used to know. Instead they were the eyes of a scared and frightened man. I was about to walk in when I heard Phil's voice coming from a corner. I froze for a moment and then peeked in and saw Phil sitting off to the side of Manny. He was reading Manny the Bible, his voice droning softly over the hum of medical equipment. And Manny was giving him full attention, his eyes wide open and scared to death. Neither of them saw me and I moved quickly away from the doorway. My heart was beating like a rabbit's.

A nurse was about to enter the room. I stopped her.

'I was hoping you could help me out,' I said, my voice barely above a whisper. 'I need to talk privately with Manny. We're old friends but it's personal business and it's important. Could you find me in the cafeteria when he's alone?'

She looked like she wanted to bolt and could barely look me in the eye, but she nodded and muttered 'okay'.

I was in a daze as I made my way to the hospital cafeteria. I couldn't believe what I saw in there – that image of Manny listening attentively to the Bible, his eyes wide open and brimming with fear. Jesus Christ! That wasn't the Manny I knew. The Manny I knew would've been flipping Phil the bird and pulling out his catheter to piss on him if he could reach that far. I understood why Dan was so damned worried about him spilling his guts.

The Manny I used to know was the most ruthless sonofabitch I'd ever met. He had moved to Vermont from the Bronx when he was in his early twenties and he was like a piranha in a tank full of guppies. At the time I was arrested, he had his hands in every crooked, amoral business that went on in Vermont. Drugs, gambling, prostitution, loan sharking, extortion – you name it, Manny had his fat hands in it. And he had no problem taking care of the dirty part of the business himself. I don't think he enjoyed it – he wasn't a crazy sicko like his son – but he had no problem with it.

One time a big shot from New York tried to muscle in on Manny and open up escort services around a few of the ski resorts. This guy, I think his name was Wally Sneck, or something like that, made the mistake of showing up in Vermont to check out one of his businesses. Manny got wind of it, had me show up and put cuffs on Sneck, and drag him to the basement of one of Manny's clubs. I thought Manny was going to just scare him, but hell no. Manny ended up giving him a couple of hard kicks to the mouth. He checked to see whether there were any front teeth left, saw that there were, and kicked him a couple of more times until they were knocked out. I don't think he enjoyed it, but I know it didn't bother him either. It was simply business. In any case, Sneck sold his escort services that night to Manny for a buck.

His son, Manny Jr, was a different story. Junior was a sadistic psychopath. Manny had sent me on a collection job once with Junior. At the time Junior was seventeen and I think what Manny wanted was to give his kid some experience and to have me there in case there were problems. The guy we were collecting from was just some poor sap, and he was crapping in his pants when we cornered him one night in a parking lot. He would have paid up right away, but before I realized what was happening, Junior had taken a lead pipe to the guy's knees. He got several whacks in before I was able to pull him off. I could tell that crazy bastard enjoyed every second of it. That was the one and only time I was willing to go out on a job with him. Over the years I'd heard other stories regarding Junior – pretty bizarre stuff, and I wouldn't bet against any of them being true.

When I got to the cafeteria, I bought a cup of coffee and sat down. I now knew there was a good chance Manny would confess all to Phil and I would end up going away for a long time, maybe even life if Manny could sell that I had killed Ferguson. And as Dan had pointed out, I wouldn't be spending my days in a county jail in Bradley, but some hardcore maximum-security prison God knows where. Panic started to overtake me. I felt a tightening in my chest and could barely breathe. I knew I couldn't spend any more time locked away. It was tough enough sitting out the last seven years in county jail and spending my days realizing how badly I had wasted my life.

Crazy thoughts flooded my head, thoughts of running and suicide and other things I wouldn't want to mention. If Elaine knew me as well as she thought she did I would've driven to some quiet spot, put a gun in my mouth, and ended it right then and there. Because that would've been the easy way out. But I wasn't going to take the easy way out. I didn't know what I was going to do but it wasn't going to be that.

Running wouldn't do any good either. Even with the sixty-five hundred dollars that Dan gave me I wouldn't be able to run far enough. Eventually they'd catch up with me. And even if I could, what would I be running to? A drifting, meaningless existence? Going back on the promise I'd just made my girls? No, running wasn't an option. Neither was suicide. But I was going to have to do something, because I wasn't going to live out my days in prison.

At one point I could feel that I was being stared at. To my left, a few tables over, a family of four sat. They were all large boned, heavy and unattractive. All of them were glaring in my direction. The father was a few years older than me, and along with the mother there was a teenage son and a pre-teen daughter. From the physical resemblance, I knew they were the family of the boy whose arm I shattered. I stared back at them until they left their table. Then I went back to my brooding.

I was deep in some dark thoughts when I realized someone was standing near me. I looked up and saw it was the nurse from before. She was a small, mousy woman in her mid-thirties, with thinning brown hair and large nervous eyes. She was trying to clear her throat to get my attention.

I looked up at her and forced a smile.

'Mr Vassey's company has left,' she told me.

'Thank you. I appreciate your helping me like this.'

'I… I should be getting back to work.' She stood awkwardly for a moment and looked like what she really wanted was for me to invite her to sit down. I wasn't feeling up to visiting Manny yet so I asked if I could buy her a cup of coffee.

'I really should be getting back.' She could barely meet my eyes, but she didn't seem overly anxious to walk away.

I stood up and pulled a chair out for her. 'Come on,' I said, forcing a bigger smile. 'Why don't you take a five-minute break and join me?'

She hesitated for a moment but she sat down. 'I guess I can take a short break,' she admitted, showing a tiny smile.

I asked her how she took her coffee and whether she wanted anything else, maybe a Danish or doughnut, but all she wanted was the coffee. I got up and bought her a cup and also ended up buying her a piece of chocolate cake that looked edible.

I brought the coffee and cake back to the table and sat across from her. She murmured out a 'thank you', and glanced up at me while she sipped her drink. I noticed she was looking uneasily at my scratches.

'I walked into a tree branch last night and got a little scratched up,' I said.

I could tell from the change in her expression that she believed me. The scratches obviously weren't made by a tree branch, but if you want to believe something, you'll believe it. She mentioned how I needed to be more careful and I agreed with her.

'By the way,' I said as I held out my hand, 'my name's Joe Denton. I'm happy to meet you.'

She hesitated before taking my hand. Her own hand was small and disappeared in mine. Even though she looked a bit mousy and her hair was too thin, she had some nice features. Especially her eyes when they weren't nervous. They were a soft hazel color and were nice to look at.

'I'm Charlotte Boyd,' she said in a muted voice.

We had shaken hands longer than we should have. I made the first move to let go.

'I've lived in Bradley my whole life and never knew any Boyds,' I said, still forcing my smile. 'Are you from around here?'

'I moved here from Montreal three years ago,' she said. She no longer had any problem meeting my eyes.

'I've never been to Montreal. I'll have to go someday. Let me guess, you're French?'

'No,' she said, 'and it's not very nice up there if you're not. I moved to Montreal after college. I grew up in Toronto.'

'Toronto and Montreal, huh? And now you're in the middle of nowhere. Well, anyway, how do you like Bradley?'

'I like it.' She looked away from me, her tiny smile gone. 'It's fine.'

She had no engagement or wedding ring on. My guess was she

was unattached and probably as lonely as I was. 'I know, Bradley's a small town. It probably takes getting used to after cities like Montreal and Toronto,' I said. 'So you're Manny's nurse?'

She nodded. 'He's one of my patients.' She lowered her voice. 'Mr Vassey is not doing well. His cancer is at an advanced stage.'

'I know. Oh well, what can you do?' I shook my head sadly and then hesitated for a moment. 'Was that Phil Coakley I saw in there with Manny?'

'I believe so, yes. Mr Coakley visits every day. He seems like a nice man. It's a shame what happened to his face.'

I could tell from her expression that she didn't mean anything by her comment. She had no idea that I was the cause of that shame. I guess she hadn't read the papers the other day.

I muttered something under my breath about agreeing with her how much of a shame it was. I glanced at my watch and saw it was almost four.

'I better get up there and see Manny while I got the chance,' I said.

She lowered her glance from me. 'It was nice meeting you, Joe.' She spoke so quietly I could barely hear her.

'Same here, Charlotte. I hope it didn't sound like I was giving you the third degree before with all my questions. I used to be a police officer and some habits die hard. But it was nice meeting you. Maybe we'll bump into each other again.'

'I didn't mind your questions at all.'

'Well, that's good. I'll see you around.'

I started towards the elevator and stopped to give her a friendly wave. She seemed somewhat startled by it, but gave me a wave back and her soft hazel eyes held steady as they met mine.

I found Manny alone when I got to his room. His eyes were partially open but he seemed to be sleeping. It would've been so easy to grab a pillow and end it right there. I wondered briefly whether at this stage they'd bother with an autopsy. But I knew they would. Phil would hear that I was in the hospital asking about Manny and he would demand one. And even if nobody mentioned anything about me being there, Phil would still suspect that I was involved and demand the autopsy anyway.

I could see Manny was on oxygen and there were intravenous tubes stuck in his arms. One of the tubes was connected to a morphine drip. As I was studying it, I heard Manny stir.

'Who's there?' he asked.

I pulled up a chair and sat down next to him. 'How you doing, Manny, it's been a long time.'

He stared at me and blinked several times before he recognized me. 'They let you out already? Too bad,' he noted without much enthusiasm.

'A damn shame,' I said, agreeing with him. 'You're looking better these days. You finally find a diet that works? Good for you.'

'What you talking about? I got cancer. I'm dying. They give me a month, two months tops.'

'I heard about your condition, Manny. I'm sorry.' I moved closer to him and lowered my voice. 'And I was sorry to hear that you reneged on our agreement and took every dime Elaine had.'

He flashed me a nasty smile and it was the first time I recognized him as the Manny of old. I had seen that smile dozens of times before after he had screwed someone. The smile all but said *what are you going to do about it, cocksucker?*

'Joe,' he said, still showing that smile, 'you were on the books for over a hundred large. I took less than twenty out of her. You're lucky I didn't make her work her ass off for the rest of your balance. Besides, you made me make that deal under duress.'

He turned from me, his smile fading. 'What do you want?' he asked.

'I just wanted to see an old friend.'

'You're full of crap.'

'Okay, I want to know why you're lying here every goddam day listening to Phil Coakley read you the Bible.'

'How's that your business?'

'It's my business when Phil's bragging to me that he's going to convert you to Christ and have you confess all so he can put me away.'

That comment should have enraged Manny, at least it would've enraged the old Manny. This one just stared at me blankly, his shriveled face sagging into his pillow.

'Well, Manny, you see why it's my business?'

His eyes wavered and he looked away from me. 'He gives me comfort,' he said at last.

I just gawked at him, incredulous. 'What the hell are you saying? That you've found religion? That you're going to confess all your sins so you can go to heaven? You realize how ridiculous that sounds? Damn it, Manny, is that what you're saying?'

'I'm not saying nothing. I'm not going to rat anyone. But even if I did, what difference would it make? It can't be used in court. It's hearsay.'

'You're a lawyer now? I got news for you, Manny, a deathbed confession is an exception to the hearsay rule. Any confession you make can be used in court regardless of how dead and buried you are. I don't know what crap Phil is filling you up with, but he's bullshitting you.'

'I'm not going to rat,' he said, but he couldn't look me in the eye. I knew he was lying. His mouth screwed up as if he were about to start bawling. 'I'm a dying man, Joe. What do you want from me?'

'I want you to keep your mouth shut. If you talk, it's not just me. You'll end up putting a lot of people away, including your own son. I guarantee you Junior would go away for a long time.'

He gave me a look right then that told me he'd already made a deal. The look only flashed on his face for a second, but it told me everything. If he talks Junior gets protected.

'I don't feel good, Joe. Why don't you get out of here.'

I leaned very close to him. 'Look, Manny,' I whispered into his ear, 'I kept my mouth shut for the last seven years while I sat in jail. I could've talked and put you away with me. Right now you'd be rotting in a prison hospital if I hadn't kept quiet.'

'Yeah, so?'

'So? Goddam it, Manny, confessing your sins to Phil won't change anything. You're still going to end up burning in hell.'

'No I won't,' he argued stubbornly.

From behind me I heard a loud voice booming, 'Hey, Pop, who's that with you?' I turned and saw Manny Jr with what must have been two of his sons. Junior had grown to look a lot like his dad used to; a heavy, thick man with a complexion like chipped glass and a hardness about him. His two boys were probably under seven but both looked like miniature versions of him. Junior stood staring at me for a long moment before he recognized me. Then a vicious smile crept onto his face.

'Hey, look what the cat dragged in here. Joe Denton, what the hell are you doing here?'

'Old business with your dad.'

'Yeah, well, I think your business is over. Don't let the door hit you too hard on the way out.'

He started towards me, his smile stretching until his lips nearly disappeared. I got up and walked close to him. 'You and me have business,' I said. 'Star Diner out in Chesterville. Meet me there at seven.'

'Nah,' he said. 'Why don't you meet me at the house. I got a new game room in the basement. We can have some fun.'

'I don't think so. Star Diner at seven. You better be there, Junior.'

I turned back and told Manny I'd be seeing him, and then I walked out of there.

Chapter 8

It was twenty past seven and I was halfway through my turkey hotplate special before Junior showed up. He had a couple of thugs with him; hard humorless types who used to work for his dad. Junior spotted me at my booth, leered in my direction, and came over and sat down. The diner was mostly empty and his two thugs sat at an empty booth near by.

'Hey, what's going on, Joe?' he said. 'You invite me to dinner and you start without me? Don't you got no etiquette?'

He signaled the waitress over. 'Sweetheart,' he said, 'bring me a steak, well done, and a glass of wine, something red.'

'We offer Chianti, Cabernet and Merlot by the glass, sir. Which would you prefer?' she asked.

'Whichever's better, your choice, sweetheart. Just make sure it's your best.'

He waited until she left and then turned to me. 'I try to drink more red wine these days.' Then lower and more surly, 'I don't appreciate you trying to order me around, Joe, but it's been a while and I figure I give you a break for old time's sake. What business you and me got?'

I took my time chewing and swallowing my food before telling him that I needed to talk to him about Manny.

'Yeah, what about Pop?'

'Why are you letting Phil Coakley work on him?'

'I don't know what you're talking about.'

'You don't know Phil is visiting your dad every day?'

'Yeah, so?'

'So? Phil was bragging to me that he's going to put the fear of God in your dad and squeeze a confession out of him.'

Junior gave me a slight smile. 'Let him try. Pop's no rat. He's not going to talk.'

'I think you're wrong there.'

'I think you better shut up.'

His leer had shifted into something more violent. I took a deep breath and let it out slowly. 'Look, Junior,' I said, 'I think we've got a real problem here.'

'I don't think we got any problem. Pop's not going to rat anyone. You don't need to worry about nothing.' He leaned forward, a glint in his eyes. 'And I never liked you calling me Junior. Got it?'

I sighed. 'Sure. Manny. All you have to do is send your dad to a hospital out of state, maybe to Boston or New York. Your dad will get better care and we won't have to worry about Phil trying to trick him into a confession.'

Junior was shaking his head. 'I can't do that,' he said. 'Pop wants to stay put. He don't want to go nowhere.' He rubbed a thick hand over his jaw and showed me an embarrassed smile. 'Besides,' he said, 'I like having him close by.'

'You could send him back to the Bronx. He must have old friends and family there.'

'Nah, I told you, he don't want to go nowhere.'

'Then keep Phil out of your dad's room. Don't let him visit.'

'Yeah, well, I can't do that either. Those visits are helping my pop's spirit. It makes him feel good. Besides, it don't matter. Pop's not going say a word to him.'

'How do you know that?'

''Cause I know.'

'You talk to your dad about what he's planning to do?'

A glint of violence was back in his eyes. 'I don't know what point you're trying to make.'

'That if your dad talks you're going to get hurt too. Even if he made a deal with Phil not to prosecute you, you'll still get hurt. All of your businesses will be shut down. And I guarantee you all your money will be taken away. Besides, I doubt Phil would bother honoring a deal. My bet would be as soon as your dad's dead, you'll get prosecuted along with everyone else.'

The waitress came over with his glass of wine. Junior sat frozen as she placed it in front of him. He waited until she had walked away before telling me that he'd take any bet I wanted to make.

'You got yourself such a great track record making winning bets,' he said. 'Me and Pops used to get a good laugh out of your losing streak. You couldn't win a bet to save your life.'

'I'm glad I was able to amuse both of you,' I said. 'But it doesn't change the fact your dad's telling me about hearsay exclusions and other things he doesn't have a clue about. The only way he could possibly have heard about any of that stuff was from Phil. His new buddy is trying to sell him a ticket to heaven, filling him up with a bunch of crap about how he can cleanse his soul with a deathbed confession that can't be used in court.'

'Pop tell you that?'

'Just about.'

Junior's eyes dulled a bit as he thought over what I said. Then he shook his head. 'No fucking way. You're delusional. Your stint in jail made you soft in the head, Joe. There's no way Pop's saying a word to nobody. No fucking way. And I'm getting sick of you saying otherwise. I came here tonight 'cause of old times and you're going to give me this shit?'

Junior pointed a thick, stubby finger at me and lowered his

voice. 'You know what pisses me off about you? You think you're so goddam smart. If you're so brilliant how come you ended up in jail? If it was me, there's no way I walk out of that building with Coakley still breathing. You do something that stupid and you're going to start questioning me?'

'I wasn't questioning you, I'm just trying—'

'Yeah, well, shut up. From now on I'm doing the questioning and you're doing the answering, understand? And first thing I want to know about is an old friend of ours that I'll call Billy F. Do you remember Billy F.?'

I didn't say anything.

'Billy F., come on, think back. You were supposed to collect thirty grand from him. Remember him yet?'

'I was never sent to collect from Ferguson.'

'That's not what Pop says.'

'I don't give a shit what your pop says.'

'Not a good attitude, Joe.'

'This is what the two of you cooked up, huh?'

'I don't know what the fuck you're talking about. All I know is what Pop told me. That, and that Billy F. emptied out an IRA account before seeing you. Oh yeah, one other thing, we never got a dime of our money.'

'Fuck you.'

'Not a good attitude, Joe, 'cause I'm putting you on the hook for the thirty grand. For old time's sake, I'll give you a break on the interest. Five percent a week. First payment due Wednesday. That gives you four days. And I want at least three grand. You know Jamie and Duane over there?'

Junior waved a hand in the direction of his two thugs. Jamie, who was sitting closer to me, winked. Duane paid no attention and sat as still as a granite block.

'They'll be collecting from you,' Junior went on. 'But being as we're old friends I'll give you another break. You got a twenty-grand line of credit if you want to place any bets. Hey, a couple of good picks and we'll be even by Sunday night. What do you say, want to take any action this weekend?'

Junior showed me an ugly smile and then he started laughing. After a while I joined him.

'Yeah, what's so funny?' he said.

'That you think you're going to collect a dime from me,' I said when I could.

'Don't worry. I'll be collecting it.'

That just made me laugh harder.

'Jamie and Duane are tougher than those two boys you put in the hospital,' he said.

'You heard about that, huh? Well, they might be but you sure as hell aren't. They come after me and I'll be seeing you afterwards.'

Junior's mouth twitched. He sat frozen, breathing hard, his black eyes shining with malice.

'What's to stop me right now from taking you out of here and driving you someplace private?' he asked.

'Well,' I said, 'I guess us being old friends and all.'

He didn't say anything. He just sat staring at me and breathing hard.

'And I guess because if I were to disappear you'd be going away to prison for a long time.'

'Pop told me about your so-called safety deposit box. I think you're bluffing.'

'There's only one way to find out.'

The waitress came over with his dinner. After she put it in front of him, Manny called her back. 'Hey, darling,' he said, 'I kind of lost my appetite. Why don't you wrap this up for me.'

He waited until she went back to the kitchen before standing up. 'You keep away from Pop, understand? He's a sick man, he don't need your shit. If I hear anything about you bothering him again, I promise I'll call your bluff. And don't worry, Joe, you'll be hearing from my boys Wednesday. And you'll be paying up. One way or another I'll be collecting from you.'

'I'll be looking forward to it,' I said.

'You think you're so fucking smart.' He shook his head. He started walking towards the counter and his two thugs got up to join him. The waitress came out of the kitchen with his steak wrapped up and he took it from her.

'Thanks, darling,' he said, 'dinner's on my buddy sitting over there.' One of his thugs, Jamie, got a chuckle out of that. I watched as the three of them left the diner, got into a Range Rover and drove off.

I finished my dinner and then called the waitress over and asked for a piece of pecan pie with a scoop of vanilla ice cream and a cup of coffee. She was about to walk away, hesitated, and showed me an awkward smile.

'Those are some friends you've got,' she remarked.

'They sure are,' I agreed. The thought hit me that Manny and Junior and Dan Pleasant were the closest things I had to friends these days, and I started laughing. It wasn't really funny, at least not entirely, but it was something. She must have thought I was nuts.

Everything would've been solved if Junior had been willing to either move Manny out of state or to keep Phil from visiting him. But I knew no amount of convincing would change Junior's mind. It would have to be something else. I was sure Manny was working out a deal with Phil. There was no doubt about that. I wondered briefly whether Junior was in on the discussions and decided he wasn't. He enjoyed what he did too much and wouldn't want to give up what he had. When Manny confessed it would come as a surprise to him. It would probably shatter him to find out that his old man was a rat after all. At least I'd be able to get a little consolation out of that.

I wasn't too worried about his boys trying to collect from

me. I had gone out on jobs with both of them in the past, and while they were tough and vicious, they weren't used to their victims fighting back. You get somewhat spoiled when the guy you're beating is always cowering on his knees. Maybe I'd surprise them – take one of them out quickly and then deal with the other. What bothered me more was the whole setup. It smelled like something Manny would come up with to tie me to Ferguson's murder. I wondered briefly about it, but then decided it didn't matter. I had more important things to worry about and, anyway, Wednesday was a long way away. Hopefully, I'd be far from Bradley by then.

I finished my pie and ice cream and lingered somewhat over my coffee before heading out. I had only driven a mile from the diner when someone flashed their lights behind me. I looked in my rearview mirror and saw Dan Pleasant in his pickup truck waving me over. I pulled over to the side of the road and waited for him to pull up behind me. He got out of his truck, casually walked to my passenger side, rapped on the window, and then opened the door and sat inside.

'Why don't you drive around,' he said.

I shifted the car into first gear and pulled back onto the road. 'How'd you know where to find me?' I asked.

Out of the corner of my eye I could see Dan smiling pleasantly. 'One of my deputies, Hal Wheely, spotted you sitting in the Star Diner with Junior and gave me a call. I've been waiting out here close to a half-hour for you to finish up. I'll tell you, Joe, that was an interesting situation you got yourself into last night. The police report read like a bad Hollywood script. I would've thought you'd try to be smarter and keep a low profile.'

'It was just one of those things,' I said.

'Just one of those things?' Dan chuckled softly. 'I guess that's one way of describing it. So tell me, Joe, did it happen the way you said it?'

'Yeah, pretty much.'

He seemed somewhat amused as he studied the area where I had been scratched. 'Looks like she did a pretty good job on you,' he said.

'It's not too bad. I'll live.'

'I can just picture it.' He chuckled again. 'Little Clara Coakley luring you with her nice ass and small tits and you falling for it hook, line and sinker. Even with her small tits she's a good-looking girl, but let me explain the ropes to you. You're forty, a disgraced ex-cop, a felon, no job, no prospects, and at best average looking. There're not too many twenty-something-year-old girls, especially attractive ones like Clara, who'd have any interest in you.'

'Thanks for the pep talk. Did one of your deputies spot her car parked near my parents'?'

'What do you think, Joe?'

'Pretty much that.'

'After those two boys were brought to the emergency ward, the hospital called my office. Our DA friend should have called me also, but I guess it slipped his mind. Any case, I dragged myself out of a warm bed for you, Joe. I visited your Bradley police station, read the police report, and thought I'd help clear the matter up quickly. Let me tell you what I was hoping. That you'd be smart enough to make a deal with our DA friend. Nothing outrageous, just something fair like you don't file charges against his little girl and he leaves sleeping dogs lie. Or in our case, cancer-ridden dogs. Tell me you did that.'

'I thought about it, but no, I didn't.'

'Damn it!' He punched the dashboard. His face screwed up into a snarl, the type you'd see on a wounded animal. Just as quickly it was gone and his pleasant smile was back. He sighed, still smiling pleasantly, 'Joe, Joe, Joe. Why didn't you do that? I really thought you'd be smart enough to do that.'

'Because it wouldn't have done any good,' I said.

'I think it could've done a lot of good.'

'No, it wouldn't. He would've brought charges against his daughter without blinking an eye. If I had offered him a deal it would have only made him dig harder. Besides, he knows no jury around here would convict her.'

Dan thought over what I said and shook his head. 'I think you're outguessing yourself. You're probably right about Clara walking with nothing but a slap on her pretty behind, but it would still be a nasty business and I don't think he'd want to put her through that. Why don't you do us both a favor and visit Coakley tomorrow and threaten to press charges against Clara.'

'Trust me, I was there with Phil last night. I saw the way he was taking it. If I tried suggesting a deal, he'd bring me up on obstruction of justice charges.'

'Well, Joe,' he said, 'you know that I like to play the percentages. I thought this would be a simpler and less risky way to resolve our problem, but it's your call. As long as you resolve it, I'm satisfied. I have to tell you, though, time is ticking away. I'd really like to see our problem resolved with Plan A, but I'm afraid I might have to go to Plan B soon.'

'I wasn't bluffing years ago when I told you about my safety deposit box.'

'I didn't think you were.'

'You'll do jail time if anything happens to me.'

'I know I will.' He gave a heavy sigh. 'But, Joe, as I told you before, I like to play the percentages. If Manny talks, which I consider a certainty, I'll go away for a very long time. From what you've told me about the contents of your safety deposit box, I think the only thing that can hurt me is that tape. I've talked to a lawyer and I'm pretty sure your journal won't be able to cause me too much damage. Some, but not much. In any case, purely from a percentage point of view, I'm better off with that scenario than with Manny talking. From a personal point of view, I'd hate to do it. I like you, Joe, and I'm not terribly fond of either our DA or Manny.'

'And you think you can get away with murdering me?'

He made a sour face and shrugged. 'Again, I'd hate to go in that direction, but yes, I think so. You get picked up by my deputies, a struggle ensues, and then we have the inevitable outcome.'

'And you've had practice with that.'

'Joe, I'm not saying one way or the other.'

'You're not thinking clearly,' I said. 'If I were to drop dead right now it wouldn't stop Phil from trying to coax a confession out of Manny.'

Dan was still smiling pleasantly, but his smile seemed frozen on his face. 'I'm playing the percentages with that also. I think if you're out of the picture, Coakley will let things drop. I might be wrong. We'll see. On another subject, you visit Manny yet?'

I nodded.

'And did you reach the same opinion as me – that he's about to screw us?'

'I saw him while Phil was reading him the Bible. You're right, he's not the Manny I used to know. He's a scared man who's trying to bargain his way into heaven. My guess, he's trying to work out a deal with his lawyer to protect Junior.'

'Sonofabitch!' Dan exploded. 'I saw Harold Grayson a few days ago and he couldn't look me in the eye. Damn, I should've known better. Joe, as a friend, I'm telling you to make a choice and get it over with. Manny or Coakley, either one. Just get it done. Time's running out, understand?'

I didn't say anything.

He took a deep breath and let it out loudly. 'Even without Plan B, I know you wouldn't want to spend the rest of your days in prison. So act smart now, okay? If you don't think you can make a deal with our DA friend, then choose between them and get it done.'

We drove in silence for a while. I turned my car around and headed back to his pickup truck. He let out another heavy sigh and asked me about my dinner with Junior.

'I thought I could talk sense into that psycho. All he has to do is either move his old man out of state or keep Phil from visiting him, but he won't consider it. According to Junior, his old man's not a rat and that's all there is to it.'

'I could've saved you the trouble. I tried talking to Junior a few weeks ago. He's not right in the head. And he's certainly a one hundred percent certifiable psycho. Of course, that's nothing we didn't already know.'

'He could barely control himself when I pushed him about Manny confessing,' I said.

'I can imagine that.' His eyes crinkled with amusement. 'Junior's got some complex concerning his old man. You should see it, Joe, if Manny so much as raises his voice to him or reprimands him, Junior goes pale as a sheet. Probably wets himself also. He's not capable of standing up to Manny about anything, especially questioning who can visit him or where he's going to live out his final days. If it were that simple, I would've taken care of this weeks ago.'

I decided it wouldn't be a good idea to mention about Junior siccing his thugs on me to collect thirty grand. Instead I told him how Junior had invited me to his basement to show me a new game room.

'He did that, huh?' Dan said, laughing slightly.

'Yep.'

'I guess for him it probably is a game room,' he said.

'What's he got down there?'

'Junior's built himself a soundproof room with two items in it; a butcher's table and a furnace.'

Dan rubbed a hand across his eyes. I glanced over and saw that his smile had faded. He looked different, weary, his boyish features gone.

'Manny's been sick for about a year now,' he said. 'He was always a ruthless, tough bastard, but he was sane and his bottom line was business. You could work with him. Since Junior's taken over, it's been different. The guy's a sadistic nut job who gets off on showing the world what a badass he is. Money's secondary with him. If I didn't have to worry about consequences with Manny, I would've taken Junior into the woods months ago and put a bullet in his head.'

Dan stopped to push a hand through his hair and scratch the back of his head. When he looked back at me, he gave me a faint, almost apologetic smile.

'Let me tell you about this special room he built,' he continued. 'This college kid up in Burlington was supposedly manufacturing and distributing crystal meth without Junior's blessing. A few months ago this kid disappears without a trace, and then a rumor starts circulating about Junior's special room and how Junior had this college kid brought there and tied to the butcher's table. According to the rumor, Junior chopped the kid up with a meat cleaver and burned the body parts in the furnace. I had to investigate it. Even though I knew it could end up biting me in the ass with Manny, I had to look into it. So I got a search warrant and sure enough I found a soundproof room with nothing in it but a butcher's table and a furnace. Forensics went over it with a fine-tooth comb but Junior must have scrubbed it clean.'

'And you would've arrested Junior if you found anything?'

'I would've had to,' he said. 'I know this must sound out of character for me, but I would've had to take my chances with Manny. Some things you just can't ignore. But I promise you this; when Manny checks out Junior will be following close behind.'

I had gotten back to Dan's truck. I swung a quick U-turn and pulled up behind it.

He turned to me and placed a hand on my arm in a brotherly sort of way. His pleasant smile was back on, but it didn't quite erase the weariness around his eyes. 'Look, Joe,' he said, 'I know it's been almost eight years. As a friend I've taken care of things. Go to Kelley's, have yourself a good time.'

He started to get out of my car but stopped and faced me again. 'You've got two days left, Joe. Take care of it, okay?'

I half heard myself asking how I was supposed to get to Manny while he was being monitored twenty-four hours a day in the hospital.

'You're a smart man, think of something. If you can't there's always our DA friend.'

'If anything happens to Phil I'm the first guy they'll go after,' I said.

He stared at me for what seemed like minutes. 'Worst case get yourself a hunting rifle and wait outside his door Monday night. I'll make sure my boys bungle the investigation.'

I knew he was lying. I also knew the Bradley police would take charge of any murder within the city limits. If the Bradley police got a strong whiff that I was involved, which they would, then his deputies would step in and take care of me. Maybe he wouldn't even take that chance and would have his deputies waiting near by to deal with me on the spot. He was simply improvising on Plan B where Phil and I both ended up dead.

As he was getting into his truck, I yelled out to him, asking him what Manny had on him. He ignored my question. Before driving off he rolled down his window and gave me a half-hearted wave.

I sat in my car numb. I don't think I ever felt the level of despair that I felt right then. Not even after my sentencing. Not even after Elaine had dumped me and had my divorce papers delivered by courier while I sat locked away in jail. I felt like I could barely move, as if all my strength had bled out of me.

The other day when I left jail I was determined not to cause any more damage in my life. But that was short lived. In less than a day I put two boys in the hospital and God knows what I did to Clara Coakley. And now all I could think about was murder. Because Dan was right, that was the only way out, or at least the only way out I could see. It had to be Manny or Phil. The problem was I didn't see any way to get to Manny and I'd already done so much damage to Phil. The idea of doing any more just made me weaker.

At that moment, sitting in my car, I don't think I ever felt lower in my life. It all seemed so pointless. If I had a gun I probably would've used it. And during that moment of great despair all I could think about was Kelley's; as if they could offer me some sort of salvation. At least help me get through the next few hours.

Chapter 9

Kelley's was in the middle of nowhere, sitting on the edge of Bradley off Route Six. It was maybe eighty yards from the road and if you didn't know it was there you'd probably pass by without realizing it. Even if you did see the building you wouldn't know what it was. And that was the way it was supposed to be. Nothing about the concrete exterior would give you any idea what went on inside. As long as they made their monthly payoffs and kept things quiet, the local police and sheriff's office left them alone. My guess was there were a good number of people who'd lived in Bradley their whole lives and didn't know Kelley's existed.

Before my arrest I used to spend a lot of time at Kelley's. It was a good place to hang out. Good music, good booze, and an easy source for cocaine. Most nights I'd just sit and talk to Earl and not even pay attention to what was happening onstage. All the time I spent there, I never once ventured out of the main club area. I never went into the back rooms or took any of the girls up on their offers. I guess back then I was just looking for ways to stay out of the house and Kelley's was as good as any.

I ended up driving past its entranceway several times before I found it. It was dark and it had been a while, but eventually I found the narrow dirt path that made up its driveway. The parking lot was less than half full, which was slow for a Saturday night. A biker type guarding the door gave me the once-over as I made my way in, but didn't say anything. There was no cover charge at Kelley's. They had plenty of ways to take money off you without needing a cover charge.

I saw Earl working the bar. Earl owned the place and most nights doubled as bartender and bouncer. He looked like a lot of bikers I've known – a big bald-headed guy with a mustache and goatee and thick arms that were decorated with tattoos. He did a double take when he saw me.

'Holy shit,' he said. 'Joe, Joe Denton. Howya doin', man? Get over here!'

I took a seat at the bar and we shook hands. He had added a couple of tattoos to the side of his neck and a necklace tattoo made up of intertwined serpents that went around his collarbone. He gave me a big grin.

'Shit, it's been a long fucking time. You surviving okay on the outside, man?'

I was going to give him some bullshit answer but I was feeling too low for that. 'It's been rough,' I admitted.

'Yeah, I hear you.' He gave me a sympathetic nod. Lowering his voice, 'You need anything? Coke?'

I hadn't thought about drugs until that moment, but as soon as he mentioned coke I found myself weakening. A couple of lines would help clear my head and put me in a better mood. It scared me to realize how badly I wanted to do some lines right then. It was a struggle, but I shook my head. Almost as if it were a dream I heard myself tell him no thanks.

He seemed somewhat surprised, but nodded. 'Hey, man, you change your mind, let me know. At least let me buy you a drink. What will you have?'

'Just a beer,' I said.

'You got it, buddy.'

He opened a bottle of imported ale that I used to drink

exclusively and handed it to me, still showing a friendly grin. Bob Seger's 'Her Strut' was blasting out behind me. I turned around and saw a slender, dark-haired girl onstage naked except for garter belts and high-heeled shoes. She was moving quickly to the music, but stopped to squat down so that an overweight slob signaling with a dollar bill could have a better look. The dollar bill was slipped into one of her garter belts and she held her position for a few more seconds before moving off. Vermont's a topless-only state, but the rules for the most part were ignored at Kelley's.

'We've got a new crop of girls since you've been here last. That's Cindy on stage. Man, I tell you, she could hurt you.'

I looked around the room. There were maybe a dozen guys sitting around the stage and another ten scattered at tables. I didn't spot anyone I knew. I took a long drink of my ale and then turned back to Earl. 'You're still playing good music,' I said.

'Yeah, what can I tell you? I'm stuck in the early eighties. The girls, man, they're constantly giving me shit about playing their own music for their sets. Fuck that. I'm playing what I want to listen to. But for you, any request – just name it.'

'Seger's good,' I said. 'I wouldn't mind listening to some ZZ Top. Creedence. Maybe some Stones. Dire Straits.'

'You got it, man.' He gave me a sheepish look. 'Shit, you were gone for a long time. How'd you spend your time while locked up?'

'I thought a lot, read a lot, and played a lot of checkers. I just kept trying to make it to the next day.'

'I hear you.' He pointed a thumb at my gut. 'Man, I'll tell you, you look like you got out of jail in great shape.'

'I did five hundred pushups and two thousand sit-ups every day.'

He cocked an eyebrow, not quite believing me. 'Five hundred pushups at one time?'

'Five sets, one hundred pushups and four hundred sit-ups to a set.'

We both turned and watched the dancer finish her last song. When I turned back to Earl, I could see his eyes brighten. 'What about those Pats, huh?' he asked. 'Who'd ever thought they'd win a Super Bowl?'

'I never would've guessed it,' I said.

'You get to watch the game?'

'Yeah, the warden loaned me a thirteen-inch black-and-white set. The reception wasn't too good but I was able to make it out.'

'Man, that sucks having to watch the game like that. Hey, look, I got the Super Bowl on tape. I also got a forty-two-inch plasma TV. Anytime, come over to my place and we'll watch it and have a few beers.'

'Thanks, I appreciate the offer.' I laughed. 'If I was on the outside I would've lost a bundle on that game. I never would've picked the Pats to cover.'

'Yeah? Guess what? I put twenty grand on them to win. I like to think having to pay off had something to do with that sonofabitch Vassey getting the big C. It's just too bad his punk kid didn't get it with him.'

He was still grinning but his eyes dulled and his color dropped a shade, making the blue-green ink of his tattoos stand out starkly in contrast.

'How's life been under Junior?'

'Not good, man. I'm thinking of selling out.' He started drumming his fingers hard along the bar.

He lowered his voice and edged closer to me.

'The old man was bad enough, but that punk kid of his is killing me.'

'Yeah?'

'Shit, yeah. Vassey was hitting me for fifteen hundred a week. The first thing this punk kid did when the old man goes into the hospital is bump it to thirty-five. I can't afford that, not with the police contributions I got to make. This kid is squeezing me to death. I've been having to take bigger cuts from my girls to make his payoffs, and they don't like it – I've already lost three of them because of this.' He leaned even closer to me. 'The last few months I've been talking with some of my biker buddies. I'm thinking of standing up to that punk.'

He gave me a weak shrug as he leaned back and lowered his gaze. 'But I'm not sure I want to go to war right now. Probably better to sell the place and move on. Of course, that punk is only offering me a tenth of what Kelley's is worth. I'll tell you, man, my pop would be rolling over in his grave if he saw what was happening.'

'I'd stand up to him if I were you,' I said.

'You would, huh?'

I took a long drink, finishing off the ale. 'Yeah, I would,' I said. 'I know the sheriff's office isn't too thrilled with Junior right now. I think they'd back you up on it. I think there are a lot of people around here who'd like to see Junior disappear.'

Earl thought it over, and as he did, he showed me a weak smile. 'Man, you're probably right. I don't know. I'd probably just end up seeing my place torched and some of my girls hurt. What sucks is if I sell out to that punk, he'll just drive Kelley's into the ground. My girls wouldn't stand for him.'

'Maybe you should try holding out for a while. Things might change.'

'Nothing's going to fucking change,' he spat out bitterly. 'I'm not the only one he's squeezing out. That punk's pulling the same shit with a bunch of college clubs. One of them has already sold out. He now owns the Blue Horn out in Eastfield. From what I hear he only paid twenty thou for it.'

'That's probably just Junior bragging.'

'No.' Earl shook his head, his eyes cold blue steel. 'I heard that straight from the guy who used to own it. He was lucky he could talk with the way he'd been worked over.'

'Why would Junior want to own a college club?'

'Because he's a greedy fucker. That's all there is to it, man. And it's not just one. As I was saying, he's squeezing a bunch of them.'

Earl noticed my bottle was empty and replaced it. I lifted my ale towards him. 'Well, anyway,' I said, ' here's to better days.'

Earl nodded. 'I hear you, man.'

We sat and bullshitted for a while longer before I moved to one of the tables facing the stage. There was a thin redhead who had taken her T-shirt off and was dancing topless to Creedence's 'Bad Moon Rising'. As I watched her, I found my mind wandering. I was too preoccupied wondering what interest Junior had in college clubs to pay much attention to her. It didn't seem to be in Junior's character to want to own legitimate businesses. Clubs like the Blue Horn are nothing more than hangouts for college kids. They'll bring in a band, charge cover, and sell food and soft drinks. Most of these clubs don't have liquor licenses. None of them makes much money. It didn't seem to be something that would be worth Junior's trouble. After a while I decided to give up worrying about it.

'Bad Moon Rising' ended and the redhead walked around the stage to let guys slip dollar bills in her G-string. She had nice green eyes and a sweet smile. She also didn't look much older than eighteen. Even with her mostly naked, I couldn't help thinking she seemed more like a high school cheerleader than a stripper. The DJ announced, 'Susie Q for our own little Susie,' and the Creedence song by the same name started. The redhead, Susie, slipped off her G-string and started moving rhythmically to the music. I noticed a ratty-looking guy with a thick mustache staring at her intently. He had kind of a slight to medium build, but was wearing a muscle shirt and was trying to puff himself out. Every time someone would slip a dollar bill under her garter, the muscles along his jaw would bulge. One guy let his hand linger a little too long on her thigh and Muscle-shirt started to push himself out of his chair, his body tense and his eyes filled with violence. The hand was removed, and Muscle-shirt, with what looked like a great deal of effort, forced himself back down, his eyes still seething.

When the song was over, the redhead collected the dollar bills that had been thrown onstage and then flashed a sweet smile before walking off. As soon as she was gone, Muscle-shirt left his seat and got in the face of the guy who had let his hand linger. This guy looked like a truck driver. A big burly fellow with thick ham-hock hands. At first it looked like they were going to get into it, but the big burly guy lost his nerve. Muscle-shirt had his finger in the guy's face and you could see the life just go right out of his eyes. All he wanted was to get the hell out of there. Muscle-shirt jabbed him hard in the chest with his forefinger and then walked back to his seat, more puffed up than before.

I had finished my ale and made my way back to the bar to buy another one, but Earl wouldn't take my money.

'Hey, man,' he said as he opened up another bottle for me, 'tonight it's on the house. Consider it a welcome-home party.'

'About time I had one,' I said. I accepted the ale from him and pointed a thumb at Muscle-shirt. 'What's the story there? How come you let him get away with that type of behavior?'

Earl showed an uneasy smile. 'Well, you know how it is. I like having Susie dance here. She's a sweet kid and she's nice to look at, you know? Kind of makes me feel good to have her around. If I throw the Rooster out, I think I'd lose her.'

'The Rooster, huh? That's a great name for him.'

'Yeah, it fits, don't it?' Earl made a face as if he were suffering a bad case of gas. 'I probably should have a talk with him.'

I went back to my table and watched as Earl approached Muscle-shirt. He put a hand on the guy's shoulder and moved his face so it was inches from Muscle-shirt's ear. I could tell he didn't like what he was being told. He tried to argue, but the more he did, the more pressure Earl applied to his shoulder. He seemed to be struggling to keep himself sitting straight in his chair. After a short while, Muscle-shirt shut his mouth and nodded, the muscles along his jaw bulging heavily. Earl forced a handshake out of him and then went back to the bar, giving me a wink as he went by.

The next dancer was introduced as Toni. My jaw dropped when I saw her. She couldn't have been more than five feet tall and was at most ninety pounds, but she was a knockout. Maybe the most gorgeous woman I had ever seen. Long curly black hair, big brown eyes, and lips that could stop your heart. She wasn't exposing anything for her first song, wearing a belly shirt, hot pants and high heels. The Stones' 'Angie' blasted out from the loudspeakers and as she started dancing she caught my eye and gave me a smile. Her smile did something to me. It made me feel a little funny inside. I know it sounds ridiculous, reacting that way because a stripper deemed me worthy of a smile, but that was the effect she had.

I heard someone call my name. A heavyset man in his late forties had sat down next to me and was offering me his hand. He looked somewhat familiar but I couldn't place him.

'Joe?' he asked again. 'Joe Denton?'

I shook hands with him, puzzled, trying to figure out why his small bloodshot eyes and doughy features seemed familiar.

'I'm sorry,' I said. 'Do I know you?'

'We know each other. I'm a few years older than you, but I grew up in Bradley. You were closer in age to my brother, Billy.'

I could see the resemblance then. 'I'm sorry,' I said. 'You're Scott Ferguson.'

'That's right.'

'You joined the army or something, didn't you?'

'Yep. I joined up when I was eighteen. I didn't move back here until two years after my brother's death.'

We both sat quietly for a moment and nursed our beers. It was as if everything around me at that point were a million miles away. The music, the heart-stopping little dynamo on-stage, the club, everything.

'That's a shame about what happened to your brother,' I said.

He nodded in agreement. 'You investigated Billy's murder, didn't you?'

'That's right, I did. That was a while ago, though.'

He sat silently for a long moment, brooding. Finally, he asked, 'It was brutal, wasn't it?'

'I'm sorry, yes, it was.'

'And you never had any suspects?'

'There was no physical evidence and no witnesses. No, we never had any suspects. You should probably talk with the Bradley police. I'm sure your brother's case is still open. Maybe they've found something over the years.'

'I've talked with everyone involved. You're the only person I haven't talked to yet.'

'I'm sorry, I don't know anything that could help you.'

He was staring straight at me. I could feel his small bloodshot eyes boring into me.

'Billy had taken thirty thousand dollars out of an IRA account the day he was murdered,' he stated.

'Yes, I know.'

'You do?'

'Yeah, I didn't know it at the time I was investigating your brother's murder, but the DA, Phil Coakley, mentioned it to me recently.'

'How come none of you cops bothered to check into something like that?' he asked. 'Nobody knew about Billy's IRA until I settled his estate two years after his murder. How come?'

'Again, I'm sorry. It was sloppy police work on our part. We should have found that out.'

'When did the DA mention my brother's IRA to you?'

'Yesterday.'

'Why'd he do that? You're not a cop anymore.'

'I guess he wanted to know if I had any ideas about it.'

'Do you?'

I turned to him. 'Scott,' I said, 'that was a long time ago. At least eight or nine years. I really haven't thought much about it. I'm sorry for your loss, but I've had problems of my own.'

'If I'm bothering you I'll leave,' he said.

I didn't say anything.

'So I'm bothering you?' he asked, his expression growing more sullen.

'You're not bothering me. I wish I could help. I just don't know anything.'

He nursed his beer for a moment, his small eyes staring off into the distance. 'Do you have any idea why Billy took out thirty thousand dollars?' he asked.

'Sorry, nothing more that what the DA probably already told you.'

'You know, you've been apologizing a lot to me.'

I turned and stared at him. He tried to meet my stare, but after a while he lowered his eyes. 'I was trying to be understanding,' I said. 'I know it's got to be tough having your brother murdered like that. And Scott, it was worse than brutal. I don't think I ever saw anyone beaten that badly. But to be honest, even though Billy was in my high school class, I never really knew him well. He was just some fat slob druggie that I'd see around town. What Phil told me was he owed thirty thousand in gambling debts.'

'The DA told me he was gambling with a local bookie named Vassey.'

I let out a short laugh. 'Manny is, or at least was, a lot more than just a bookie. Yeah, if Billy owed him and was stubborn about paying, Manny would've sent muscle to collect. But I don't think he'd go as far as to kill any of his customers. Not out of any moral sense. Just because Manny was too smart a businessman for that.'

'Maybe Billy was going to pay Vassey. Maybe someone else found out he had the money.'

He was looking at me as if I were that someone. After all, I had no problem stabbing a DA thirteen times in the face, so why in the world would I have a problem beating a man to death for thirty grand? It shook me up a little inside to realize how easy a sell it was. Somehow I kept myself under control and pretended to give the matter some thought.

'I don't think so,' I said after an appropriate amount of time. 'Manny always kept his business pretty tight. I don't think anyone would have known about it from him. If your brother talked about it, maybe. But I remember interviewing his friends. They were a bunch of lowlife hicks and druggies, but none of them struck me as having the balls to do something like this.'

'Someone must have known about Billy having that money,' he insisted, his tone accusatory. Again, I pretended to ignore it.

'Maybe,' I said. 'This was eight or nine years ago. Back then Manny had started sending his son, Manny Jr, on collections. I think he was trying to break Junior into the business. The thing is, though, Junior's a psycho. He likes to injure people. He gets off on it. I remember one guy who stumbled into the emergency room after his hand had been chewed up by a garbage disposal. The poor sonofabitch was in shock. Somehow he had driven himself to the hospital, and, if you can believe it, using a stick shift.'

I paused for a moment. It was a true story, and thinking about it made me a little queasy. I tried to remember his name and finally came up with it. 'John Shortsleave,' I said. 'That was the poor sonofabitch. He used to live near Willows Pond, but he packed up and moved after this happened. I knew Junior was involved, but I couldn't get Shortsleave to talk. He was too scared. Even though Junior had ground up his hand with a garbage disposal, Shortsleave wouldn't talk. There were others also. After a while Manny got smart and stopped sending his son out on jobs, but I think that was some time after your brother was murdered. Maybe Junior was sent to collect from your brother. If it was Junior, we never would've gotten him.'

All the conviction and certainty drained from Ferguson's eyes. His pale doughy face was now clouded by doubt. I guess my story rang true to him. And if Junior had been sent to collect from Billy Ferguson it well could have turned out the way it did.

'You think Vassey's son could've killed Billy?' he asked, his attitude and manner now completely changed, almost subservient.

'It's possible,' I said. 'But as I say, if he did, we never would have been able to prove it.'

'Why?'

'Manny's just too smart. He would've cleaned it up and bought an airtight alibi for his son.'

Ferguson seemed to shrink inwards as he digested this. Large creases of doubt formed along his forehead.

'So how long were you in the army?' I asked.

'What? Oh, uh, twenty-two years,' he answered, distracted.

'Really? I'll tell you, Scott, that's something. You must've gotten a chance to see quite a bit.'

'Yeah, well, I guess so,' he muttered, only half hearing me.

'Where were you stationed?'

'What? Oh, the last five years in Heidelberg.'

'No kidding? You know, I've never been more than a few hours from Bradley. I really should go to Europe some time. You know, see the world. Maybe you could let me know places I should visit—'

'Yeah, sure,' he said. 'Look, I have to go.' He got to his feet and looked as if he had forgotten where he was. He stared blindly at the entrance before recognizing it. As he walked away I yelled out to him to take care of himself. He half-heartedly put up a hand to wave, but didn't bother looking back.

I tried to settle back into my chair, but it took a long time before I could pay attention to what was going on around me. By the time I could, Toni had finished her last set. She had only stripped down to a bikini top and a G-string, but a thick pile of dollar bills had still been thrown onstage and slipped under her garters. Guys had surrounded the stage and were begging her to take something off. She quieted them by flashing her heart-stopping smile. As she collected her money, she glanced in my direction and gave me a look of disappointment.

I finished my ale and visited Earl to get another one. When I got back Toni was sitting at my table. She was now wearing a football jersey. My guess, she probably had nothing but panties underneath it.

'I'm mad at you,' she said, playfully, her eyes sparkling.

If it were anyone else I probably would've told them to take a number. Instead, I sat down in the chair next to her and asked why.

She got up and sat on my knee. The feel of her body was electric.

'Because,' she said, 'I danced my heart out and you didn't even pay attention.' She leaned over so her mouth was against my ear. 'Sheriff Dan told me to take good care of you, Joe.'

'You recognize me, huh?'

'You're quite a celebrity. Your picture in the paper and everything.' She placed a finger on one of my scratches and traced it lightly. 'What happened?' she asked softly. 'You put your face somewhere it didn't belong?'

'Yeah, back in Bradley.'

She laughed at that. 'You're a funny guy,' she said.

'I usually leave them in stitches.'

She laughed again. 'That's not a nice thing to say, is it, Joe?' Then her mouth up against my ear again, 'You want to see me privately?'

I found myself nodding. She got off my knee and took hold of my hand and led me past the stage and to a curtained area in the back. Past the curtains was a long hallway with four small rooms on each side. Kind of like we were in the dressing area of a clothing store. Toni picked one of the rooms, led me in, and closed the door behind us. The room was bigger than a clothing store's dressing room, but not much. She had me sit on a carpeted bench and then she sat on my thighs, straddling and facing me. Her hands were clasped behind the back of my head and she gave me that heart-stopping smile. I lowered my eyes and focused on the soft curvature of her throat, and as I did, I felt something funny in my own throat. She smelled so fresh and sweet that it made me dizzy.

'Hey, what are you staring at down there?' she asked, laughing.

I looked back into her eyes.

'That's better,' she said. 'I'd like you to know that I'm very particular who I come back here with.'

I started laughing. I couldn't help myself. 'You can't be that particular,' I said.

'Why's that?'

'Because you're with me,' I explained, the laughter dying somewhere deep within me.

'Now stop that!' She waved a finger in front of my nose, scolding me. I noticed how small her hand was. Two of them would barely make up one of mine.

She placed her hand along my jaw and caressed it. 'I asked Earl about you, and he told me you were a great guy. He said you used to be a regular at Kelley's, that you used to come here almost every night, but you never once stepped back here with any of the girls. Why was that?'

'I was married then.'

'Are you still married?'

'No.'

'See?' she said. 'You were being faithful, you weren't going to betray your wife. Most guys who come here couldn't care less about that. And I read all about you. What you did was not so nice, but you took responsibility for it. And Joe, most of the guys I know wouldn't have had the guts to have pled guilty.'

I didn't say anything. Her logic was twisted, but I wasn't going to argue with her. Of course I betrayed Elaine and my daughters. It didn't matter whether I had sex with any of the girls at Kelley's, just spending most of my nights at a strip club was betrayal enough. Even though I never paid much attention to the strippers, I still abandoned my family. I abandoned them so that I could sit and bullshit with Earl and listen to music and snort cocaine and try to hide from them what I had become. And as far as Phil Coakley was concerned, I didn't have the guts to do anything other than plead guilty. Elaine was right, back then I wouldn't have been able to sit in a courtroom and listen to the accusations against me. I would have done anything to avoid that.

Toni reached down and started to unbuckle my belt. I stopped her. She gave me a tender smile. 'I know, it's been a long time,' she said.

'I'm just not ready right now.'

'Would you like some coke?'

I found myself nodding. She leaned forward and planted a kiss on my cheek. Then she got up and left the room. It had been a long time, but it was more than that. Elaine had been my first and only girlfriend. I dated her through high school and married her right afterwards. She was the only woman I had ever been with. But it was more than that.

All the hopes I had for turning my life around were turning to dust. I felt like I was balancing on an icy precipice and that any wrong move would send me tumbling off into oblivion. What I was going to have to do in the next few days was bad enough, but at least when it was done I could put it behind me and move on. Now, though, I was back at Kelley's, and not only that, but in one of their private rooms with a girl half my age and paid to be with me. I was falling back into my old habits. Drifting back into whatever was easy. Worse actually. But I was too paralyzed to move. Toni was too beautiful and I wanted too much what she had to offer. Still, it made me sick inside.

There was a light knock on the door, and Toni came back into the room and sat on my lap. She had a vial and a coke spoon with her. She opened the vial, filled the coke spoon, and snorted it. I could see the rush hit her, I could see the effect it had on her eyes and mouth. I wanted to bolt, but as I said before, I was paralyzed. When she offered me the spoon I took it. The rush hit me hard. I could feel the cocaine stinging the back of my eyes. I could taste it deep in my throat. We both did several more hits. She put the vial down and started to take off her football jersey. I stopped her.

'Either you're a really big football fan or you're shy,' she said, laughing, her expression quizzical.

'Let's sit for another minute.'

She tried moving my hand to her breast, but I moved it back to her small slender hip. She started giggling.

'It's funny your being so shy,' she said.

'Why's that?'

'Because of someone else. Someone you sort of know. He can barely even look at the girl he's with.'

'And why is that funny?'

'I don't know. It's just that the two of you are connected, kind of.'

Her eyes sparkled with amusement. I could tell she was just dying to tell me her private joke. But I could already guess it.

'Phil Coakley comes here, huh?' I asked.

That seemed to sober her up. 'I really shouldn't be talking about this,' she said.

'Don't worry, you didn't tell me anything. I guessed.'

'Well, he doesn't really come here. Not exactly. He couldn't even if he wanted to.'

'Yeah, it wouldn't look good for the DA to be frequenting a place like Kelley's.'

'I guess that's part of it.' She let out a laugh. 'But only a small part. Trust me. The girl he's seeing has to meet him at a motel. It wouldn't matter who she was seeing. It's funny, she thinks it's sweet that he can barely look at her. I don't know how she stomachs looking at him. Can you imagine what his face must look like when he's climaxing?'

She let out a shudder. I could feel it shake her whole body. I didn't say anything.

'That was pretty mean of me, wasn't it?' she said. Then, after a hesitation, 'I've heard that he used to be good looking.'

I nodded.

She gave me a long curious look as she studied me. 'There I go again,' she said, giggling. 'I'm bumming you out. And I was told to take good care of you. You just might have to put me across your knee.'

She giggled again and then filled up the coke spoon and inhaled it deeply. The cocaine was starting to affect her skin color, making it slightly jaundiced. Small droplets of perspiration hung from her forehead. As she smiled at me now it seemed a bit plastic. She was still beautiful, but not as stunning as when I first saw her. The coke spoon was refilled and handed to me. As I held it I felt my arm tremble. I wanted the coke, I wanted the rush that it would give me, I wanted to feel more alive than I was feeling, but I could see the effect the coke was having on Toni. I could see how it was marring her appearance. In my mind's eye I could see myself staring out with the same dumb glassy expression. I dropped the spoon back into the vial. My head was pounding. I felt like if I didn't get out of there my heart was going to explode.

'I think I better get going,' I said. I slid her off my lap and stood up at the same time.

'You're kidding?' She seemed genuinely surprised, not quite believing what she heard.

'I'm sorry, this just isn't right. Not for me anyway.'

She just stood hands on hips, staring at me with disbelief. 'Joe, why don't you sit back down and enjoy the ride. This is all paid for.'

'I'm not feeling good. I think I'd better just leave.'

'You're kidding, right?'

'I'm sorry, I've got to go.'

'Then go. 'Bye now.'

As I opened the door, I glanced behind me and saw Toni staring at me with utter disgust, her lips pressed tight into a rigid smile. Then I was out of there. ZZ Top's 'Legs' blasted me as I pushed through the curtains and stepped in front of a loudspeaker next to the stage. A healthy-looking blonde took her top off as she swayed to the beat of the music. I rushed past her and the stage, and nodded towards Earl on my way out. I felt as if I was suffocating. As I got outside, I sort of collapsed, standing bent over with hands on knees, trying desperately to breathe in the cool night air. After a few minutes of that, my head started to clear and I could breathe normally.

I guess I had a panic attack. It was probably triggered by the cocaine. The attack left me feeling shaky, but I was for the most part over it. I made my way over to my car, got in, and sank into my seat as I tried to clear my head. I felt disgusted with myself.

Elaine had been right, I always took the easy way. I always looked for short cuts. If things had continued with Toni I would've been following the same pattern that I always followed. At some point I had to break it. I sat for a long time, maybe a half-hour, maybe longer, before I was able to gather up the strength to drive away from there.

Chapter 10

It was almost midnight before I got back to my parents' house. I was surprised to see my dad still up. He was standing by the kitchen sink making himself some tea. He turned and gave me a self-conscious smile when he heard me.

'You left in quite a huff this morning,' he said.

I slid past him and filled up a glass of water and drank it down. I did that two more times and then washed out the glass and put it back on the shelf. After that, I turned sideways to face him.

'What did you expect?' I asked.

'We're not trying to fight with you, Joey. We're only trying to talk with you, that's all.'

He looked old standing there with his shoulders stooped and his face drawn and haggard. It softened my attitude.

'I'm sorry, Dad,' I said.

'I'm sorry too, son.' His eyes widened with concern as he looked at me. 'Joey, are you feeling okay?' he asked. 'You're sweating.'

'I'm okay, I've just had a busy day.'

'My God, you're pale as a ghost.'

'Don't worry about me, I'm fine.'

'How about I make you something to eat. Would you like some scrambled eggs?'

'Sure, Dad, that'd be good.'

I sat down at the kitchen table and watched as he got two eggs from the refrigerator, cracked them into a bowl, mixed in some milk and black pepper and then stirred them with a fork. When he was done, he put a frying pan on the stove, melted some butter and then poured in the eggs.

'I got some ham, Joey, would you like some thrown in?'

'That sounds great.'

He took a slice of ham, broke it into pieces, and dropped them onto the eggs before scrambling all of it. He then scraped the eggs onto a plate and placed it in front of me.

'How about some toast?'

'Sure.'

After he made me some toast and coffee, he sat down across from me with his tea. He sipped his drink slowly as I ate the eggs.

'What did you do today on your first day out?'

'Visited some friends. Nothing much else.'

I felt awkward sitting there with him. We were never very close. When I was a kid he used to spend a lot of his time at the firehouse and I never saw him much. Later, when I was in high school and starting as quarterback, we got a little closer. He'd show up for my games and take me out to dinner afterwards. Still, we never connected. Now it was as if we were strangers. He was just some old stooped man drinking a cup of tea. And I could tell he was as uncomfortable as I was.

He cleared his throat and waited until I looked at him.

'Joey, have you thought about what you're going to do?'

'What do you mean?'

'I was hoping you would think about college.'

'I'm too old for that,' I said. 'I'm forty. I'm not going to sit in a classroom with a bunch of eighteen-year-olds.'

'Other people have done it.'

'I'm not going to. Besides, how would I pay for it?'

'I'm sure you would find a way.'

If I kept the police pension I'd be able to, but I wasn't going to do that. Besides, I needed to get a real job so I could do something for my daughters. I couldn't wait four more years for that. 'Even if I wanted to, I don't think too many colleges would take a forty-year-old ex-felon. What I was thinking was that maybe I'd go to a trade school and become a plumber, or maybe an electrician.'

His face deflated with that. 'You could do that, Joey,' he said, 'but I hope you consider college. I'm sure if you set your mind to it you could find a good school that would take you. I think that would be the best thing for you.'

'I appreciate your concern.'

He gave me a sad, wistful kind of smile. 'Do you remember what you got on your SATs?'

Of course I remembered. My SAT scores were a sore subject that we had gone over time after time in the past. I shook my head and pretended I didn't.

'Eight hundred math and seven-sixty English,' he said. 'The only thing that I demanded of you when you were in high school was that you take the SATs. You didn't even study for them and you got those types of scores. Even though your grades weren't too good, with those scores and the way you excelled in sports you could've gotten into a good college. I should've pushed you harder. I shouldn't have let you just drift along and become a cop.'

'And why was that?'

He let out a loud sigh. 'Joey,' he said, 'I'm going to speak frankly with you. I'm not trying to start a fight or upset you. Can I do that?'

'Go ahead.'

He seemed stuck, his face locked in a pained expression. As he sat there with his hands resting lightly on the table, I couldn't help noticing all the liver spots decorating them. There were more spots along his forehead where his hair used to be. Finally, his internal struggle broke and he made a decision.

'I shouldn't have let you because I knew how it would turn out,' he said at last, his manner more relaxed. 'I knew you'd get bored, and I knew with the way you, uh, are, you'd end up getting in trouble. I knew all that and I did nothing about it. Just as I know you'll get bored as either a plumber or an electrician and that you'll end up falling into the same old patterns. I don't think you could help yourself. I think college could change that. At least it could give you a chance.'

As I sat and stared at him, I could feel my throat tightening and a hotness spreading along my face and ears. Part of what he said was true, but only a small part of it. Yeah, I got bored as a cop, but that had nothing to do with what followed. The fact that he thought he could sit there and judge me when he didn't have a clue was infuriating. And the fact that he was so damn sure of himself only infuriated me more.

'Dad, it's almost funny you showing all this concern now,' I said. 'You couldn't even visit me once in seven years.'

'I'm sorry about that, son.'

'Forget it.'

'No, I'd like to explain. About not visiting you in jail—'

'At this point I couldn't care less.'

'Now, Joey, don't be like this!'

'Don't be like what?'

'I'm trying to talk to you as a man,' he said. 'I'm not trying to upset you and I'm not trying to pick a fight. But I do want to talk to you. And I want to explain why we didn't visit. This isn't easy for me, but I want to explain. I think I should. Joey, what you did was so, um, so…' He seemed lost for the right word.

I volunteered, 'Unforgivable?'

He nodded. 'It was. I don't know if you knew, but I was there that night. I saw you when you walked out of the courthouse covered with blood. You were still holding that letter opener. I saw first hand what you did to Phil.'

He seemed lost in thought for a moment. Then his eyes focused back on me. 'You got to remember, Joey, I've known the Coakleys my whole life. Barry Coakley, Phil's uncle, was a buddy of mine in the department. I had worked alongside him for over twenty-five years. I couldn't face the guys after what you did, I had to retire. And then I started finding out more about you. About your gambling and drug addictions. I also had a long talk with Elaine. She told me how you used to spend almost every night at that strip club having sex with prostitutes.'

'I never cheated on my wife.'

He showed me a frail, sad smile. 'Joey—'

'I'm not lying about that. I did have a gambling and cocaine problem. And I did spend a lot of time at Kelley's. But I never once cheated on Elaine.'

He shrugged weakly. 'Maybe you didn't,' he said. 'Anyway, it took me a long time to come to terms with what you did, especially my role in it. It took a lot of soul searching on my part. The toughest thing for me, Joey, was that nothing you did came as any surprise to me. To be honest, I think I almost expected it.'

All I could do was stare at him. Stare at him and hate him for being so damn sure of himself. Finally I muttered something about was that so.

'Yes, Joey. I've read a lot of books and talked to a lot of people.'

I didn't say anything. I just stared at him and hated him all the more.

'I talked to psychiatrists, Joey.' His mouth moved for a moment as if he were stuck. Then he said, 'You've got what would be called a narcissistic personality disorder.'

'You're making psychiatric diagnoses now, huh?'

'Joey, please listen to me. Please. I know it fits you. I've talked to enough people and read enough about it to know that. Back then, of course, I didn't know what your disorder was called, but I knew what was in you. And I did nothing about it. I'll never forgive myself for that. I think that was part of why I couldn't get myself to visit you.'

I could feel myself trembling as I stared at him. My voice sounded odd to me when I asked whether my mother felt the same way.

'I'm not going to lie to you, your mother was hit very hard by what you did. She'd never wanted to believe me when I'd try to talk to her about you. She'd always defend you, Joey, always ignoring what was right in front of her face. Then after you tried to murder Phil, she couldn't ignore it any longer. I think that's why she spends almost every day volunteering. She's trying to make up for all those years of ignoring what she shouldn't have ignored.'

I had only finished half my food, but I'd lost my appetite for what was left. I pushed the plate away. 'Well, thanks for the eggs and the psychoanalysis. I think I'm going to head off to bed.'

'Joey, I'm trying to talk honestly with you.'

'Yeah, I guess there's got to be a first time for everything. But I appreciate your taking the time to figure out my personality defects. It was very thoughtful of you.'

'I wish you'd think over what I said and not be so dismissive.'

'Look,' I said, feeling the hotness intensify along my neck and ears, 'you don't have a fucking clue. Go play psychiatrist with someone else. You don't know me and you never did.'

'Then explain to me why you did the things you did.'

'Because I screwed up. Because shit happens. Nothing more and nothing less.'

'Son, how many close friends do you have?'

'What?'

'Humor me, please, how many close friends do you have?'

'What's that supposed to prove? I just spent the last seven years in jail.'

'Before that. You can go back to when you were in high school. Name me one close friend.'

'I had plenty of friends on the force before I was arrested. And I had plenty on my football and baseball teams back in high school.'

'I know, son, but name me one that you ever considered a close friend and not just an acquaintance.'

'Look, I'm tired of this. I'm not playing this game anymore.'

'Son, I'm bringing all this up for a reason. Partly so you can try to get help, but also for your daughters' – and my granddaughters' – sake. You've been talking about custody, but you got to understand how harmful that would be. You got to understand what that would do to Melissa and Courtney. I know deep down you don't want to hurt them. But you got to understand, Joey.'

I was too angry at him to explain that I knew that as well as him. That any talk of seeking custody changes was so that him and my mom could see my kids. 'You think I could hurt my daughters?'

'I don't think you'd want to intentionally, but be honest, son, what real feelings do you have towards them?'

'What the hell are you talking about?'

'If they were to die tomorrow how would you really feel?'

'I've had enough of this.' I pushed myself away from the table. I turned my back on him. I had to. I couldn't look at him anymore. As I made my way towards my room I heard him stammer out from behind how he had books on the subject in his den and that I should try to read them. That was the only thing he would ask of me. I got to my room and slammed the door shut.

I stood frozen for a long time and then I started sobbing. I couldn't help myself. It wasn't out of hurt or pain, but because I was so damn angry. I wanted to hurt him for being so damn cocksure of himself about me and for twisting me – in his mind anyway – into some kind of monster. And for questioning whether or not I had genuine feelings about my daughters. For doubting whether I truly loved them.

Of course I didn't have a chance of sleeping. Not with the cocaine in my system and not with the thoughts that were racing through my head. Sometime around three in the morning, I went to the den and found his psychiatry books. Several of them were nothing but general layman's books. One was on personality disorders and another dealt with surviving a narcissistic personality. I thumbed through the general books, and then took the other two to my room.

I had both of them finished by five in the morning. From what I could tell a narcissistic personality was a form of a sociopath. They had similar characteristics: an exaggerated sense of self-importance, a complete lack of empathy towards those around them, and they were exploitive in their interpersonal relationships. True sociopaths, though, were better at hiding what they were and could be charming, while narcissistic personalities, because they were so caught up in their grandiose views of themselves, stuck out like sore thumbs. They tended to be arrogant and shallow, with an unreasonable sense of entitlement and a need to be admired; kind of like spoiled brats. There were other things that I found that were interesting; their drugs of choice were alcohol and cocaine, they seldom formed close friendships, and they were driven by power. All in all it was interesting reading, but that's all it was.

You could probably point to any person alive, take enough stuff out of context, twist it around, and use it to prove they had any personality disorder you wanted to. I guess with my dad he couldn't accept the fact that there was no real reason why I did the things I did. He needed an explanation, he needed some underlying disease or mental defect to point to, so he found one.

It didn't matter whether it made any sense or not. The alcohol and cocaine use was an easy match. And he probably worked out in his mind that my motivation for being a cop had something to do with power. He was right about my not having any close friendships, but there were reasons for that. Back when I was in eighth grade I started spending a lot of time with Elaine. Probably the only time I wasn't with her was when I was in class or playing sports. That went on all through high school. I didn't have any time left over to develop close friendships. And I guess it wasn't important enough to me to care about it.

As far as wanting to be a cop, well, there were a lot of reasons for that also, and none of them had to do with me seeking out some form of power over those around me. Yeah, the idea of it attracted me as a kid, especially the way the cops were shown on TV, but there were other reasons. I didn't want to leave Bradley after high school. I was comfortable there, and besides, Elaine couldn't leave since she had to take care of her sick mother. I didn't have a lot of choices. I wasn't going to be cooped up in an office making minimum wage, and I didn't want to work in a garage or do construction. Yeah, I could've worked an assembly line, either building military aircraft in Bradley or computer equipment in Chesterville, but I didn't think I could deal with the drudgery of that. And maybe I wanted something with some respectability, but that didn't make me a narcissistic personality.

The thing is, none of the major characteristics matched. I certainly didn't have any great love for myself, I couldn't care less whether anyone admired me, and as far as a sense of entitlement, well, I'd have to think the opposite was true. I started taking the payoffs because I didn't want to make waves. I never wanted the money, I didn't feel entitled to it, but it was easier to just take the payoffs and keep my mouth shut. The money, though, made me feel rotten, and at some subconscious level I must have wanted to get rid of it as quickly as I got it. That had to be why I started with the gambling and cocaine. It had nothing to do with a narcissistic personality. But there was more to it. Loving myself? Shit, no, I had to have been trying pretty damn hard to hurt myself, and the reason had to have been because in fact I hated myself. Hated myself for just going along and taking money I didn't want. For doing things I didn't want to do. For once again just taking the easy way out.

As for lack of empathy, I had to believe I felt bad about what I did to Phil. At least I think I did. It's hard to say exactly. I know I felt uneasy about it, but it could be because he was walking around so that everyone in Bradley could look at him and remind themselves about what I did. If he had died that night and I had gotten away with his murder, maybe I'd feel differently now. It's hard to say. Of course, what I did to him was in some ways worse than murder. Making him into a freak, driving his wife away, and leaving him as nothing more than a bitter shell of what he used to be. How could I not feel guilty about that?

The one thing my dad said that stuck in my craw was how he had almost been expecting the things that I had done. The hell with him. If he wanted to invent personality disorders for me that was his business. If he wanted to write me off, fine, let him. As far as my daughters went, he could read himself psychiatry books from now till doomsday for all I cared. He had no idea what was in my heart. He never did and he never would. I wasn't going to waste any more time worrying about what he thought.

As I mentioned before, it was five in the morning. It had been days since I'd had any real sleep and my head was feeling kind of fuzzy. I went into the kitchen and made myself some coffee. I decided none of what was going to happen was worth worrying about. I would do what I had to and then move on. Just like anyone else in the world would.

Chapter 11

I made sure I was out of the house before my parents woke up. I had my suit on. It was loose on me, especially around the stomach and thighs, but it looked okay. I got in my car and sat motionless for a few minutes. All I could think about was getting my hands on some cocaine and doing a few lines. I almost drove to Earl's house, but I stopped myself. I had slipped the night before and I knew I couldn't slip again, at least not if I wanted any chance of keeping the promise I made for my girls. As bad as the craving was, as fuzzy as my head felt, I knew I had to fight it. I checked the time and saw it was six thirty. I needed something so I drove to a twenty-four-hour convenience store and bought a box of powdered doughnuts and a large black coffee. The doughnuts and the coffee helped somewhat. At least they made my head feel a little less fuzzy.

While I sat in my car, I checked the scratches along my cheek in the rearview mirror. The swelling had gone down. They were still noticeable, but they didn't look as bad as they had.

It was almost seven. Still an hour before church. It had been years since I had been to services, the last time probably being right after Courtney was born. I couldn't say exactly why I had decided to go today. It was just something that I felt I needed to do. Something that was driving me at a gut level.

I finished off the powdered doughnuts. I still had fifty minutes to kill. My shoes were looking scuffed, so I went back into the convenience store and found a shoeshine kit. After I had worked on them for a while, they looked better. I still had twenty minutes to kill. I went back into the store, bought a paper, and read it until it was time to leave. Then I drove over to the church and found a spot in the parking lot.

The attendance was better than at Kelley's the night before, the church about three-quarters filled. Minister Charles Thayer was standing behind the pulpit announcing news about different members of the congregation. I took an empty seat in the last pew. One of his eyebrows rose as he recognized me.

I noticed Phil sitting in the front with Clara, and his younger daughter, Megan. Clara had makeup caked on, but even so, dark purple bruises stood out along the side of her face. Somehow Phil sensed that I was there. He glanced back at me quickly, his expression completely blank. Other members of the congregation started to look back at me, some of them glaring openly. I guess Thayer decided to address the situation. He made an announcement welcoming me, stating that while I had committed a terrible crime I had confessed freely in open court, and if God could forgive and love a repentant sinner, so could my neighbors. There was some mumbling after that, but there was also head-nodding. Phil Coakley sat stone faced. I could see Clara squeezing his hand. I could see Megan fighting back tears. After that I only half heard what Thayer had to say. I was too busy watching Phil, trying to make up my mind about something.

When Toni had leaked out her secret about Phil it got me thinking about how I could use it. Now I had an idea worked out. Nobody would end up dead from it, nobody would even get badly hurt. It wouldn't solve my current problem, but it would buy me some time, maybe a week, maybe longer. And maybe given the extra time my problem would resolve itself. Who knows how much longer Manny really had? Maybe he had a month or two like the doctors were telling him, but with some luck maybe he only had a week or less. If I could keep finding ways to buy myself time I had a chance of getting out of this mess without having to kill anyone.

What troubled me about my idea was that while no one would get physically hurt, it would end up humiliating Phil, and would also damage and possibly even destroy his career. From the hints Toni had dropped I had a pretty good idea who Phil was seeing. Better than even money it was the redhead, Susie. I didn't know for sure, but I had a pretty good feeling that's who it was. With Muscle-shirt strutting about there was no way she could entertain anyone in one of the back rooms at Kelley's. She'd have to meet Phil in a motel. Also, I know it's kind of a cliché saying this about a stripper (and more times than not it turns out to be the exact opposite), but she seemed like a genuinely sweet girl. I could see her looking on it as an act of mercy. But still, if Phil and she were caught in a motel room and a morals charge was brought against him, it would sideline him, and maybe for a good deal longer than a week. I was still trying to make up my mind when Thayer's sermon ended. People started to mill out of the church, a few of them nodding to me as they went by.

As I got up to leave, I heard Thayer call my name. He was walking briskly to catch up to me, a broad smile on his round red face.

'I was glad to see you here today, Joe,' he said as he took my hand with both of his.

'Thank you, Reverend.'

'I hope this is going to be a weekly occurrence?'

'I hope so.'

'Good, good.' His eyes moistened as he gave my hand a couple of friendly pats. 'I am so glad for this change of heart in you, Joe. Remember, in the eyes of God, we're all sinners. But for the truly repentant, it's never too late for redemption. Remember that. I'll be looking for you here next week. And hopefully your parents also. If you could, tell them for me, we've missed them here.'

He let go of my hand and gave me a warm pat on the back before turning to talk to one of the other members of his flock. I knew I wouldn't be seeing him again. At least not in church.

When I got to my car I found Phil leaning against it. The way the sunlight hit his face made it look like some crazy grotesque quilt that had been stitched together with red and blue thread. As I approached him, he showed me a little smile.

'I can't help wondering what con you're trying to pull, Joe,' he said.

'What do you mean?'

'Why you would bother showing up at church? Because, Joe, you're about as repentant as a rabid dog.'

'And why's that?'

He shook his head sadly, still smiling. 'If you were truly repentant you'd confess to all your crimes, not just the one you were caught red handed in.'

'I don't know what you're talking about.'

'Of course you do. Before you set fire to the documents that I had collected, I was building a case against you for money you had stolen from the evidence room. There were a number of thefts and burglaries along the way, weren't there, Joe? And maybe worse crimes than that?'

He stopped, his eyes narrowing as he studied me. I saw a brightness flash in his eyes and then a crazy smile twisting his lips. Before I realized what was happening, he jumped forward and grabbed me, trying to pin my arms behind me. A few of the churchgoers stopped to gawk at us. More started to come over. Thayer wandered over, a look of bewilderment spoiling his round red face.

The last thing I wanted to do was scuffle with Phil in the

church parking lot. I let him pin my arms back. 'Let go of me,' I said, trying to keep my voice calm.

He ignored me. 'Call the police,' he demanded to the crowd that had formed. I heard someone calling with a cell phone.

Thayer stepped forward. 'Phil, what in the world is going on?'

'This repentant sinner of yours was snorting cocaine before services. You can see the residue on his nose, chin and suit jacket. I'm holding him until the police come.'

I started laughing. Normally I would have just stood still until the police arrived, but I didn't want to risk a drug test and have cocaine from last night show up. 'Reverend,' I said, 'whatever powder is on me is from powdered doughnuts. You'll find an empty box in my car.'

Thayer walked over to my car, peeked in, and then walked back to me. He dabbed his finger against my chin and tasted it.

'Phil, let go of Joe immediately,' he said. 'I saw an empty box with my own eyes and this is nothing but powdered sugar.'

Phil didn't move, at least not at first, and then he reluctantly let go of me. I took a step away from him, making a show of grimacing and rubbing my arms. As I turned to face him I could see nothing but loathing in his eyes.

'I'm sorry,' he said, without much feeling.

I held out my hand to him. He had no choice, he had to accept it.

'I am so sorry for what I did to you eight years ago,' I said, hamming it up, but for the most part meaning what I was saying. 'I wish to God there was some way I could take it back, that I could've been the one stabbed instead of you. But there's nothing I can do, Phil, except pray that you can find it in your heart to forgive me.'

It was all true, but I still I laid it on pretty thick. All he could do was stand there and take it. I let my eyes wander to the crowd that had gathered around us and could see that I'd won over a few of my fellow townspeople. Not all, but a few. At that moment I made up my mind. If that sanctimonious holier-than-thou sonofabitch was going to screw around with prostitutes and then try to act morally superior to me, the hell with him.

A police cruiser pulled up with its siren blaring. Tony Flauria stepped out of it. 'Okay,' he said, bulling his way forward, his eyes focused on me, 'someone call in an emergency?'

Thayer stepped forward. 'Nothing but a misunderstanding, Officer.'

Flauria looked towards Phil. 'Is that right, Mr Coakley?'

Phil stood silently for a moment and then nodded.

Flauria gave me a long hard look before turning back to his cruiser. The crowd started to disperse. Phil hung back until we were alone.

'Hey, Joe,' he said as he walked off. 'What can I say? I made a mistake. Don't worry, next time I'll be more careful. Next time my evidence will be rock solid. I promise.'

I watched as he walked away and got in his car. His two girls were sitting there waiting for him. All three of them looked like ghosts as they drove by. I waited until they were out of sight and then walked a block to a payphone. I then called and left a message for Dan Pleasant, telling him where I would be.

It was ten thirty. After seven years of watching his routine, I knew Morris Smith would be in his office reading the Sunday paper. I headed over to the Bradley county jail. When I got there I found Morris with his feet on his desk, leaning back and doing the Sunday crossword puzzle. He seemed surprised to see me.

'Well, hello there, young fellow,' he croaked. He struggled to pull his feet off his desk and then extended a hand to me. 'To what do I owe the pleasure of your company?'

'I thought I'd swing by and see if I could interest you in a game of checkers.'

'Why, certainly. I'm always up to teaching a youngster like you a lesson or two.'

His soft rubbery face seemed to light up as he took the checkerboard from his desk drawer.

'How's business been?' I asked.

'Oh, very light,' he said. 'No steady customers since your recent departure. Only a few temporary guests. A few drunks and disorderlies. Nothing too interesting. So, Joe, Sunday's my day off. How'd you know I'd be here?'

'Come on, Morris. Who are you trying to kid? If you're going to read the Sunday paper, you might as well collect overtime while doing so.'

He chuckled at that. We had the pieces set up and his rubbery, jovial face became deadly serious as he made the first move and stared intently at the board.

I was just killing time while I waited for Dan to show. I wasn't paying enough attention and before I knew it I had a sure win. There was no way out of it without making an obvious blunder, so I took the game. Morris's mood seemed to darken with the loss.

'You caught me off guard,' he noted sourly.

'Sooner or later I was bound to get lucky.'

'Quit gloating and set them up again.'

I let him win the next three games and his mood brightened.

'Your luck's left you, young fellow,' he said as he tried to suppress a smile.

'I've got to learn when I've met my match,' I said.

Halfway through the next game, I let myself accidentally blunder into a combination that would leave me being double-jumped. Morris spotted it and couldn't keep the smile from his face. He moved quickly, pouncing on the move, and then settled back in his chair, his hands folded across his thick body, a thin Cheshire cat grin playing on his lips.

'So, Joe,' he said, 'have you given any thought about leaving Bradley?'

'I've been thinking about it.'

I pretended to notice the double jump I was being forced into. I winced, swore, and then grudgingly made the move I had to. I could tell Morris appreciated the show. He carefully double-jumped me and picked up my checkers.

'I heard about what happened a couple of nights ago,' he said. His thick eyelids were raised as he watched me. 'With Phil's daughter and those two boys. You almost ended up back here. Or worse.'

'I should have recognized her,' I said. 'I hadn't seen her since she was fourteen, and she was wearing dark glasses, but I should have recognized her.'

'Maybe so. But I think, Joe, your luck has run out in these parts. You'd be better off with a fresh start someplace else. As much as I'd miss these games and the sterling competition that you offer me, I think that would be the best thing for you.'

There was a knock on the door. As it swung open, Dan Pleasant leaned in.

'I was hoping to catch you here, Morris,' he said, and then he did a double-take as he pretended to be surprised by my presence.

'Speak of the devil,' he said. 'Joe, I was just talking about you.'

He ambled over to me, a pleasant smile stretched across his face. After we exchanged handshakes, he shook his head as if in amazement.

'How long has it been, Joe? Years, huh?' Then to Morris, 'What are you doing letting this miscreant hang around here? He'll set a bad example for our other tenants.'

Morris seemed a bit taken aback by Dan's arrival. 'I've been teaching this young man a lesson in humility,' he croaked out in that gravel voice of his.

Dan pulled up a chair and sat down, leaning back with his hands clasped behind his head. 'I'm glad I found you here, Morris. I need an inventory of the stockroom.'

Morris made a face. 'It's Sunday. Can't it wait until tomorrow when I can put one of my staff on it?'

'I'm sorry. I'm working on a budget proposal and I need this right away. Of course, since you're here putting in overtime, I figured it wouldn't be too much of an imposition.'

'And you need the inventory right this moment?'

'I would like it, yes.'

Morris raised his eyelids as he glanced suspiciously at both of us. With a great deal of effort he pushed himself out of his chair. As he made his way across the office, he stopped to waggle a finger at me.

'Don't go moving those checkers around. I have the position right up here.'

He tapped his skull and gave us both one last suspicious glance before leaving the office and closing the door.

Dan turned to me, smiling as pleasantly as ever.

'I wasn't kidding before about just talking about you,' he said. 'What happened this morning?'

'I ate some powdered doughnuts before church. Some of the powder must've gotten on me and Phil thought it was cocaine residue. He jumped me right there in the church parking lot.'

'You're kidding?'

'Nope.'

Dan chuckled at that. 'I guess our DA friend is chomping at the bit to nail you any way he can. Let me ask you a question. What the hell were you doing going to church?'

'I don't know.' I looked away. 'I guess I was trying to fill some spiritual void.'

'Yeah, well, you should've tried filling it last night at Kelley's.' He was still smiling, but it was thinner and less pleasant. 'I talked with Toni. I don't understand you, Joe. That was all the spiritual enlightenment you needed right there. And an exclusive and expensive one at that. A hell of an expensive one. Here I go out of my way to help you out and what do you do? You walk out on her?'

'I wasn't feeling good last night.'

'You weren't feeling good, huh?' He started laughing, but it came out kind of brittle and harsh. 'I don't know. You've been acting soft in the head ever since you got out of jail. All I asked of you was to keep a low profile, do what needs to be done, and then move the hell away from here. Instead you go to Zeke's just begging for trouble—'

'I didn't go to Zeke's looking for trouble.'

'Of course you did. The same reason you went to church this morning. It's making me wonder whether I can count on you. It's really causing me to think, Joe, especially about your Tuesday deadline.' He paused to study me, his smile now completely gone. 'So what's so important that I had to be dragged here?' he asked.

'I found out something about Phil last night.'

'Yeah?'

I hesitated, feeling a little sick inside thinking about what I was doing.

'Hurry it up. I don't have all day.'

I took a deep breath and told Dan about Phil's weekly trysts.

'No kidding?'

'No kidding.'

His smile came back. 'Well, it explains why you walked out on Toni.'

'Why's that?'

'Never mind,' he said, chuckling to himself. He seemed to enjoy whatever private joke he was having. He wiped a tear from his eye and asked, 'What girl's he seeing?'

'I'm not sure, but I think it's the redhead.'

'Susie?'

'Yeah, I think so.'

'What do you know,' he said. 'He's got good taste, I'll give him that. So why's this so important?'

I hesitated again as I felt my stomach twist into knots. I waited until the discomfort passed. 'If your boys can catch them in the act, you could have the county bring a morals charge against Phil. That would sideline him for at least a week and buy us some more time.'

He sat like a mannequin as he stared at me, his smile frozen into something not quite human. He was like that for a good several minutes.

'Why am I wasting my time with you,' he finally said.

'We're playing a waiting game now with Manny,' I tried to explain. 'If we can buy enough time this problem is going to resolve itself and—'

'There is no problem if you take care of either Manny or Coakley. That's all that has to be done. It's so damn simple, but you want to make it into some big complicated mess. I really think you have gone soft in the head, Joe. I'm serious about that.'

He got out of his chair and took several angry paces before turning back to me. 'Quit trying to be so fucking smart,' he forced out. His skin color had dropped to a sickly white. He was breathing hard and I could tell he was making an effort to control his emotions. 'You think you're so goddam brilliant, and maybe in some ways you are, but in other ways you're the stupidest motherfucker I know. This is simple. So very fucking simple. Just take care of it and get it done before Tuesday. This is the last time I'm going to tell you that.'

'Dan, why don't you think about what I said—'

'Shut the fuck up.' He pointed a finger at me. 'Just shut your mouth and think. Quit acting like a goddam moron.'

He started towards the door, but stopped to face me.

'I'm pissed off right now,' he said. 'So don't get too offended, okay? Just fucking think and do what needs to be done. And when Morris comes back, tell him I'll pick up his inventory later in the week.'

After Dan left, I sat alone and generally felt lousy. It just seemed like such a rotten thing to do, telling Dan about what Phil was doing. If I hadn't maimed him, he wouldn't be seeing a prostitute. And here I was trying to expose him even further. I felt some relief that Dan wasn't going to use what I told him, but it still made me sick to my stomach thinking about it. At that point I made a decision. Whatever was going to happen was going to happen, but Phil was going to be left out of it. I wasn't going to cause him any more damage. I wasn't quite sure what I was going to do, but I knew that much.

When Morris came back with his inventory, I gave him Dan's message. It left him in a foul mood. I let him beat me a few more times and it mollified him somewhat. A little before twelve thirty I stood up and offered him my hand.

'I've got to get out of here while I still have a little dignity intact,' I told him.

'Well, young fellow, thanks for stopping by to see me,' he said, his eyelids half raised. 'At least, I think so.'

I wasn't quite sure what he meant by that. I murmured something about seeing him around.

'Funny about Dan showing up for that inventory,' he noted.

'Yeah, that did seem kind of odd to me also. Well, so long.'

Morris let his eyelids droop a bit more. 'As far as seeing me around,' he said, 'I certainly hope not. At least not here in Bradley. I hope by this time tomorrow you're walking along the sunny beaches of the west coast of Florida.'

'It's a nice thought, Morris, but I got a meeting with my parole officer tomorrow. But I'll be thinking about it.'

'I hope you do more than think about it. I'd hate to see you back here.'

'Don't worry, you won't.'

Morris walked me out of the building and we shook hands again before parting. I walked over to my car and sat inside, not sure what to do next. There had to be a way out, I knew there had to be, but I couldn't come up with it. If only it could be as simple as driving to Florida.

I tried picturing what it would be like living in Florida. Having white sand beaches and the ocean and hot weather. Drinking nothing but margaritas and daiquiris, and eating fresh key lime pie, stone crabs, and shrimp the size of my fist. I tried to imagine what it would be like living somewhere where nobody knew me and where nobody had any vendettas against me. The idea of it sounded so damn nice. If I took off I'd probably have six months, maybe as much as a year, before they caught up to me. I thought about it. It was tempting, but then it hit me how useless my life would end up being. And then I started thinking about my daughters. After a while they were all I could think about. More than anything I needed to hear their voices. Five minutes, that would be all I needed. It just didn't seem too much to ask for. I sat for a while longer and then drove to downtown Bradley, parked in front of the drugstore, and got five dollars' worth of change.

When I had gotten Elaine's address I had also gotten her phone number. There was a payphone outside the drugstore. I walked over to it, took out Elaine's phone number from my wallet, and stared at the jagged scrap of paper until I made up my mind. I felt jumpy inside as I dialed the number. While the phone rang I felt as if my heart was going to bust out of my chest.

A girl's voice answered, 'Hello?'

I tried to ask if she was Melissa but my voice cracked.

She asked again, 'Hello, who's calling?'

This time I was able to get my question out. My voice sounded odd to me. I realized I was trembling.

In a guarded voice, she said, 'No, I'm Courtney. Who's this?'

'I'm your dad.'

'Who?'

I cleared my throat and tried to talk louder. 'I'm your dad, sweetheart,' I said, my words sounding hollow as they echoed through my head. 'I know it's been a long time. And I know you probably don't remember me, but I wanted to call to tell you that I've always been thinking of you and that I love you.'

She must've put down the phone. I don't think she heard most of what I said. I heard her yelling, 'Mom, there's a strange man on the phone who says he's my dad.'

I heard a more distant yelling, probably from Elaine. I couldn't make out what she was saying. Only that her voice sounded frantic. Then I heard a rumbling noise, probably somebody running.

Elaine had picked up the receiver. 'I don't want you calling again,' she said.

'Elaine, all I want to do is talk to my daughters—'

'You're not going to.' Her voice had become deadly calm. It kind of surprised me how calm it was. 'Tomorrow I'm going to get an unlisted phone number. I'm not going to let the girls answer the phone until we have the new number, so don't bother wasting your time.'

I heard a click as she hung up.

I stood there feeling as if I barely had the strength to move. Somehow I hung up the receiver and got back into my car. It hadn't fully hit me how important my girls were to me until I tried talking to Courtney. I had to find a way to live for my two girls. I had to give my life meaning for them. Otherwise, what the hell was the point of anything? The thought of that overwhelmed me. I sat still and forced myself to concentrate. Eventually I came up with a plan. It was a long shot, but given that Phil was off limits, it was the best I could come up with.

Chapter 12

I stopped off at the information desk to ask whether Charlotte Boyd was working. The woman at the desk seemed familiar. She was about my age, attractive except for some small red blotches around her nose and premature gray hair. I saw from her name tag that she was Alice Cook. I remembered an Alice Harrison from high school and was pretty sure it was the same person. Fortunately she didn't recognize me. She couldn't have – she was being too nice. After she checked the hospital work schedule, she told me that Charlotte had this Sunday off.

'Are you a friend of Charlotte's?' she asked.

'I only met her the other day,' I said. 'We had coffee together and I was hoping to see her again.'

She gave me a smile as if to say isn't that sweet. 'Charlotte's such a nice girl. Quiet, but very nice. If she used some makeup and did something with her hair, she'd be quite pretty.'

That was stretching it. She'd still have those nervous eyes and a mousy look about her. Still, I appreciated the effort. I agreed with her and asked if she could give me Charlotte's home number and address.

'I'm sorry, but that's against hospital policy,' she said. I could tell she wasn't happy with the policy. Her eyes brightened. 'Charlotte might be listed in the phonebook.'

She found the Bradley phonebook and started searching through it. 'Here it is.' She pointed the listing out to me. I borrowed a pen from her and wrote the address and phone number on the back of the scrap of paper on which I'd written Elaine's phone number.

'I hope she's home,' she said.

'I hope so too,' I agreed. 'She's all I'm able to think about right now.'

She gave me another of those isn't that so sweet smiles. I nodded to her as I headed off in the direction of the terminal patient ward. She looked a little confused. I guess she had expected me to run off and try to find Charlotte. But there was something else I needed to do first.

When I got to Manny's room, I found him alone. He was propped up on his bed watching TV. His eyes shifted to the side as he noticed me, but he didn't say anything.

'Jesus Christ,' I said. 'I thought you'd be keeled over and dead by now. So much for wishful thinking.'

He scrunched up what was left of his face and made an expression as if he had tasted something foul. 'You kiss your ma with a mouth like that?' he asked. His expression shifted to something ill tempered. 'And don't worry about me,' he added. 'I got two months left and I'm going to be here every goddam second of it.'

I walked over to his bed and sat on the side of it. I could tell he didn't like me sitting there, but he didn't say anything.

'What are you watching?' I asked.

'Pats–Jets game,' he muttered, half under his breath. Then his body started to convulse with what must've been laughter. It sounded more like a broken garbage disposal. 'You want any action on it, call my son,' he said when he could. 'Any amount you want to put down.' Then he started laughing some more. When he finished, he asked, 'What the hell you want?'

'Nothing much. I just thought I'd visit an old friend.'

'I got news for you, I never thought of us as friends.'

'Yeah, well, neither did I.'

'What do you know? You're not as dumb as I thought you were. So what you here for?'

'It kind of bothered me the way we left things the other day,' I said.

He didn't respond. He just shifted his cold, dead eyes sideways so he could watch me.

'After all,' I said, 'I have no right to tell you what you can and can't do. If you want to confess all your sins to Phil that's your business. I just don't see what good it would do you. I'm curious, why not make a confession to a real priest? Phil's not even Catholic.'

'Who says I want to confess jack to anyone?'

'Come on, Manny, I'm just talking hypothetical. I don't blame you for wanting to unburden yourself. But why not do it right and use a priest? I can help you find one if you want.'

His wasted face puckered up into something akin to aggrievement. 'I never liked priests much,' he said.

'Look, Manny, have you talked this over with your son? He's not going to be happy with this. Even if Phil honors the deal you make, Manny Jr is going to lose everything he's got. And he'll be watched by the law every second of the rest of his life. You'll be forcing him into a mundane, blue-collar existence. He'll probably end up having to bag groceries at Food Mart.'

As I stared at him, as I watched him shift uncomfortably in his bed, I realized that he wasn't just trying to save his own soul. That part of his rationale for making a deal with Phil was to force Junior out of the business. That he was trying to save Junior's soul also.

I started laughing. I couldn't help myself. As Manny stared back at me, I could see in his eyes that he knew that I knew what was really going on. There was no kidding each other anymore.

'You should think about getting your affairs in order, Joe.'

'I appreciate your concern.'

We were both quiet then, both deep in our own thoughts. After a while Manny announced that he was feeling tired and he wanted me to leave.

'And don't bother blabbing your ideas to my son,' he warned me. ''Cause I admitted nothing.'

As I looked at him, I felt a blind fury overtake me. This sonofabitch was all set to ruin me because of some bullshit notion of saving his psychotic lunatic son.

'It's not going to be as simple as you think, Manny,' I said.

'I don't know what you're talking about.'

'You don't, huh? You think everything a criminal like you says is going to be taken at face value?'

'Look Joe, you're the convicted felon here, not me. And I'm not saying I'm confessing anything. But if I do, it's going to be the truth.'

'The truth according to who? A piece of scum like you?'

'The truth, Joe. Like how you were the guy who beat Billy Ferguson to death.'

He showed me that 'go screw yourself' smile of his that I knew so well, and as I watched him gloat I could feel a hotness flush my face. He got to me. That was still no excuse, but he got to me.

'So that's going to be your story?' I half heard myself asking. 'The thing is I remember playing poker that night and I'm sure I can line up friends who'll vouch for me. So who did you really send to collect? Junior? Is that what this is all about?'

His body started convulsing again, making that same broken-down garbage disposal noise. When he was done laughing, he looked me straight in the eye. 'What friends you got these days, Joe?' he asked, and then he started laughing again, his body convulsing harder than before.

I had to get out of there. I knew I made a mistake talking about

Billy Ferguson with him, but as I had said, he got to me, and the words just slipped out. I couldn't help myself. Everything was a haze as I made my way towards the elevator and then down to the main lobby. I could sort of make out Alice Cook as I walked past her desk. I think she said something to me, but I'm not sure. I just had to get out of there. I had to get that noise of his convulsing laughter out of my head. When I got to my car I sat for a long time. There was no doubt about any of it anymore. There was no longer even a tiny glimmer of hope. If I didn't shut Manny up I was going to be spending the rest of my days in prison.

Charlotte Boyd lived in the Maple Farms apartment complex off of Route Two. The apartment complex was built in the early sixties and was an eyesore. A four-story concrete structure housing close to eighty apartments. Each unit had its own balcony where the outer wall was made up of colored sheet metal, the colors ranging from purple to lime green to a dull yellow. I don't know what the architect could possibly have been thinking.

I found Charlotte's apartment number and dialed it up on the intercom system. After about a minute I heard some static and then what I thought was her voice, but I wasn't sure. I pressed the talk button and announced who I was. Another thirty seconds and I was buzzed in.

When I got to her door I knocked. I heard some movement from behind it and could tell she was using her peephole. The door opened a few inches and I heard her soft voice asking me to come in.

'I have several cats,' she explained in what was barely over a whisper. 'I don't want to leave the door open because they might run out.'

I squeezed through the opening and shut the door behind me. Charlotte was standing in front of me, her large hazel eyes holding steady on mine. Her hair was pulled back in a ponytail and she was dressed in jeans and a University of Toronto sweatshirt. She looked younger than when I saw her the day before. She also looked prettier. Her nurse's uniform had hung on her like a curtain. With her jeans on, I could tell her body had more of a definition to it than I would've thought. Also, her eyes didn't seem all that nervous anymore.

'Hi, Charlotte. I was hoping to find you at home.'

'Would you like to sit down?'

Off to the side of the entranceway was a small living room. There wasn't much furniture in it; a small antique-looking chair and a matching loveseat, a coffee table, and a stereo bench with a TV. A neatly arranged stack of magazines lay on the coffee table, and there were books and small knick-knacks on a few built-in shelves. While there wasn't much to the room, it had a nice feel. Charlotte took the antique chair and I sat on the loveseat. On the coffee table was a photograph of three very odd-looking cats, all with pushed-in faces and dour expressions.

'Are these yours?' I asked.

'Yes. That's Lady Margarite in the middle. Next to her on the right is Princess Anne, and on the left is Simone.'

For the life of me, I wouldn't have been able to tell one from the other. All three of them looked like carbon copies of each other.

'Three ladies, huh?' I said. I looked around to see whether I could spot any of them.

'They're skittish with strangers,' Charlotte said. 'Could I get you something to drink?'

'No thanks.' I showed her an apologetic smile. 'I've been thinking a lot about you since yesterday. I was hoping I could talk you into taking a ride with me to Burlington and joining me for a late brunch. I know I'm putting you on the spot by showing up like this.'

From the way she hesitated I knew she had already eaten

lunch. But she nodded. 'I'd like that, Joe. Let me change clothes and I'll be right with you.'

She disappeared into her bedroom. As I waited I flipped through the magazines on her coffee table and found a couple on cats, one on antiques, another on knitting, and a final one on travel. I thumbed through the travel magazine until I came across an article about Italy. I wasn't entirely kidding Scott Ferguson about wanting to see the world. I was forty years old and had so far seen almost none of it. It struck me that I had never even been in an airplane. As I looked at pictures of the Colosseum in Rome and the canals of Venice, I started daydreaming. With some effort I shook myself out of it and put the magazine down.

I got up and took a look at what she had on her shelves. There were a number of porcelain figurines; mostly either ballerinas or cats, with a couple of birds mixed in. As far as her books went, there were half a dozen on Victorian England, a handful of what looked like medieval romance novels, and a couple on the Diana and Prince Charles wedding. There were a few other miscellaneous books that you'd probably classify as literary. Out of boredom I had actually read most of them while in jail.

I noticed one of my eyes had started itching like crazy, and as I rubbed it, I saw one of her cats peeking at me from around the corner. I guess it was trying to decide whether I was worth the trouble. Its expression looked even more dour in person. It must've made up its mind that I wasn't, because it darted back around the corner and out of sight.

By this time both my eyes were tearing and my nose had started running. Then I started sneezing. It came out almost like machine-gun fire. Charlotte came running into the room. She had changed into a sweater and a skirt and had pulled her hair out of its ponytail, but with the sneezing and the way my eyes were swelling up I couldn't pay much attention to her. I could tell, though, that she had a worried look on her face.

Between sneezes I told her that I thought I was allergic to her cats.

'I'm so sorry.'

'There's nothing for you to be sorry about.' I stopped to fire off a couple more sneezes. 'I was the one who dropped by out of the blue.' I had to stop again. When I could continue, I told her I was going to buy some allergy medication and that I'd meet her out front in fifteen minutes.

'If we go to the hospital, I can pick you up a sample of a prescription allergy medication that will be more effective than what you can buy over the counter.'

'Okay, sure.'

I was anxious to get out of there. She still needed a few minutes so I told her I'd meet her in the lobby. I just couldn't catch a break. I actually found myself feeling comfortable in her apartment, but it couldn't be that simple – I couldn't be given a few minutes of peace. Something had to screw it up, so of course I had to find myself allergic to her cats. And of course she couldn't just have one. She had to have three of them spreading dander throughout her apartment.

I found a rest room in the lobby and splashed cold water on my face and in my eyes, but it didn't help much. My eyes still felt itchy as hell and my nose was running like a faucet. I went through a dozen paper towels before my nose started to dry out. I forced myself to look in the mirror and couldn't help laughing at what I saw. I looked pathetic. My eyes were almost swollen shut. As it was, I could only keep them open to narrow slits. My nose looked raw from blowing it out with all those paper towels. Here I needed to win Charlotte over in a quick whirlwind romance, and I looked like this? As I said before, I couldn't catch a break.

I found Charlotte waiting for me in the lobby. The concern in her face seemed to have deepened and there was some nervousness back in her eyes.

'I didn't know where you were,' she said.

'I was trying to wash out my eyes.' I forced a laugh. 'I'll tell you, that hit me pretty hard. I never knew I was allergic to cats before.'

She seemed deep in thought as we walked to my car. When we got there she asked whether she should drive.

'Do you know how to handle a stick shift?'

She shook her head.

'Don't worry,' I said. 'I'll be okay driving.'

I put the top down and we headed off towards Bradley Memorial. With the way my eyes had swollen up, it was a struggle keeping them open against the sunlight. They just kept trying to force themselves shut. The fresh air, though, felt good against my face. Somehow, even though I could barely keep my eyes open, I got us to the hospital in one piece. Charlotte got out of the car and told me she'd be right back.

While I waited for her, I spotted Junior leaving the hospital with his two pint-sized miniature versions of himself. He saw me sitting in my car, and as he did, an ugly grin spread across his face. He changed direction and started walking towards me, ignoring his two boys as they punched at each other's arms.

'Well, look who's here,' he said. 'Whatsa matta, Joe, you been crying or something? Big bad world getting you down?'

'Junior, you better look after your two kids before they kill each other.'

He turned sideways to see his two boys smacking each other. He raised his hand as if he were going to slap both of them, and barked at them to stop it. They obeyed his order, both staring back with sullen, dull expressions.

'They're chips off the old block, huh, Junior?' I said.

He turned back towards me, his grin stretched tighter across his face. 'What I tell you before about calling me Junior,' he said.

'Sorry, old habits die hard.'

'You think you're so fucking smart. You're a fucking moron, that's what you are. What I tell you before about bothering my pop?'

'He told me why he's working out a deal with Phil.'

'You're fucking delusional.'

'You want to know why he's going to be spilling his guts? It's partly because of you, Junior. Woops, there I go, calling you that again.'

He didn't say anything, he just stared at me with his dark black eyes, his grin all but disappearing as it stretched even farther across his face. I noticed I even had his two boys' attention.

'He wants to save your soul. He thinks if he can force you out of your life of crime he can convert you into a devout, God-fearing member of society.'

'You've gone completely nutso, pal.'

'You think so, huh? Why don't you go back in there and talk to your dad about it. See what he has to say.'

'I don't have to go bothering Pop because of your bullshit delusions. But I tell you, Joe, there's going to be a price you're gonna pay for disturbing Pop. Beyond and above the thirty grand you owe me.'

'You got me shaking here, Junior.'

He took a step towards my car, his face flushed with violence. 'If you had any brains you would be shaking. You and me will settle this later, Joe. I promise you that.'

'If you have any issues with me,' I said, 'we can settle them now.'

'Nah, later, when we have some privacy.'

'We don't have to wait. If you want I can get out of the car now and kick the crap out of you in front of your two kids. Would you like me to do that?'

He started walking away from my car, his ugly grin back in place. 'That's okay, Joe. We'll settle things later. I guarantee it.'

I watched as Junior and his two kids walked across the

parking lot and got into his Range Rover. I was so caught up watching them that I wasn't aware that Charlotte had gotten into my passenger seat until she closed the door shut. It damn near gave me a heart attack.

'Here you go,' she said as she handed me a bottle of water and a pill. As I swallowed the pill, I noticed Junior's Range Rover slow down and could see him getting a good long look at Charlotte. Both his boys were also staring at her, both with their pug noses pressed hard against the same back passenger window. Junior lowered his window and waved at the two of us.

'See you around, Joe,' he yelled out before speeding off.

'I think that was Mr Vassey's son,' Charlotte said.

I nodded. I didn't like the fact that Junior saw the two of us together, but there was nothing I could do about it and it probably didn't matter.

'He doesn't seem like a very nice man,' she remarked quietly.

'I'd have to agree with that.'

She peered at me for a moment before turning away with a slight blush. 'Your swelling has gone down. Are you feeling any better?'

'I think so.'

I gave a quick look in the rearview mirror and could see she was right about the swelling. It was easier to keep my eyes open against the sunlight. As I pulled out of the parking lot and headed towards Burlington, Charlotte seemed lost in her own thoughts. She sat quietly, her brow furrowed, her small hands clasped tightly together.

At one point I thought I saw her shivering. I asked whether she was cold. She hesitated for a moment before telling me that she was fine. I pulled the car over and put the top back up.

'If the wind's bothering you, it's okay to tell me,' I said.

'It really wasn't bothering me,' she said. I could tell from how withdrawn she had gotten that something was on her mind, but

I didn't push it. After several minutes she interrupted our silence to ask me why I came to see her today.

'Why?' I laughed. 'I wanted to take you out on a date.'

'Why, though?'

'Because it was nice having coffee with you the other day. Because I find you attractive. And I guess because I wanted to get to know you better.'

She sat quietly after that, seeming to sink deeper into her private thoughts.

When we got to downtown Burlington, I parked in a garage and we set off on foot. It was one of those perfect fall days that send couples flocking to the stores and restaurants in the downtown area. It felt good just strolling about outside. As we were checking out the different restaurants around town, Charlotte's mood perked up. Whatever funk she had been slipping into was gone. She became more talkative and it took only a small effort on my part to squeeze a smile out of her.

We found a small French bistro that we decided to settle on. It was two thirty in the afternoon and the place was still crowded. A little after three we were seated. Charlotte ordered an apple crêpe and a glass of white wine. I ordered beef bourguignon. I tried asking for a bottle of beer to go with my meal, but Charlotte became concerned about my mixing alcohol with the allergy medication she had given me, so I ended up sticking with coffee. While I wanted the beer, it was kind of sweet that she showed the concern that she did.

Charlotte started to fidget as we waited for our food. The nervousness had come back to her large hazel eyes. I could tell she wanted to ask me something. She looked away from me and stared down at her small clasped hands. I couldn't help noticing how tiny and white her knuckles were.

'Joe,' she asked, 'you're not married, are you?'

I couldn't keep from smiling. So that was what had put her in a funk earlier. 'No,' I said. 'I was married once, but we divorced over seven years ago. And I don't have a girlfriend. To be honest, you're only the second woman I've ever dated.'

She looked back up at me. I could almost see the thoughts running through her head.

'It's true,' I said. 'I knew my wife when we were kids. We were together through high school and got married right afterwards. I've never dated anyone else, and you're the first person I've gone out with since my divorce.'

'Joe, the only thing I'll ask of you is that you don't lie to me.'

'Everything I've told you is the truth.'

Her eyes held steady on mine again. We sat like that for a while, just kind of looking at each other. I was actually beginning to feel pretty good, almost forgetting what I needed from her. A small, easy smile had made its way onto her face. We sat like that, not really aware of anything else, until our waiter broke the spell by bringing us our food.

I didn't realize how hungry I was until I smelled the food. The only thing I had eaten that day was the powdered doughnuts, and my stomach was now rumbling. Still, though, I forced myself to eat at a leisurely pace. I watched as Charlotte cut her crêpe into tiny pieces. After every few bites, she would stop to dab her mouth with her napkin. It was kind of cute, I guess. I never saw anyone eat that way before.

She coughed lightly to get my attention. 'Joe, do you have any children?' she asked.

'Two girls. Melissa's fourteen and Courtney's twelve.'

'Do you see them much?'

From her expression, I could tell what she really wanted to know was whether I still saw my ex-wife much. I shook my head. 'They're out of my life now,' I said. 'I won't be seeing them in the future.'

She tried to give me a sympathetic look, but I could tell there was some relief mixed in. To be polite, because it wasn't really any surprise to me, I made a comment about how I was surprised that she wasn't already married or involved in a relationship.

'I've never been married,' she said. She seemed to shrink inwards as a darkness passed over her face. 'I haven't dated much.'

After that I kept the conversation light, asking her about what she liked to do and stuff like that. When she wasn't working, she was usually at home reading a book or watching TV. I had a feeling that since she'd moved to Vermont her company had been almost exclusively her three cats. I could tell that I impressed her when I was able to discuss several of the books that were on her shelves. I didn't tell her that during the last seven years I probably emptied out the Bradley library – or to be more specific, Morris had emptied it out for me. Every week he'd check out between five and ten books for me. It got to the point where during the last year he'd almost always brought me several books each week that I'd already read.

I could see that there was another question dying to bust loose from her. I sat back and smiled and waited for it.

'Joe,' she said, 'you mentioned yesterday that you used to be a police officer?'

'Yeah.' I took a deep breath and made a decision. 'I did something pretty bad and was kicked off the force.'

An odd look flashed on her face. It wasn't surprise or shock or anything like that. I wasn't quite sure what it was. In any case, she didn't seem taken aback by my answer. She seemed almost satisfied with it, her eyes calm and holding steady on mine.

'What do you do now?'

'I'm in transition.' I let loose a short laugh. I couldn't help myself. 'My dad wants me to go to college. Who knows, maybe I could major in history or literature and become a professor someday. I don't know, I still haven't figured out yet what I'm going to do with my life.'

It was funny; she didn't press me about what I did to get myself thrown off the force, or why I hadn't dated during the last seven years. For the rest of the lunch, we stuck with small talk, only superficial stuff. When I tried asking her why she left Montreal she changed the subject to how nice the weather was, then her face darkened as she stared at her hands. I moved the conversation to her cats and that brightened her back up. She told me they were Persians and that she had brought them with her from Canada. Before too long she was smiling again.

After lunch we strolled around some of the stores. At one point she took hold of my hand. It felt nicer than I would have expected.

We made our way down to Lake Champlain. After walking for a few minutes along the shore, we sat on some rocks and looked out at the water. I saw a couple of seagulls flying overhead, and as I watched them, I found my thoughts drifting. I felt calm sitting there. The noises that had been buzzing through my head for the past several days were silent. Charlotte brought me out of it by asking how I knew Manny Vassey.

'I got to know him when I was a cop,' I said.

'Wasn't he a criminal?'

'Yeah, he was.'

'And you're friends with him?'

'Not exactly.' I hesitated as I tried to think of a way to broach the subject of what I really needed from her. Because what I really needed from her wasn't a girlfriend or a relationship, but for her to overdose Manny – maybe with morphine, maybe with something else. As I thought about it, I realized how crazy the idea was. It was more than a long shot, it was nuts. Completely, absolutely nuts. I felt cold all of a sudden, especially in the head.

The coldness was penetrating deep into my eye sockets. Kind of like when you eat ice cream too fast, except worse. I had to look away from her. But I had no other choice – no other way out that I could see – so I stumbled along, my voice sounding strange and foreign to me.

'I guess over the years I've grown to respect him, at least at some level, and maybe somewhat begrudgingly,' I said. 'He was always a tough, hard sonofabitch. But no one should have to die the way he's dying.'

I could feel the words drying up in my throat. I shifted my gaze back to her. Charlotte sat silently watching me, her color having dropped to a pasty white. Her mouth looked so small, her lips almost disappearing into her face. I forced myself to push forward, ignoring the queasiness that was working its way into my stomach.

'It just doesn't seem right.' I coughed and cleared my throat, my voice growing hoarse as I continued. 'Especially when it would take only a little extra morphine to put him out of his misery.'

'Is that why you asked me out?'

'What?'

'I asked you if that was why you asked me out,' she said.

There was no nervousness in her eyes. There was really nothing there. Her expression had hardened into something not quite human. I barely recognized her. I found myself shaking my head.

'I don't get what you're asking,' I said.

She just sat staring at me. After a while she told me that Alice Cook at the information desk had stopped her when she had gone back to the hospital to get my allergy medication.

'Alice told me that you were asking about me,' Charlotte said. 'She told me what you did to Mr Coakley. She told me how you went to prison. Please, Joe, don't lie to me. Tell me why you asked me out. Was it to get me to overdose Mr Vassey with morphine? Because I would never do that.'

So Alice had recognized me after all. Probably hit her after we had talked. Now I knew the reason for Charlotte's funk earlier and it left my head spinning. I heard myself mumble something about how I had no idea what she was talking about. 'I was only making an observation,' I forced out. 'Why would you think I'd want something like that?'

'Mr Coakley spends a lot of time visiting Mr Vassey.'

'So? What does that have to do with me? And I told you before why I asked you out. That was the only reason.'

We sat quietly after that. I'm not sure how long. It might've been ten minutes, maybe fifteen, but it seemed like an eternity. After a while she leaned against me. I looked over and saw her expression had softened. She moved closer and rested her head against my shoulder.

'Aren't the clouds lovely,' she whispered.

It was weird. She acted as if nothing had happened. There were no questions about what I had done to Phil, or about my being in jail, or my interest in Manny Vassey. She just sat quietly, occasionally making comments about how nice a day she was having or how beautiful the lake and sky were. Later, when we drove back to Bradley, it was more of the same. On the way back she told me she'd like something to eat so we stopped off at a diner. I could barely stomach anything and only had a few spoons of rice pudding. I watched as Charlotte took bird-sized bites from a grilled cheese sandwich. During it all my mind raced as I tried to understand how my conversation with her went the way it did, and more importantly, what I was going to do next.

When I got her back to her apartment, she hesitated and moved awkwardly towards me.

'Would you like to come in?' she asked.

'I'd like to,' I said, 'but your cats and my allergies—'

'Your medication should be good for twelve hours.'

'I'd better not risk it, at least not tonight. I still feel a little shaky from before.'

I wasn't exaggerating. I did feel shaky. Maybe not from my earlier allergic reaction, but I still felt shaky as hell. I could see a thought start to formulate in her eyes about us maybe finding someplace else to be alone, so I moved quickly and gave her a long kiss. When I moved away I asked if I could see her tomorrow when she got off work.

'I could pick you up here,' I said.

She nodded. 'I'd like that. I finish work tomorrow at seven. Why don't you come by at eight?'

I told her I'd see her then and gave her a quick kiss before leaving. As I drove back to my parents' house, I kept playing the scene at the lake over and over again in my head. Maybe my comment about putting Manny out of his misery was out of line, but how could she make the leap from that to guessing that I only asked her out so I could manipulate her into overdosing Manny? The only thing I could come up with was she must have overheard Manny and Phil talking together. Maybe she overheard Phil trying to convince Manny to incriminate me. Anyway, I couldn't get that out of my head, that and the fact that even though she knew what I had done, she was willing to go out with me and pretend that none of it ever happened.

What really got to me was the look on her face when she was waiting for me to explain myself. It was the type of look you might see at an accident site when a bystander catches a glimpse of something he wishes to hell he never saw. And she knew damn well I was lying! She knew it, but went straight into denial, pretending everything between us was hunky-dory.

By the time I got to my parents' house, I was feeling worse than shaky – kind of weak in the knees, like all I wanted to do was get to bed, lie down and hide from the world. When I opened the door I saw both my parents sitting in the den. They had the TV set on, but it was obvious they weren't paying attention to it. When they turned to me, my mom's mouth started to move as if she were chewing gum and my dad looked as if he dreaded what was about to happen.

'Can you sit down, Joey?' my dad asked.

'What's this about?'

My mom's mouth was closed but it was still moving furiously. It seemed like an effort for her to stop it. 'Do what your father tells you to do,' she demanded sharply.

I took a couple of steps into the room. 'Look,' I said, 'I'm tired and I don't have time for this nonsense. What do you want?'

'Sit down!' my mom ordered, her voice shrill and bordering on hysteria, her mouth once again chewing away on her imaginary gum.

'If this is about what happened at church—'

'Elaine called us today,' my dad said. He had slouched forward and was wringing his hands. He could barely look up at me. 'She told us how you drove to Albany the other day and how you called this morning. Courtney's been upset all day about your call.'

At first I was numb. Then as I looked at them, at my mom's raisin-like face rigid with fury and my dad's hangdog beaten expression, I could feel the blood rush to my head.

'You lied to me before,' I said. 'You knew where my daughters were and you lied to me about it.'

'Son, listen to me—'

But I didn't. I turned and raced out of the room.

The blood was now boiling in me. I was actually seeing red, honest to God. I started choking on the treachery and unfairness of it; that my own parents would conspire with my ex-wife to keep me away from my daughters.

My parents must've sat in their chairs stunned. I don't

think they had any idea where I was headed until I locked the door to their bedroom. Then I heard some activity from them, but I ignored it. I started pulling drawers from the dressers and dumping their contents onto the floor. My dad knocked meekly on the door, asking me to unlock it, and then my mom joined in, rapping on it frantically, but I ignored them. And then I found the pictures.

There were maybe fifty of them in total. They were all of Melissa and Courtney taken at different ages. As I looked at them, I felt the rage that had been burning inside me fizzle away. Both my girls looked a lot like Elaine. They were both petite and blonde. They both had such thin legs and arms. As I went through the pictures and saw my girls as they grew older, I could see some of me in Courtney, at least around the eyes. And there was a little bit of me in Melissa too; this sorrowful little smile that she had. Both girls had grown up to look a lot like Elaine; they were both pretty as hell, but there was just enough of me in both of them to keep them from being beautiful.

The rapping on the door had grown harder and more frantic. My mom yelled at me not to dare go through her things. The combination of it – her yelling and the rapping – knocked me out of my thoughts. I felt a heaviness settle in my throat. I closed my eyes and tried to swallow back the emotion that was fighting its way forward. I was damned if I was going to let the two of them see me cry. It took some effort, and some deep breathing, but I got myself under control.

I went over to the door and opened it. The two of them stood there, shocked, their eyes first going to the mess on the floor and then to the stack of photos that I was holding. My dad looked like death warmed over, my mom's shriveled face was livid.

'You had no right going through my possessions,' my mom squeezed out in a tight, cold voice.

'Shut up.'

'Don't you dare talk to your mother like that,' my dad said without much conviction.

'You two can go screw yourselves,' I said. 'You're going to lie to me about my daughters? You couldn't even let me see pictures of them? Go to hell.'

'Give me those pictures,' my mom demanded. And then she made a grab for them. I backed away and raised my hand so I was holding them above her head. She started hopping up and down trying to reach for them.

'You give those back to me or I'll call the police on you,' she forced out between hops. She was breathing heavily now. 'What you're doing is stealing.'

'Go right ahead and call them,' I said.

The whole situation was so laughable that I couldn't help myself. I just started laughing like a crazy man. Maybe I was having some sort of minor breakdown, I don't know, but I just kept laughing away as my mom hopped up and down trying to grab those photos from me.

The gunshot brought me out of it. That one shot was really made up of almost four simultaneous noises – the gun blast, glass breaking, a whirling rush past my ear, and then the bullet thudding into the wall. Four distinct noises all within the span of less than a second. I pushed both my mom and dad down and then dove to the floor.

Just before I hit the floor there was another shot and the sound of another window shattering. Then I heard tires squeal as a car raced away. At first my mind was completely blank, and when it started working again, all I could think was that sonofabitch Junior had tried making a go at me. I got to my feet and raced to the front door, but the car was long gone.

I went outside and could see from the street the two windows that were shot out. I had a pretty good idea where the shots came from. A car must've stopped in front of the house and fired the shots before speeding off. The first one had missed me by inches. It had been too close to have been meant as a warning. Whoever fired the shot was trying to blow my head off.

As I was standing there a couple of the neighbors poked their heads out. I yelled to them, asking whether anyone saw anything, but they just shook their heads and went back inside.

I ran back into the house and to my parents' room. Both of them were still on the floor. My dad looked out of it and my mom was making little mewing noises as she clutched at her hip. I saw where one of the bullets had hit the wall, and dug it out with a penknife. My guess, it was a seven millimeter, probably fired from a hunting rifle. I got on the phone and called the police and asked them to send an ambulance. Then I went over to my parents.

My dad was sitting up, but was still completely out of it. I helped him to his feet and walked him over to the bed. After I had him laid down I went over to my mom and knelt next to her.

She looked like she was in a great deal of pain as she clutched at her hip and made tiny sobbing noises.

'Mom, do you think you can stand up?' I asked.

'Get away from me, just leave and get away from me!'

'You don't mean that. You're in pain. Let me—'

'I said get away from me! And get out of my house! I don't ever want you back here.'

She had her eyes shut and tears were streaming down her small withered face. As I knelt next to her, she let go of her hip with her right hand and swung out, catching me on the side of the face. There wasn't much to her blow, probably weaker than what a three-year-old might do, but the shock of it sent me to my feet and stepping away from her.

The hell with it. The hell with both of them.

I looked around and saw that when I had dove to the floor after the first gunshot, I had flung the photos and they were now scattered across the room. I bent over and started picking them up. I was only partially paying attention to my dad, but noticed he had gotten off his bed and was standing beside me. All of a sudden, he started pummeling me, hitting me with both fists – not hard enough to do any real damage, but hard enough to hurt. And hard enough to almost send me to the floor. I caught my balance and moved back a few steps before turning to face him.

'You heard your mother,' he cried. He had his fists clenched and was waving them at me. 'Get out of our house!'

'Dad. Come on—'

'You're not welcome here! Get out!'

He took a step towards me and I just shook my head and left the room and kept walking until I was out of the house. When I got to the curb I sat down. As I waited for the police to show up, I looked over the photos that I had grabbed. I had only been able to pick up six of them. Still, it settled me down to look at images of Melissa and Courtney as they smiled shyly at the camera.

The cruiser came quickly. It's not every day in Bradley you have shots fired at a residential home. The siren turned off and Bill Wright and a younger cop that I didn't know got out of the car.

Bill stood for a moment and peered at the two broken windows before addressing me.

'What happened here?' he asked.

'Someone took a couple of shots at me from outside. The first shot missed me by inches.'

Bill turned his gaze back towards the windows. 'You called for an ambulance. Is anyone hurt?'

'I pushed my parents to the floor after the first shot. I think my mom might've broken her hip.'

'It was just you and your mom and dad inside?'

'Yeah.'

Bill turned to the younger cop. 'Mike, go inside and see how they're doing. Take their statements, and also, give the station another call, make sure an ambulance is on its way.'

The younger cop, Mike, gave me a funny look before leaving us. Bill stood awkwardly for a moment and then looked back again towards the house.

'The ambulance should've been here by now,' he muttered under his breath. Then to me, 'Did you see anything?'

'No. After the shots were fired I ran outside, but whoever did this was long gone.'

'Any idea who might've shot at you?'

'No idea. As I told you, I didn't see anyone.'

Of course, that wasn't what he asked. Annoyance disturbed his long narrow face. He turned to stare at me for a few seconds before looking away. In any case he let it drop.

'Why were you waiting outside for us?'

'My parents didn't want me in their house.'

He nodded as if that made perfect sense. He asked, 'You haven't looked around for shell casings, have you?'

I shook my head. 'I dug one of the bullets out of the bedroom wall. It looks like a seven millimeter. I left it on top of the dresser.'

'I'll see if I can find any casings.'

He took out a flashlight and started searching the ground. I watched as he walked back and forth. After a few minutes he found one and held it up with a pencil. At that moment an ambulance pulled up. Two EMT workers jumped out of it.

'You took your time coming here,' I said.

Neither of them bothered to look at me. One of them told me they left as soon as they got the call. The other one addressed Bill. 'What do we have here?' he asked.

'An elderly woman might've broken her hip.'

Without being asked, I told them that my mom was sixty-three. The EMTs ignored me and opened the back of their ambulance and took out a stretcher. Then they made a beeline to the house, leaving me and Bill Wright alone. I just sat and stared at him. Eventually, he flinched under it.

'You were holding up the ambulance,' I said.

He pretended not to hear me.

'What were you hoping for?' I asked. 'That I had gotten hit and would bleed out before help could get to me?'

'I don't know what you're talking about.'

'Bullshit.'

He turned and glared at me, but it was forced and unnatural. Then he looked away. We stood silently for what seemed like minutes before he muttered something about me waiting where I was. 'I'll be right back,' he said.

I watched as he walked away, his gait self-conscious. He was about to enter the house, but he backed up to let the two EMTs out. They held a short conversation before he slid past them and went inside.

The stretcher the EMTs were carrying was empty. As they were loading it into the back of the ambulance I asked how my mom was.

'I think her hip is badly bruised, but not broken,' one of them said to me.

'Shouldn't you be taking her to the hospital?'

He shrugged. 'If they don't want to go, you can't make them.'

The two of them finished loading up the ambulance and then drove off. I sat for another few minutes on the curb and then stood up and got into my car. While I sat there I thought about the police holding up the ambulance on me. When I had called, I had spoken to the switchboard operator, and she had probably relayed my message to the desk sergeant, Schilling. It had probably been his idea. Still, I was sure Bill knew about it. As I thought about it, I realized I didn't care. Just as I realized I didn't care that my parents had thrown me out. Let them all do whatever they wanted to. As soon as I could, I'd be out of Bradley. Then none of it would matter.

I had my eyes closed and head tilted back when there was a short rap on the driver's side window. I opened my eyes and saw Bill leaning over, frowning. I rolled down the window.

'You weren't planning on driving off, were you?'

I shook my head. 'I was just waiting here for you.'

'That's quite a mess in there,' he said.

I didn't bother answering him.

He waited for a few seconds, realized I wasn't going to say anything, and then continued. 'Your parents claim you have photos that belong to them. They want them back.'

'They're pictures of my kids.'

'They say they'll file charges against you if you don't return them.'

'Let them.'

'If that's what you want.'

He started fingering his handcuffs. He had them half slid off his belt before I stopped him.

'This is ridiculous,' I said. 'I'll go in and talk to them.'

He shook his head. 'They don't want you in their house. Why don't you hand me those photos. It would be a pretty stupid thing to have to arrest you for.'

'Yeah, it would be,' I agreed. 'Especially since if I was brought in tonight, I'd make a stink about that ambulance being held up on me. Someone might actually care about it.'

I could see his eyes dull a bit, but he didn't say a word. I let out a lungful of air. 'Why don't you go back in there and tell them that if they want I'll give them their pictures back, but if I do, I'll also be driving to Albany tonight so I can take my own in the morning. Let's see what they say to that.'

Bill's mouth twisted into a smirk as he shot me a disgusted

look, but after a ten-count, he turned and went back into the house. When he came back he told me I could keep the photos.

'You need anything else from me?' I asked.

He shook his head, his eyes as lifeless as glass.

'I've got a duffel bag with my clothes in there. It's in my bedroom. You want to accompany me while I go in and get it?'

'They don't want you in there.' I could see in his eyes the last thing he wanted to do was run another errand for me. It just about killed him, but he gritted his teeth and told me to wait where I was while he went in and retrieved my bag for me.

As he went back into the house, I got out of the car and stretched. My muscles ached and I was dead tired. As I stretched, Bill came out of the house with my duffel bag. For a moment it looked as if he were going to hand it to me, but as I reached out for the bag he dropped it at my feet.

'About your being shot at,' he said, 'here's a suggestion. Why don't you get in your car and keeping driving 'til you get someplace where somebody gives a damn?'

Chapter 13

I found a roadside motel in Eastfield to spend the night. The room they gave me had a dirty, stale feel to it and seemed more like a bunker than a motel room. The walls were concrete, the flooring a mix of industrial carpeting and cement, and the mattress had to have been at least thirty years old and in worse shape than the one I had in jail. It was the type of place where you kept your shoes on, and still checked where you stepped so you wouldn't walk on any left-behind hypodermic needles or used rubbers. Still, I was out before my eyes closed. Completely out, no dreams, nothing. It was as if a switch had been thrown.

The room was still dark when I opened my eyes. My neck and joints ached and I had a rotten taste in my mouth and generally felt lousy. With some effort, I contorted my neck and upper body so I could look at the two-dollar alarm clock next to the bed. It was only a few minutes past five. I pushed myself out of bed, got into the shower and tried to get as clean as I could. It wasn't easy; the shower wasn't the type you could really get clean in. The soap they gave was a small sliver, the water stayed mostly cold and only at the end made it close to lukewarm, and the lone towel that was left folded in the bathroom couldn't have cost more than fifty cents and was about as thick as tissue paper.

I wanted to get out of there quickly and escape the griminess of the place, and was dressed and in my car by five thirty. The first thing I did was drive to an all-night gas station and buy some doughnuts, aspirin and road maps. I brought all the stuff out to my car, and after wolfing down the doughnuts and chewing on a few aspirin, I unfolded the road maps and planned out a trip to Montreal. Before heading off, I called my parole officer, Craig Simpson, on a payphone and left a message that I had to miss our meeting because of a job interview. I knew Craig well enough to know that while he'd be annoyed by my canceling our appointment, he'd let it slide.

I had thought long and hard about seeking out Junior for the stunt he pulled the night before, but I had this nagging feeling about Charlotte that I couldn't shake. When I thought back about our day together and how she had acted after she'd left the hospital, it seemed bizarre to me. Almost as if she suspected me then of wanting her to overdose Manny. I had this image of her in my mind, of when we had driven to Burlington, how she sat closed and withdrawn, and how she'd occasionally peek at me when she didn't think I was looking. I shuddered involuntarily as I thought about it. It was more than that, though. It didn't make any sense for her to jump to that conclusion as quickly as she had. There was something not quite right there and I was going to find out what it was. As much as I wanted to pay Junior back, this seemed more important.

Even though it was only six in the morning and the sun hadn't yet had a chance to rise, the air had a clammy feel to it and you could tell the day was going to be overcast. It was the type of weather that would get into your bones. I put the top down anyways. I don't know, I guess after seven years cooped up in jail, I now wanted as much air as I could get. Driving to Montreal was only a half-hour longer than the ride to Albany, but I didn't get any sense of peace from the trip. I had too many thoughts and worries nagging at me.

I reached customs by nine thirty and got to the first hospital a little before ten. It took some persistence and wheedling on my part, but the woman working in the records room was too polite to stonewall me for long. After a while she checked their files and told me that Charlotte never worked there. I went through the same deal with three more hospitals until I found one that Charlotte had worked at. When I asked the clerk in their administration office whether I could speak with someone familiar with Charlotte's work history, she asked me to wait a few minutes, and then got on the phone and tried to locate someone for me. Less than ten minutes later I was brought into the office of the Chief of Surgery.

The Chief of Surgery, Dr Henri Bouchaire, was a cheery-looking fellow, about thirty-five, with light brownish hair and long sideburns. He stood up immediately to shake my hand, and when he sat back down, he pressed both his hands flat together so they formed an apex, and rested the tip against his chin.

'I'd like to thank you for taking the time to see me,' I said.

'That's quite all right.' He paused to show me an anemic smile. 'I understand you have several questions that you would like to ask concerning a nurse we once employed. Charlotte Boyd, is that correct?'

'That's right.'

'And you are?'

I fished my driver's license out of my wallet and handed it to him. Fortunately, I was able to renew it while in jail. He gave it a cursory look and handed it back to me.

'My name's Joe Denton,' I said. 'I'm a retired police officer from Vermont and I'm investigating Ms Boyd for a hospital that she is currently employed at. To be honest, I'm surprised to be talking to you. I expected to be meeting with her past supervisor.'

'Yes, normally that would be the case.' He seemed to lose his train of thought for a moment. As he looked at me, the thin smile he was showing weakened. 'Is your investigation for a general background check or did, uh, a specific incident occur?'

'A specific incident occurred.'

'Which was?'

'A patient died who shouldn't have.'

All his cheeriness left him. He looked down at his desk for a few seconds before meeting my eyes. 'Did this, uh, patient die of respiratory failure?' he asked.

I wanted to kick myself for not researching this better, but I took a gamble and nodded. He separated his hands and started slowly massaging his temples.

'Are you okay, Doctor?' I asked.

He nodded and dropped his hands to his desk. 'I've been afraid of this,' he said.

'So you had some unexplained deaths here also?'

He both sighed and nodded at the same time. 'Mr Denton, could you please tell me what your hospital's medical staff suspects?'

It looked like not only did I hit a long shot, but one that was going to pay off big. 'Morphine overdose,' I said as calmly and evenly as I could.

'Dear Lord,' he murmured.

'And you think the same thing happened here?'

'We had four patients who died of respiratory failure which I found suspicious,' he said. 'Let me explain. Overdosing a patient with morphine will cause respiratory failure. During the post-mortem the only change is diffused cerebral edema, and the problem is that it is very nonspecific to link to a morphine overdose.'

'But you suspected Ms Boyd?'

'Yes.' He sighed. 'Their deaths did not seem consistent with their medical conditions. They were all her patients. And her demeanor afterwards seemed, uh, unnatural to me. But there was no evidence, at least none that could be used in court, to support my suspicions. The morphine levels in the IV bags were where they were supposed to be and I don't believe the instrumentation was tampered with. But after the first three deaths, I personally marked all the morphine IV tubing. I found with the last patient that it had been changed.'

'What does that mean?'

'That she could have used a syringe to inject morphine into the IV tubing and replaced the tubing afterwards. Later, there would be no evidence of what she had done.'

'Why would she bother replacing the tubing?'

'In case we looked for a needle hole.'

I leaned back in my chair and thought about it, and tried to muster as indignant a look as I could. 'So you confronted her and forced her to leave your hospital?'

He nodded. He was beginning to look a little green around the gills.

'You did more than that, didn't you,' I said. 'You forced her to leave Montreal.'

'I wish there was something else I could have done,' he said. 'We had no concrete evidence that she poisoned her patients. I felt fortunate simply to have her leave the province.'

'So as long as she moved to another country and murdered her patients there, that was okay with you?'

He shook his head. 'No, of course not. But what else could I have done?'

He seemed like a decent enough guy and I didn't get any enjoyment out of putting him through the wringer, but I needed to make my performance look authentic. The last thing I wanted to do was make him suspicious and have him check up on me.

I gave it some time to make it look like I was mulling things over. 'Well, Doctor,' I said after a while, 'I guess I can appreciate how difficult the situation must've been for you. I guess if I were in your shoes, I don't know what I would've done.' I paused, because there was something else nagging at the back of my brain. 'Were the four patients all terminal?' I asked.

He shook his head. 'No, in fact only one of them was.'

I must've, at least at some level, been suspecting that, but it still came as a surprise. I guess when the idea first came to me, I had assumed Charlotte had been acting out some sort of angel of mercy thing. But it wasn't that. She had other reasons for doing what she did. And this image of her sneaking through the hospital with her morphine syringe started to creep me out.

I had another question that was nagging at me. I asked him whether Charlotte had any close friends at the hospital that she might've confided in. He told me he had asked around at the time and couldn't find anyone who considered themselves more than an acquaintance of hers. And not many considered themselves that.

I stood up and thanked him for his time.

He seemed taken aback by my abruptness, but took my outstretched hand and mumbled out an apology for what happened. I then left him deep in his own thoughts.

At a subconscious level, I must've suspected something like that of Charlotte all along. I had to have. That had to have been why I came up with the plan that I did, because otherwise it would've been completely nuts. Maybe it was the way she avoided talking about Montreal, or maybe it was some look or expression of hers that I'd caught a glimpse of, or maybe it was simply the whole package, but something about her had caused that seed to be planted in my mind.

I could understand now why she had jumped to the conclusion that she did. When I had made my offhand remark about overdosing Manny, she must have panicked and thought that I had already dug around her past in Montreal and suspected what she had done. I thought about her and the repressed life that she lived. It must've been worse when she was in Montreal. I could just imagine how all that repression would weigh on her. How it would press on her chest. How tough it would be to breathe against. And how she'd find relief by unloading a morphine syringe into a patient's IV tubing.

Well, anyway, she was going to use a morphine syringe one more time.

It was only a quarter to twelve. I drove around until I found a diner, and then went inside and ordered lunch. My waitress was a cute little thing; blonde, perky, big dimples, and friendly as all hell. She had one of those smiles that made you feel good just looking at it. I kidded around with her after she brought me my food and had a feeling that if I asked her to come back to the States with me, she would've jumped in my car. In any case, the check was six bucks and I left her a ten-dollar tip.

After lunch I thought about driving around the city and seeing the sights. I thought about it, but decided to head back to Vermont. I still had plenty of things that needed to be done. When I reached the US border and the customs officer asked how my trip went, I couldn't help myself – I just showed him a big smile and told him it was the best damn trip I ever had. I was feeling too good to have said anything else. Hell, I was just about beaming. I hadn't realized before how much stress had bottled up in my neck and back and joints, but it was all gone now. I was feeling loose. Maybe a little anxious, but not much. All in all I felt good.

As I drove, at times my mind would just drift along, not aware of anything but the road and the scenery. At other times I found myself thinking about what was going to happen. Charlotte was going to shoot enough morphine into Manny's IV tubing to kill him and that would be the end of it.

When the idea had first come to me, I was concerned whether a morphine overdose could be detected by an autopsy. Now, though, thanks to the good Dr Bouchaire, I knew that it couldn't be. I knew that there was nothing to worry about. Soon Manny would be checking out and that would be that. Dan Pleasant would be off my back, Phil Coakley would be left empty handed, and Junior, well, that was still a problem. Something was going to have to be done about him. There'd have to be payback for his taking a couple of shots at me. But I knew I'd come up with something, and when it was all over, I'd move somewhere and start fresh. And then I'd start doing what I needed to for my girls.

During my ride back an idea popped into my head on how I could take care of Junior. Over the next half-hour or so, the idea gelled nicely, and the more I thought about it, the more I liked it. It would be a fitting epitaph to my life in Bradley. After a while my mind started drifting along with the scenery again. And then I just settled back into my seat and enjoyed the ride.

Chapter 14

I was on Route Six as I entered Chesterville, and as I passed the Green Valley Motor Lodge, I saw half a dozen police cars and three sheriff's vehicles in the parking lot, all with their lights flashing. I almost stopped to see what had happened, but I knew my presence wouldn't be appreciated. Still, my palms felt itchy as I drove by.

Two miles down the road, I spotted a bar and pulled over. From the outside, the place looked like a typical small-town dive. It was four thirty and the bar was busier than it had any right to be. Inside, it looked just as divey. At that hour it should've had only a few hardcore and unrepentant drinkers scattered about. Instead it was nearly wall to wall people and there was a buzz running through the room.

I squeezed my way to the bar, got the bartender's attention, and ordered a Guinness. Next to me on my right was a stubby guy with a thick beard, wearing a Red Sox cap and a plaid hunting jacket. He was holding a pint as he talked to one of his buddies, a look of both amusement and disbelief mixed on his face. I leaned closer to eavesdrop on their conversation. They didn't seem to notice or care.

I was able to get that the stubby guy's name was Carl. I didn't catch his buddy's name.

Carl: 'I can't believe he didn't kill him.'

Buddy: 'Shit, all he did was shoot him in the arm.'

Carl: 'And that was from only five feet away. My two-year-old can shoot better than that.'

Buddy: 'He killed the girl, though.'

Carl: 'Yeah, he killed her alright. I heard they took her out in a bag. Is that what you heard too, Sam?'

An old guy with a sour face who stood next to them turned and nodded. Carl and his buddy stopped to finish their beers. They waved the bartender over for another round. I was still waiting for my Guinness.

Buddy: 'I wonder where he shot her?'

Carl: 'Don't know.'

Buddy: 'Did you ever see her dance?'

Carl: 'Yeah, if you could call what she did dancing. What a rotten shame. She was one of the nicer girls there. And you didn't have to tip her much to get her panties off.'

Buddy: 'I always thought Paul was nuts.'

Carl: 'Yeah, I don't know. He did catch them in bed.'

Buddy: 'So what? She was a stripper. What did he expect?'

Carl: 'Yeah, I guess. Jesus, I don't know.' He broke out laughing. 'That DA's going have a tough time showing his face around town after this.' And he kept laughing at his own joke.

I could feel my heart pounding. I tapped him on the shoulder. He stopped laughing and turned slowly to face me, bleary eyed from what must've already been several pints of beer.

'What happened here?' I asked.

He peered at me for a moment before answering. 'We had a double shooting at the motel up the street,' he said. 'A guy caught his stripper girlfriend in bed with the DA, Phil Coakley – you know, the guy whose face is all fucked up? He killed his girlfriend but only shot Coakley in the arm. What I hear, Coakley tackled him and knocked him out. Police have the guy now.'

'The dead girl's a stripper named Susie?'

'Yeah, Susie Baker. The guy who killed her is Paul Frechotte. You know them?'

'Sort of. Not really. Any idea how Frechotte knew they were in the motel room?'

He shook his head slowly. His eyes narrowed as he looked at me.

'You look familiar,' he said. 'Do I know you?'

While we were talking, his buddy stood behind him grinning like an idiot. At some point, I guess he recognized me. His grin disappeared and he seemed to sober up. He nudged Carl and leaned over so he could say something in his ear. I could see recognition flash in Carl's eyes. Without saying a word, the two of them moved away from me. As I looked around the bar I could see others had recognized me. They weren't staring at me outright, but I could see them sneaking glances at me. I could see other people being nudged and whispered to.

The bartender had just brought me my beer. I dropped five bucks on the bar and got out of there.

When I got to my car my hands were shaking. I had to sit for a few minutes before I could pull out of the parking lot. I kept thinking of Susie, of how sweet and innocent she had seemed, and how much, even with her clothes off, she had looked like a high school cheerleader. I imagined how the scene at the motel went down. I could imagine Frechotte breaking in on them, gun already drawn, shooting Susie first, and then shooting wildly as Phil rushed him. It probably didn't take much for Phil to knock him out. I knew, at least at some level, that I was responsible for what happened. I knew how Frechotte found out about that motel room.

I drove straight to the county jail in Bradley. A roaring in my head drowned out the road noise. I could barely hear anything above it. And I could barely see where I was driving. It was as if I had blinders on. As if I had no peripheral vision. The little

I could see was clouded by a red haze. Somehow, though, I got there without cracking up. When I got out of my car, I stood and waited while the roaring in my head subsided and the haze faded. Then I went inside and searched for Morris.

I found him in his office. He was leaning back in his chair with his feet up on his desk and his eyes closed. When he heard me, his eyelids lifted so he could peer at me.

'You know where Dan is?' I asked.

'Probably at the crime scene. Things didn't work out the way you planned, did they, Joe?'

'Morris, I had nothing to do with this. I swear.'

His eyelids dropped a bit, but otherwise his expression of complete indifference remained unchanged.

'Susan Baker was only twenty-two,' he croaked out in a tired voice. 'Are you happy with yourself?'

'Morris, I swear, I didn't know any of this was going to happen—'

'Of course you did, Joe. Phil has something on you and Dan, doesn't he?'

I shook my head.

'That's why you arranged to meet Dan here yesterday,' he said.

'I didn't arrange that—'

He held up a hand to stop me. It looked like it took all the strength he had.

'No, please,' he said. 'Don't embarrass yourself like this, Joe. Somehow you found out about that girl and Phil. You arranged to meet Dan here. Then the two of you planned what happened today. Except all you accomplished was causing an innocent girl to be killed. Because Phil survived with only a flesh wound.'

'Morris, I had no idea about any of this.'

'Joe, please.' He showed me a sad smile. 'I actually thought of us as friends. I actually thought that there was something of substance inside you, that you could reform yourself and live a decent life. But I was wrong. We're through, Joe. We're not friends anymore.'

He let his eyelids close. As far as he was concerned I wasn't there.

I stood frozen, wanting to explain to him how wrong he was, but I realized there was nothing to explain. I turned and left.

I didn't know what else to do so I drove back to my motel room, dialed Dan's beeper, and left a message. The waiting was murder. I was feeling so jumpy and sick inside. All the damage I was causing was adding up. I had already put two boys in the hospital and now this. Because of me a young girl lay dead in the morgue. And of course there was more than that. There was Phil. And I guess in some way, Clara. Even my own parents...

I tried watching TV to get my mind off it all, but I couldn't lie still. I had too much nervous energy. Every few minutes I'd have to get off the bed and do pushups or pace the room. I needed to get a hold of Dan and have him explain what happened. Of course I knew what happened, but I needed him to explain it.

Around a quarter to six there was a soft knock on my door. I opened it and saw Dan standing there. He stepped into the room quickly, closing the door behind him. I watched as he walked over to a chair and sat down. He tilted the chair back so it leaned against the wall, and loosely clasped his hands behind his head. As he looked up at me, he smiled pleasantly, but his coloring was pasty and he looked worn out around the eyes and mouth. He remarked about what a fleabag I had picked.

'You think with the money I gave you you could've picked a better place, Joe. Jesus, I've been in gas station rest rooms that I'd rather sleep in,' he said.

I could feel myself trembling as I stared at him. I had an urge to kick his chair legs out from under him and send him crashing to the floor. I started to say something, but forced my mouth shut. I didn't trust myself yet to talk.

'You probably heard about what happened today,' he said. 'What a mess. I've been up to my ears in it all day. I got here as soon as I could.'

I asked him how Frechotte ended up at that motel.

He made a face. 'Come on, Joe, after what you told me? You should know the answer to that.'

'I'd like to hear it anyway.'

'You would, huh? Okay, Joe, I'll tell you what you already know. I had one of my boys follow Susie this morning. When she went to the motel, and later when Coakley showed his ugly face, I called Frechotte and told him about it. Anonymously, of course, and from a payphone. If he wasn't such a fucking jerk-off our problems would be over now.'

'You sonofabitch.'

'And why's that?'

'You had no goddam right.'

'What are you talking about? Joe, I did only what you wanted me to do.'

'I never wanted you to do that.'

'Really?'

I didn't answer him. He was still smiling pleasantly, and as he looked at me, a glint of genuine amusement shone in his eyes.

'Joe,' he said, 'who are you trying to kid? Why'd you tell me about Coakley banging that broad?'

'I already told you why the other day.'

'Yeah, right. You expect me to believe that cock-and-bull story you gave me? That you only wanted me to follow Coakley around so I could catch him in the act and file a morals charge against him? You think I'm an imbecile?'

Whatever was in his eyes died. As he looked at me, his smile tightened into something vicious. He stood up and moved close to me. Close enough that I could smell his breath.

'You want to take a swing at me, is that it, Joe?' he asked, his voice barely above a whisper. 'Well, go right ahead, but I promise you I want to kick your teeth in a hell of a lot more than you could imagine. What happened today is your fault. Don't kid yourself otherwise. If you had taken care of things like you were supposed to, I wouldn't have had to send that puffed-up piece of crap Frechotte to that motel room.'

He was breathing heavily, his breath stale and oppressive, a bit like rotting garbage. I had to force myself to keep from stepping away from him. Then the moment passed. His eyes came back to life and his smile loosened into something more recognizable. He shook his head as if to indicate that I was nuts, and then sat back in the chair and crossed his legs.

'You were right about Grayson,' he said. 'I cornered him this morning and got him to tell me that he's meeting with Coakley and Manny Wednesday to iron out a deal. And you're right, the deal's going to protect Junior. So Joe, I'm expecting you to take care of this today. How are you going to do it?'

'I'm not telling you shit.'

'No, that's not a good answer. Three of my boys are waiting outside. Unless I hear something more convincing, I'm going to bring them in here and we're going to take care of things here and now. So Joe, how are you going to take care of this?'

As I looked at him I knew he meant what he said. He casually took his revolver out of its holster and rested it on his knee. I knew I was a breath away from being a dead man.

My throat had dried up on me. I had to clear it before I could talk.

'I'll take care of this,' I said, my voice cracking.

'What did you say? I couldn't hear you. Your voice kind of faded on you.'

I went into the bathroom and poured myself a cup of water. I couldn't have gotten a word out without it. I drank it slowly and walked back to him. I stopped when he moved his hand to get a better grip on the gun.

I told him again that I'd take care of things.

'That's not good enough, Joe. You've been letting me down for three days now. I want to hear details. I want to be convinced.'

'I can't tell you,' I said. 'Someone else is involved. But it's all worked out. Manny will be gone by morning.'

'Joe, come on, you should know there are no secrets between us. I want to know every little detail.'

I could feel the sweat building on the back of my neck. I shook my head.

He pursed his lips as he studied me. I could tell he was trying to make up his mind, and I could see it in his eyes when he settled on a decision. He put his gun back in its holster and smiled as pleasantly as I ever saw him.

'Okay, Joe, you have until tonight. But I hope you understand, I'm not playing anymore. You understand that, right?'

I nodded.

'So tell me, this other person, you didn't by any chance mention my name to him?'

'No. No one else has been mentioned.'

'That's good, Joe. You're using some brains for a change. Keep it up. Maybe we'll all be able to look back at this someday and get a good laugh out of it.'

He stood up, gave me a wink, and headed towards the door. I tried to keep my mouth shut, but I couldn't help myself.

'It doesn't bother you what happened to that girl?' I asked.

He turned to me and shrugged. 'Of course it does,' he said. 'If it were up to me, Frechotte would have unloaded a full clip into Coakley's face and left her out of it. If he had done that, this would be over now and we'd have the added benefit of a closed casket.'

His smile turned wistful as he thought about it. He shook his head sadly. 'But it wasn't up to me, Joe,' he continued, 'just as it wasn't up to me that you've been fucking around with this the last three days. But I will miss her. She was a sweet girl, and you don't get a chance to see a nice little red bush like hers every day.'

He left then.

The back of my shirt had soaked through with sweat. I got out of my clothes, took a quick shower, and dried off the best I could with the dishrag that had been left in the bathroom to masquerade as a bath towel. Afterwards, I got dressed and sat on the bed and looked at the pictures I had of Melissa and Courtney. When I felt strong enough, I threw whatever I had into my duffel bag and checked out of the motel. As I drove to Bradley Memorial Hospital, I spotted one of Dan's deputies, Hal Wheely, following me in an unmarked Chevy.

I made no attempt to lose him. He did a pretty clumsy job of tailing me, and he must've known that I spotted him. But I guess he didn't care.

Chapter 15

It was twenty to seven by the time I pulled into the hospital parking lot. When I got to the lobby, I noticed Alice Cook behind the information desk. She avoided my eye as I walked past her.

I thought I'd catch Charlotte before her shift ended. I didn't feel that I could wait until eight to see her. As I headed towards the terminal ward, I spotted Junior and his two goons, Jamie and Duane, at the other end of the hallway walking towards me. When he saw me, a big ugly grin broke across his face.

'Hey, Joe,' he yelled out. 'Whatcha doin' here? You're not planning on bothering my pop again, are you?'

I stopped where I was. Junior and his two goons kept coming, maybe even speeding up their pace. When Junior reached me, he moved alongside me and put his arm around my shoulder.

'Get your hands off me,' I told him as I braced myself.

'Hey, I'm just talking friendly-like to an old friend, that's all,' Junior said. His two goons had positioned themselves so I was sandwiched between all three of them.

'I told you to get your hands off me,' I said.

'Lighten up. We're all friends here, okay? Now I asked you, are you here to bother my pop again?'

'Junior, I'm going to tell you for the last time to get your hands off me.'

I had taken my car keys out of my pocket. I could feel my muscles tensing. Even with his two goons standing next to me, I'd be able to get a couple of shots in. I'd make sure that Junior was bleeding from somewhere before they pulled me off him. I guess Junior realized that also. His ugly grin dulled a bit and he removed his hand from my shoulder. He backed up half a step. His two goons stood where they were.

'Hey, don't go psycho on me, okay?' Junior said. 'I'm just talking to you as an old pal, that's all. Want to know something, Joe? I hung out with Pop later than usual today hoping you'd show up.'

'I'm glad I didn't disappoint you.'

'You think you're so goddam smart, but guess what? You're not as bright as you think you are. I knew sooner or later you'd try bothering Pop again with your bullshit.'

'Is that so?'

'Yeah, that's so. And I want to tell you I figured out how you're going to pay for bothering Pop the other day.'

'I thought you told me last night.'

He looked away from me to his two goons. 'What's he talking about?' he asked them. 'Anyone say shit to him last night?'

Both Jamie and Duane shook their heads. Junior looked back at me. 'I don't know what the fuck you're talking about,' he said.

'You took a couple of shots at me last night.'

'I did, did I?' he asked. He turned to his two goons and asked them, 'Either of you know anything about this?' Neither of them said anything.

He turned back to me, his grin now tight against his face. 'You're nuts, Joe. If I took a shot at you, you wouldn't be standing here now.'

'Somebody took two shots at me.'

A young doctor, probably around thirty, was approaching

from behind. He made sure to give us a wide berth as he passed by. Junior waited until he was out of earshot before he leaned closer to me.

'Look somewhere else, pal,' he said, making an effort to keep his voice low. 'I'm sure if you look hard enough you'll find plenty of other guys who'd like to plug you. But not me. Not while you owe me money. And that's what I want to talk to you about. What you owe me is being bumped to forty large.'

I couldn't help laughing.

'Laugh all you want, bright guy. The extra ten grand is the price you're paying for bothering my pop. And now I want a minimum eight grand each week.'

'Yeah, well, I want peace on earth and goodwill to all mankind. We don't all get what we want, Junior.'

'I'll get it, don't worry. I'll either get the forty grand in money or in enjoyment. One way or the other I'll get it.'

'Don't hold your breath.'

His face flushed and his eyes half-closed as he glared at me. 'You think you're so fucking smart, don't you? Let me tell you something, Joe, the difference between you and me is I don't say a word without having everything set up first. You, you go shooting off your mouth without knowing what the fuck you're saying. I got something for you to look at.'

He reached into the inside pocket of his black leather jacket and pulled out a folded document and handed it to me. It was an affidavit from Earl Kelley. In it Earl claimed the night Billy Ferguson was murdered he played poker with Junior. He also claimed he tried inviting me into the game, but that I told him I had business to take care of. There was more stuff in it but that was the gist of it.

'You can keep it,' Junior said. 'It's a copy. I got the original.'

'Thanks.'

'Pretty stupid of you shooting off your mouth to my pop,' he said. 'Whatcha thinking? That he's not going to tell me everything you said?'

'Yeah, it was stupid,' I agreed.

'So you're not so brilliant, are you?' he said. 'And Duane and Jamie will be seeing you Wednesday to collect my first eight grand. You want to know something? I'm hoping you don't have the money. Be seeing you soon, Joe.'

He started to walk away, but stopped to tell Jamie to stick with me.

'Make sure he don't go near Pop,' he said.

I watched as he and Duane walked down the hallway. Jamie stood next to me, smirking. When Junior was out of sight, I told Jamie to beat it. He seemed to find something amusing in that and got a good chuckle out of it.

I started in the direction of Manny's room.

'Hey, asshole, where do you think you're going?'

Jamie's smirk grew wider as he put a hand out to stop me. I turned and kicked him hard below the knee with what you'd call in martial arts a front snap-kick. He let out a howl and hopped on one leg, grabbing at his injured knee. Before he could do much else, I took hold of his head and slammed it as hard as I could against the wall. It made a loud clanging noise. He groaned at that. I let go and he slid down the wall. He wasn't out, not entirely, but he wasn't in either. I saw that his head had taken a large chunk out of the wall. If his skull hadn't been as hard as concrete, I probably would've killed him. I looked behind me to make sure no one saw anything and then kept walking.

Taking him out was easier than I would've expected. I guess he didn't expect me to do anything. I guess over the years he had gotten used to people just pissing in their pants at the sight of him. This time, though, it looked like I left him pissing in his own pants.

It was a few minutes past seven. I got to Manny's room and found him alone. He was sleeping with his mouth wide open, and as he breathed, he made thin grunting noises. What was lying there was only the skin and bones of what used to be Manny. It was as if all his flesh had been sucked out of him. Yet there was enough of him left to screw me over. All I could think of was why he couldn't just die already.

I was watching him from the doorway when a nurse I hadn't seen before squeezed past me.

'Visiting hours are over,' she said, shooting me back an annoyed look.

'That's okay. I was really trying to find Charlotte.'

'Charlotte Boyd?'

'Yes.'

'Her shift's over. I think she headed home.'

I thanked her. I took a few steps away from the door and watched for a moment as she took Manny's pulse, and then got out of there. Jamie was still sitting on the floor when I walked by, but he had company; a nurse and a doctor were checking him out. He looked up, but I don't think he recognized me. I don't think he knew what planet he was on. I kept going. A security guard ran past me while I walked out of the hallway.

No one bothered to stop me as I made my way through the hospital and out to my car. As I drove to Charlotte's apartment, I thought about Junior. I couldn't make up my mind whether he was putting on an act or not. He seemed convincing about not knowing I'd been shot at. I had to think if he had shot at me he would have found a way to rub my nose in it. But if he didn't take those shots at me, somebody else did. I couldn't imagine Dan doing it. If he had decided to go to his Plan B, he'd find an easier and less public way to take me out. And I couldn't imagine Phil doing it either. No matter how strongly he might hate me, I couldn't imagine him doing something like that. And it made no sense, especially if he expected to crack Manny and have me locked away for life. His daughter, Clara, though...

Yeah, she was another story. There was so much rage still in her. When I saw her in church, she was chalk white and trembling with it. I could see her trying something like that, or maybe talking a friend into it. I could see her playing up the attempted rape and showing off her bruises, and getting some dumb football type worked up enough to try blowing my head off. It could've been something like that...

Or it could've been a friend or family member of one of the boys I'd put in the hospital. Other names popped into my head, names of people who I knew would have no problem taking a shot at me.

Over the years I've learned to trust my first gut feeling, and usually nine times out of ten it's been right. But the more I thought about it, the more the shooting smelled like something an amateur would try. Someone would've had to park and wait by the curb until I was visible through a window. It was still possible Junior did it, but I was beginning to have my doubts.

As far as the affidavit went, I had been expecting something like that ever since I shot my mouth off. I knew it was a mistake as soon as I said anything to Manny about Ferguson's murder. I knew it, but I couldn't help myself. Maybe I was a little hurt that Earl went along with it, but I could understand it. Junior probably offered to lower his weekly take. I couldn't blame Earl. The only person I had to blame was myself. I never should have said a word to Manny about trying to wrap Junior up with Ferguson's murder. I knew it at the time, but I let him get under my skin. My price for that was the affidavit.

I checked several times along the way and saw that Hal Wheely was still following me. I figured it didn't matter. He'd know the apartment complex, but he'd still have no idea who

I was seeing there. And I had no plans on being seen with Charlotte anywhere in public.

When I arrived at the Maple Farms apartment complex, I waited until Wheely parked, and then drove behind his car so I would have to walk past him. When I did, I gave him a wave. That pissed him off. He rolled down his window, spat, and then looked away, pretending not to notice me.

I had to ring Charlotte's buzzer several times before she answered. She buzzed me in, and later when she opened her door, looked surprised.

'Joe, you're forty-five minutes early.'

'I've been anxious to see you,' I said, which was mostly true. 'I couldn't wait any longer.'

'Well – why don't you come in?'

I followed her into her apartment. After sitting down, I asked whether she had any more samples of the allergy medication she'd given me the other day.

'You won't need it,' she said, showing a secretive little smile. 'I put my cats in a kennel for the night. Joe, I was planning to surprise you and make you dinner. Would that be alright? If you want to go out instead, we could still do that.'

'No, dinner here would be nice. Do you want me to help?'

'Why don't you sit down and relax. You can watch TV if you like, or listen to music. Can I get you a drink? I bought a bottle of Scotch today.'

'Scotch on the rocks would be great.'

She gave me a puzzled look so I explained, 'Scotch with some ice.'

She made me the drink and brought it back to me, and then went into the kitchen to prepare dinner. I brought the drink over to her CD collection and looked at what music she had. It was mostly classical and operas. She did have one of old Frank Sinatra songs, 1940s-era stuff. I settled on that, and after putting it in the CD player, I went back to the loveseat.

I leaned back, stretching out my shoulder muscles, and then took a sip of my drink. The kitchen was open to the living room, and I could see Charlotte pounding chicken breasts with a mallet. She smiled at me when she noticed me looking at her. It was a nice smile. I smiled back.

'What are you making?' I asked.

Looking very pleased with herself, she told me, 'Chicken Cordon Bleu.'

I felt relaxed sitting there. On the surface it was nice, and I guess it was the way some people actually lived; just sitting back and listening to Sinatra as you sipped Scotch and had a pretty woman make you dinner.

Of course, the woman in this case had deep issues and probably bordered on psychotic. But as I sat there, it didn't matter to me. And I had to admit that Charlotte, at least for the moment, was pretty. I'm not saying she was beautiful by any stretch – she wasn't anywhere near in the same league as someone like Toni – but in her own way, she was pretty. Her nervousness was gone and she had fixed herself up and had put on some makeup. Her hair was set so it fell past her shoulders, and she was dressed nicely, wearing black Capri pants and a pink short-sleeve sweater. And again, she had better curves than I would've thought after seeing her in her nurse's uniform. The pants she was wearing made her hips look slender enough that I started daydreaming about what it would be like to take them off her. Maybe her coloring was a bit too pale, and maybe when I looked at her from a certain angle I could see blue veins crisscrossing her temples, but it was okay. It didn't matter. It didn't change the way I was feeling. For a few minutes I almost forgot what I was there for. I almost forgot about her murdering those people.

She seemed happy as a lark as she prepared dinner. I could

hear her humming softly to the music. Every so often she'd look over at me and smile. And I made sure to smile back.

I tried to picture her killing those people, but I couldn't do it, at least not the version of Charlotte that was now in the kitchen. The other version I could see doing it, the mousy and nervous version that I'd first met at the hospital, but not this one. The mousy, nervous one, though, I had no problem with. I could picture her holding the morphine syringe. I could see her face set in rigid concentration as she emptied the narcotic into the patient's IV tubing. I could see the relief washing over her as the patient slipped into respiratory failure. But it almost didn't seem possible that that was the same woman who was now in the kitchen humming happily to herself.

I guess I could understand why Charlotte did what she did. I committed so many crimes to keep from literally drowning in gambling debts. In her own way, she murdered those four patients to keep from suffocating. While she didn't know about all the things I'd done, she knew about Phil. I guess at some level, we understood each other.

Charlotte had left the kitchen and was bringing over a bottle of wine and a corkscrew.

'Dinner's cooking in the oven,' she said. 'Would you like to open the wine?'

'Sure.'

She handed me the bottle, and I uncorked it.

'Wait,' she said, and she went quickly into the kitchen and came back carrying a tray holding two wineglasses and a plate of cheese. She placed the tray on the coffee table.

'I thought we could sit here together until dinner is ready,' she said.

I finished my Scotch, and then poured us both some wine. Charlotte joined me on the loveseat. At first she sat with her hands clasped and her arms held tightly into her body, but after I put my arm around her shoulder, she moved close to me, curling her legs under her and resting her head against my side.

It felt nice sitting with her. I know it sounds crazy, knowing what she had done, but it wasn't as if I was much of a choirboy myself. Body-count-wise, she might've had an edge, but not by much, and not if you included the maimed and wounded. I even found myself feeling attracted to her. It made me uneasy thinking about Manny and what I was going to force her to do. I decided it could wait until later.

She brought me out of my thoughts by asking whether I liked the wine. I told her I did. Usually I preferred beer, but I did like the taste of it. I squinted at the bottle and saw that it was a French Chardonnay.

'It feels good sitting here with you,' I said, and again, I was mostly telling her the truth.

I could feel her body tense. 'You must've sat like this with your wife many times,' she said.

I thought about it and realized I never did. It wasn't as if every moment between Elaine and me was hell, but I couldn't think of one time where I felt as comfortable and relaxed with Elaine as I did right then.

'To tell you the truth,' I said, 'I don't think we ever did.'

She turned to me, not quite believing what I said, but I could see in her eyes that she was hoping I wasn't bullshitting her.

'You're lying now,' she said, half serious.

'No, I'm not. Elaine and I got together when we were teenagers. Back then we were always sneaking around and trying not to get caught. Things between us always seemed hectic and rushed. We were only nineteen when we were married, and then we were just scraping by. I had joined the force, and all the stresses of the job. And...'

And then there were the payoffs, the graft, the small crimes. At some point early on a coldness had come between Elaine and me. Not long after that came the cocaine, the gambling, and all the rest.

I shook my head, trying to shake loose those old memories. 'I guess I got married too young,' I said.

Her body relaxed after that. She put her hand on my stomach and peeked at me to see how I would react to her gesture. I reached down and kissed her forehead. As I sat with her I tried to forget everything, about who I was and what she was. I tried to forget everything that had happened and everything that was going to happen. I tried to simply enjoy the moment, because I've had so few in my life where I felt any real sense of contentment.

The buzzer for the oven timer went off.

She pulled away from me and showed me a reluctant smile. 'Why don't you bring the wineglasses to the table and I'll get dinner,' she said.

The table was in a small area off to the side of the living room. Charlotte had already set it, using a linen tablecloth and placing two silver candlesticks in the middle of it. I put down the wineglasses, and sat and waited. Not long after, Charlotte came in with the food. Along with the chicken, she had made roasted potatoes and string beans.

She lit the two candles and then sat across from me. I watched as she started cutting her food into tiny bite-sized pieces. Like before, after every few bites she'd dab at her mouth with her napkin. She was beaming. I could tell the food was good, but thinking about what I was going to do made it tasteless. Still, I ate it and remarked to her how delicious her cooking was, and that made her beam all the more.

'You really like it?' she asked.

'Could be the best meal I've ever had,' I said.

We both sat and ate quietly after that. Charlotte seemed deep in thought, as if she were trying to make up her mind about something. She didn't exactly look troubled, but her brow was somewhat furrowed and some nervousness had crept back into her eyes. She coughed lightly to get my attention.

'Mr Vassey's son asked me about you today,' she said. 'He wanted to know how I knew you.'

'What did you tell him?'

'He had seen me in your car, so I told him that I didn't know you but that you were kind enough to offer me a ride home when my car wouldn't run.'

'Did he believe you?'

'I think so, yes.' Her small, pale face darkened. 'I don't like him at all. I think he's also a criminal like his father.' She paused. 'You're not involved with him, are you?'

'No, I'm not. Anything between the two of us goes back to when I was a police officer. And you're right, Charlotte, he is a criminal and he's dangerous. You should try to keep away from him.'

She had handed me the perfect opening to bring up Manny, but I didn't have the heart to do it. The least I could do was let her enjoy her dinner. As it was, talking about Junior had darkened her mood. I tried to change the subject by asking how she had learned to cook so well.

She showed me a shy smile. 'My cooking is nothing special,' she said.

'Who are you kidding? You must've gone to culinary school.'

'Only for a year.' Then, hesitating, lowering her voice, 'My father convinced me that nursing would be more practical.'

'You don't like nursing, do you?'

She looked down at her plate. I didn't think she was going to say anything, but she told me, 'Not particularly, no.'

'You should go back to culinary school,' I said. 'We could both start fresh together. Only I have to first figure out what I could do.'

I don't know if I was bullshitting her, or playing for time, or what, but I think I actually started believing it was possible. I guess the last thing I wanted to do was think of Manny.

There was some wetness around her eyes when she looked back up at me. Not much, but some.

'Do you have any ideas what you would like to do, Joe?'

I did have one idea. Something I felt in my gut. 'I'd like to travel. Maybe go to Europe,' I said.

'Really?'

'I'm forty years old and I've never been out of the state, except for Albany, and a one-day trip to Boston.' And Canada for a couple of hours, but I didn't mention that.

I stopped to take a bite of food, and after swallowing, added, 'I used to be content with the idea of living out my life in Bradley, but those days are long gone.' I laughed. 'Kind of pathetic, huh? I don't know, I just want to see some of the world before I die.'

'I haven't traveled much either,' she said. 'I grew up in Toronto. Once, when I was a child, we went to Niagara Falls, and a few summer trips to Quebec City. But that's really been all. I haven't seen any other towns in the United States other than Bradley, and of course, yesterday, our trip to Burlington.'

'Would you like to see Europe also, Charlotte?'

She nodded.

'We could go there,' I said. 'There's nothing in the world stopping us.'

She laughed. 'Where would you want to go first?'

'I don't know. Italy, France, maybe Spain, it doesn't much matter.'

'I always wanted to see England,' she said. 'I would love to visit their castles, and see the Thames, and London, and the rolling countryside. Of course, Paris would be beautiful, too.'

'Why don't we do it, Charlotte?' I said. The idea of the two of us traveling off to Europe overwhelmed me. It didn't have to be the other way. I didn't have to force her into killing Manny. We could just go somewhere and leave Bradley far behind. Maybe they'd catch up to me eventually, but I'd get a few good months out of it before they did, and maybe more than a few. There were places where with some luck we could disappear completely. Maybe one of the Baltic states, maybe somewhere in East Asia.

I felt a dryness in my mouth as I asked her, 'What about it, Charlotte? We could drive to New York tonight and catch a plane. We'd be gone before morning.'

It got so quiet. I could hear my heart pounding as I waited for her to say something. She sat staring at me, trying to decide whether I was joking or serious. I guess she decided I was joking. She showed me a little smile as she reached across the table and took hold of my hand.

'That would be so nice, Joe,' she said. 'Maybe someday we'll be able to do something like that. I hope so.'

I forced myself to smile back. The idea had been nothing but an impulse, and a crazy one at that. Once it passed, I realized it would never have worked. We didn't have the money to make it work. And even if we did, we wouldn't have been able to survive together for very long. Not with her being the way she was and me being the way I was. The stresses of running and hiding would've been too much. As it was, I knew she was borderline psychotic.

And there were my daughters. Once I started thinking of them, the idea crumbled into dust around me.

There was only one way out for me, and as much as I hated the idea of what I was going to do to her, I had no choice.

We finished dinner, and afterwards Charlotte made coffee and brought out an Italian dessert, tiramisu, that she told me she had prepared during her lunch hour.

I waited until we had finished the dessert and coffee before asking her, 'Charlotte, how come you've never asked me about my being in jail?'

She seemed taken aback by that, almost as if she'd been slapped hard across the face. 'It's not important,' she said. 'You don't have to tell me about it.'

'It is important, and I do have to tell you about it. I did some pretty bad things years ago when I was cop. Stabbing and maiming Phil Coakley was only one of them.'

I felt something in my throat, and stopped to drink some water. There was a pleading in Charlotte's eyes for me not to say anything more, but it was too late. I looked away from her, though. I didn't want to look at those eyes.

'When I left jail,' I continued, 'all I wanted to do was lead a quiet existence and never harm anyone again. The problem is Manny Vassey knows enough to send me back to prison for a long time.'

'He might keep quiet.'

'He's not going to. I already know that. Phil has worked out a deal with him, and the arrangements are going to be finalized Wednesday.'

'But he's dying. Why would he make a deal?'

'For a bunch of reasons that don't make a lot of sense. Partly to protect his son, mostly to try to save his and his son's immortal souls.'

I couldn't help myself. I looked back over at her. Her face had become dead white and her eyes were now nothing but small gray holes. It was almost as if she was wearing some grotesque Japanese kabuki mask – one that was locked in an expression of anguish. I could see her hands were clenched into tight fists as she waited for what she knew was coming.

I took a deep breath.

'I need you to overdose Manny with morphine,' I said. 'If you don't, I'm going to go away to prison for the rest of my life.'

She just sat and stared at me.

'Charlotte, do you understand me?'

Slowly she shook her head. Almost as if she were in a trance, she said, 'I'm not going to do that.'

'You don't want me to go away to prison, do you?'

'I'm not going to do that!'

'I'm sorry, Charlotte, but you're going to have to.'

'I won't.' She was shaking her head harder, her face completely bloodless. 'How could you ask me to do something like this?'

'Charlotte, please—'

'Get out of here. Get out now or I'll scream.'

'You're not going to scream and you are going to make sure Manny dies of a morphine overdose.'

'You're insane.'

'No, not me. And please, quit this act. I know about you, Charlotte. I talked with Dr Henri Bouchaire. He told me about what you did in Montreal.'

Her mouth fell open. I watched the transformation as her face turned more into a mask of death.

She said, 'He lied to you. If he said I hurt anyone, he lied to you. They investigated those deaths. They checked the levels on the IV bags and saw that the machines hadn't been tampered with.'

'He didn't lie to me,' I said. 'He told me how you probably used a syringe to inject a fatal dose of morphine into the patient's IV tubing. I don't know if you were told this, but he marked the IV tubing on your last victim, and he knows you replaced it after the guy died.'

'He's lying.'

'He's not lying, and even if he's somehow mistaken, it wouldn't matter. If he talked to Bradley Memorial, you'd be finished here, and I guarantee you, no hospital in the States would touch you. And if any of your patients at Bradley Memorial died of respiratory failure, their cases will be reopened, and you'll be looking at murder charges.'

She started sobbing then. It was noiseless. Other than the tears and a slight heaving in her chest, I wouldn't have been able to tell she was crying. It got so quiet. As I watched, my stomach tightened into knots. I felt sick about what I was doing. I found myself wanting to comfort her. I leaned forward and tried to take hold of her hands, but she pulled them away from me.

'This is no big deal,' I tried to explain. 'You've done it before, you can do it one more time. And trust me, Manny Vassey is the most rotten sonofabitch you'll ever meet. He's not worth wasting any tears over. If anything, it's a shame you'll be putting him out of his misery.'

Through her sobbing, she forced out, 'You lied to me.'

'What are you talking about?'

'The only reason you wanted to see me was because of this.'

The knots in my stomach pulled tighter. 'Maybe at first,' I admitted. 'But Charlotte, I'm being honest now, most of what I've told you has been the truth. I have felt good being with you, better than I've felt in years. I don't know if you'll ever want to see me again after this, but if we can get past this, I think we could be good for each other. When this is all over, I'd like to keep seeing you. I promise you, everything I'm telling you now is the truth.'

'How am I supposed to get the morphine? The hospital doesn't leave narcotics lying around. You have to sign them out.'

'I figure you can siphon morphine from other patients.'

From the look that flashed across her face, I knew that's what she had done in Montreal. Then her eyes and mouth opened and her hands went to the sides of her face, and for a moment she was a spitting image of Edvard Munch's famous painting *The Scream*. She sat frozen like that for a horrible few seconds, and then she started sobbing again. Still noiseless, but more violent than before. Her whole body convulsed with it. Her face seemed to fold up into a mass of creases, her mouth now nothing more than a large gaping black hole.

'Don't make me do this,' she pleaded through her sobs. 'Don't make me do this.'

Her hands clenched again into tiny fists and she started punching her legs.

I got up and held her, trying to keep her from hitting herself. She didn't pull away or try to fight me this time. Instead, her head buried itself hard in my stomach while her tears and saliva soaked my shirt. Still she begged me, her voice muffled by my body.

'What's the big deal?' I tried asking her. 'He's going to be dead in a few weeks anyway.'

But I knew what the big deal was. For years I had promised myself that when I got out of jail I'd never cause any more harm. Somehow I knew she had made the same promise to herself. That when she left Montreal, she'd never do anything like that again. In my case, it didn't take me long to break my promise, but I was forced to. I had no other choice. And now I was doing the same to her.

Her body felt so warm and moist as I held her. I tried holding her harder. I tried to slow down her sobbing. At that moment I felt so empty inside. So rotten. As I looked at her, I realized I had no choice either. I told her I wasn't going to make her overdose Manny.

'I'll figure something else out,' I said.

Her sobbing slowly subsided. I held her and ran my hand through her hair and kissed the top of her head, and told her not to worry about anything. After a while she pulled away from me – not in a harsh way, but so she could look up at me.

'You're not going to make me do it?' she asked

'No, I won't. I'm sorry that I put you through this.' I took one of her linen napkins and used it to wipe her tears. 'I didn't think it would be that big a deal to you,' I lied.

'I never did what Dr Bouchaire told you I did. I don't know why he has to tell people I did those things.'

It was her turn to lie, but that was okay. I smiled and told her I believed her.

'I don't want you going to prison, but I can't do something like that.'

'Don't worry about me. I'm not going to prison. I'll think of something.'

'Maybe he won't say anything about you.'

'Maybe.'

She took hold of my hand and kissed it, and then held my hand against the side of her face. I stood there feeling a mix of relief and panic. I had no idea what I was going to do next.

'Look at me,' she said, showing a sad clown's smile. 'I must be a mess.'

That was putting it mildly. Her crying had left black smudges under her eyes and streaks of makeup running down her face. Somehow, even strands of her hair had gotten drenched, and were now knotted up and looking like something that might've been pulled out of a drain.

I reached down and kissed her. Awkwardly, she tried to kiss back.

'I'm sorry all this happened,' I said. 'Why don't you go get yourself cleaned up.'

'Will you stay and wait for me?' she asked.

I shook my head. 'I better get going.'

'You don't have to. You can stay if you'd like.'

'I'd like to, but I got to get some rest and figure stuff out.'

'Will I see you again?'

'Of course you will. As soon as this is over, we'll get together.'

I turned to leave and I heard her call out to me. When I looked back, she was blushing. 'Joe, if you go to prison we could still marry.'

I had to bite my tongue to keep from bursting out laughing. It was so damn funny and sad at the same time. There was no question she wasn't all there, but I smiled as sweetly as I could and told her that was exactly what we would do. And the saddest part was knowing everything that I did about her, I still found myself attracted to her.

When I got out to the parking lot, I saw that Hal Wheely was gone. I guess he decided I wasn't worth losing sleep over.

Chapter 16

I drove aimlessly. At first I was numb, no thoughts, nothing, and then a raw, cold panic overtook me. I knew Dan was serious about his ultimatum, and I knew if I was still alive by Wednesday it wouldn't much matter anyway. After Manny signed his deal and gave his deathbed confession, it would be as good as over for me.

I tried to think of some way out, but all I could come up with were nutty ideas; like sneaking into the hospital and overdosing Manny myself, or using the sixty-three hundred dollars I had left to bribe an orderly to do the job for me. As I said, they were nutty ideas, and they would've sent me straight to prison, but that was all I could come up with. After a while I started thinking of Phil, of whether there was a chance I could get away with hiding somewhere near his front door with a hunting rifle.

The panic hit me hard, harder than the other day at Kelley's. It got to the point where I could barely breathe. As I drove, a numbness spread through my legs and arms. I felt as if my limbs were dead and no longer a part of me. And the coldness, Jesus; it was like ice cubes were being pushed into my skull. Then all at once I knew I was going to black out. The world started tilting sideways on me and it was all I could do to pull over, crawl out of my car, and curl up on the side of the road.

I didn't black out. I came close, but I was able to fight through it. After a while I pushed myself up into a sitting position, grabbed my knees, and rocked back and forth until I felt I could stand. Then I got to my feet.

My clothes were drenched through with sweat. It took about all the strength I had, but I hobbled to the trunk, opened it, and pulled out my duffel bag. I found some clean clothes and changed there by the side of the road. I had to rest for a while, and then after dumping the duffel bag back into the trunk, I got into the driver's seat, and just sort of collapsed.

For a long time all I could do was hold my head in my hands. I felt so lousy. I started to think how a few lines of coke would make me feel so much better, how it would help clear out the cobwebs clouding my head. After a while that was all I could think of. It got to the point where I could almost taste cocaine in the back of my throat.

I forced my head up and looked in my rearview mirror. I looked as bad as I felt. My skin was so damn pale and my eyes so damn red. I steeled myself, and then started the car and pulled back onto the road. My hands shook as I drove. I decided I'd make a quick trip to Kelley's. And, as I told myself, I wanted to see Earl anyway and let him know there were no hard feelings about his affidavit.

Kelley's was more crowded than the other night. I ended up having to create a makeshift parking spot next to the dumpster. Before going in, I read over the copy of Earl's affidavit that Junior had given me, and then folded it into my jacket's inside pocket.

The same biker type from the other night looked me over at the door. Inside, the place was jammed. Every seat around the stage was filled and every table was taken. Springsteen's 'My Hometown' blasted over the speakers, and I glanced in the direction of the stage and saw a dark brunette slip out of her G-string. The way I was feeling it made no impact. I headed towards the bar, spotted Earl pouring some draft beers, and nodded at him. He noticed me and gave me a cold eye back in return. The bar was mostly empty. I pulled up a stool so I could sit across from him.

'How'ya doing, Earl,' I said.

He lifted his eyes towards me. 'Man, you look like shit.'

'Yeah, well, I'm feeling kind of crappy.'

'So you had to come here to spread the wealth, huh? Infect me and my girls and my customers?'

'I don't think I have anything contagious. Probably just suffering from allergies.' I lowered my voice. 'I could really use a few lines. Whatever it costs.'

'I don't know what you're asking.'

I took twenty dollars out of my wallet and placed it on the bar. 'Come on, Earl, my head's a mess right now. Three lines. That's all.'

'Wait a second. You trying to buy coke from me? That's illegal, man.'

I stared at him and he gave me a dead-eyed stare right back.

'Fine,' I said. 'Make it a beer and a shot of whiskey.'

He took the twenty bucks off the bar. When he came back, he brought me my drinks and twelve bucks change.

'Look,' I said, 'if this is about the affidavit, I have no hard feelings about it.'

'Why should you? I swore on the Bible before I filled that out. You think I perjured myself?'

'Cut the crap, okay, I know you made a deal with Junior.'

'You calling me a liar?'

A vein along his neck was twitching and the muscles in his arms and shoulders had bunched up. He had a look in his eyes that I had seen a couple of times in the past. Once, right before he cracked this guy's skull who was shooting off his mouth about different crap. Another time before he nearly beat two guys to death for harassing one of his girls. On a good day, I'd be able to hold my own against him, but as weak as I was feeling I knew he'd kill me.

I took the whiskey in one swallow and then followed that up with a healthy drink of beer. Earl stood frozen in malice, his vein still twitching away. I held the beer bottle so I could use it if I had to, although I didn't think it would do me much good.

'I swear, Earl, I don't have a clue what this is about.'

'One of my girls died today.'

'Yeah, I heard. I'm sorry.'

'Yeah, thanks. You know, that's why we're so crowded tonight. Everyone wants to pay their last respects. Is that why you're here, Joe?'

I didn't say anything. I just kept watching his vein, watching as it beat faster than a rabbit's heart.

'It's funny,' he said. 'I never knew about Susie and that DA until today, but what I've been hearing since is that this had been going on for six months. Funny thing is Rooster doesn't get a call till you've been out of jail for... how many days? Three?'

'Four,' I said.

His lips separated from his teeth, revealing a thin, bare-fanged smile. 'Yeah, four days. Why do you think that is?'

'I swear, Earl, I had nothing to do with this.'

'Why don't you guess anyway?'

I shook my head and gave a half-hearted shrug.

'No guess, huh?' He edged closer towards me. 'Hey, man, you want to know something else that's funny? Whoever called Rooster left his name as Joe.'

That sonofabitch. That was all I could think. *That sonofabitch.* I could just picture Dan chuckling to himself over that one.

'You think I'd be that stupid?' I asked, trying to look as dumbfounded as possible. 'You think I'd call and leave my name?

Come on, Earl, use your brains. You want to know why this happened a few days after I got out of jail? Because whoever did this waited until I got out of jail before calling.'

He had been edging towards me, but that stopped him in his tracks. A perturbed expression crossed his face, and then he slowly started nodding to himself as he thought over what I said. I guess he decided to give me the benefit of the doubt. He showed me a sheepish grin and refilled my shot glass.

'Hey, man,' he said. 'I could've killed you a minute ago. Damn.'

My hand shook as I picked up the shot glass. I got most of the whiskey down my throat, and only a little of it down the front of my shirt. I signaled for another shot and Earl obliged.

'Okay, so that's what's behind your affidavit,' I said. 'I can understand that, and I can understand Junior offering you a break, but you know what you wrote's a load of crap. Any way you can back out of it, claim you were coerced by Junior?'

'Hey, man, I'm not talking about that paper. I can't do anything about it now.'

'You know it's bullshit.'

'I don't know nothing like that. I'm sorry about it, but I'm not saying another word, man. Sorry.'

I started to open my mouth. I was going to say something else, but I saw it was pointless. The whiskey had taken a tiny bit of the edge off, not much, but a tiny bit. I still badly wanted the coke.

I sighed. 'Well, how about those lines, then. How much?'

He thought about it, but shook his head.

'Can't do it, man,' he said.

'Why not?'

'I have this rule. If I fuck someone, I can't give them a chance to fuck me back.'

'Wait, what you're telling me is because you screwed me with that affidavit, you're going to keep screwing me?'

'Sorry.'

A couple of guys had come over to the bar to change their tens and twenties into singles. Earl turned his back on me.

My hands were still shaking and my head was now throbbing. I got off the stool and took a couple of steps towards the exit and stopped. I remembered Toni, how she had no problem scoring coke the other night. Any of the girls could. I turned and started towards the stage area when someone grabbed my arm.

'Hey, Joe, just the man I wanted to see.'

I looked down and saw Scott Ferguson. He was wasted, his eyes barely able to focus on me. He pushed himself to his feet, and held onto my arm for support.

'I need to ask you more about Vassey,' he said.

I had no choice. I walked him back towards the bar where we would have more privacy.

'It don't make any sense,' he said. 'Why would Vassey's kid kill Billy? If Billy had the money he owed, what would be the point? It don't make any sense.'

'Maybe he was stubborn about giving up his money.'

Ferguson made a face. 'I'll tell you something about Billy,' he said. 'He was a pussy. He would've paid in a second if he thought he'd get hurt. I've been asking around, and from what I hear Vassey's kid worships his old man. He wouldn't try ripping him off. So why in the world would he kill Billy?'

'I don't know whether Junior killed your brother or not,' I said, 'but I told you the other day, the guy's a psycho. He gets off on hurting people, and if he was collecting from your brother my guess is he got carried away.'

All I could think of was getting free of him. Whatever I had to do to speed it up. I took Earl's affidavit from my jacket pocket and handed it to him.

'Read this,' I said. 'I talked to Earl and he admitted to me that he manufactured it for Junior. As you can see, Junior's already trying to cover his tracks.'

Ferguson's doughy features hardened as he stared at the affidavit. It took him a while, but he got through it.

'How come you're mentioned in it?' he asked, his expression turning more surly.

'Because Junior's creating himself an alibi, and at the same time pointing the finger at me.'

'Why you?'

'I guess he thinks it's plausible. I just got out of jail. People here in Bradley don't feel all that favorable towards me, and I guess no one would really care if I got charged with something like this. I'm as good a patsy as anyone.'

As Ferguson mulled over what I said, I took the affidavit out of his hands and slipped it back into my inside jacket pocket.

'Hey, I wanted to keep that!'

'Sorry, I need it.'

His eyes narrowed and his lips compressed, and he looked like all the other drunks I've seen over the years before they threw their first punch. He inched closer to me, his breath smelling like an open bottle of bourbon.

'How do I know there's not a good reason for pointing a finger at you?'

'If there was, I would've had Earl fill out an affidavit for me long before he did this one.'

He thought about what I said, mumbled something that I couldn't quite hear, and then seemed to lose interest in me. I watched as he staggered back to his table.

I walked around the room so I could get to the stage without having to pass Ferguson again. There were no empty seats, so I squeezed in near the loudspeakers. I took out a twenty and signaled with it. A tall, skinny blonde was now onstage. She spotted the twenty and came over. I started to slip the bill under her garter belt, but she moved my hand so I would slide it in under her G-string. Up close, she had way too much makeup on, and her face almost seemed to crack when she smiled. She leaned over and whispered in my ear about us partying alone in one of the back rooms when her set was done. I nodded. I didn't care who she was or what she looked like. All I could think about was the cocaine.

She lingered on, trying to give me my twenty dollars' worth, and trying to make sure I'd stick around after her set was over. After she moved away, she kept smiling over at me, even when other guys were slipping dollar bills under her garter belt. When she moved a certain way I caught sight of a dark bruise along the inside of her thigh. I wondered briefly what her makeup was covering up. It didn't matter to me, though. I was still going to join her in a private room. And if I had to screw her first to get the cocaine, I'd do that also.

I felt a small hand rubbing my shoulder, and then a voice next to me yelling, 'Hey!' I turned and saw Toni grinning wickedly. She looked even more stunning than the other day. She was also wearing less – only a sheer black negligee and panties.

She tried saying something to me, but I couldn't hear her over the music. She got on her toes and talked into my ear, her breath hot against me. The touch of her lips made my spine tingle.

'I still owe you something from the other night,' she said. 'What do you say, Joe? You want to go somewhere private and finish what we started?'

I reached down to ask whether she could get her hands on more coke. The scent of her made me dizzy. She told me she could. She took hold of my hand and led me around the speakers and through the curtains separating the back hallway.

The room we took was identical to the one we were in before. Toni locked the door and told me to relax. I sat back on the carpeted bench. As she came towards me, she was still grinning that same wicked grin.

'You got the coke?' I asked.

'First things first,' she said.

She reached her hand towards me. I thought she was reaching to caress my cheek, but she quickly brought her hand back and nailed me good. She couldn't have weighed more than ninety pounds and her clenched fist was less than a third the size of mine, but her punch snapped my head back. She must've got me with the side of her fist – the fleshy part above the wrist – and I was damn sure she broke my nose. She got in two more punches before I could stop her. One of them rapped me in the mouth. After I pinned her against the wall, I checked with my thumb and felt a tooth move. I was lucky she didn't knock it out completely.

She was calm, but there was a white-hot intensity burning on her face.

'You should die for what you did,' she said.

'Yeah, and what did I do?'

'You dirty bastard.'

'I've been hearing that a lot lately. So come on, what did I do?'

'You bastard. You dirty bastard. You sent Paul to that motel room.'

'Not me. I had nothing to do with it.'

She looked like she wanted to spit in my face. As I looked at her, I realized I didn't care anymore. Screw her. Screw Dan. Screw all of them. None of it mattered.

'I know who did, though,' I said. 'He's a buddy of yours. Want to guess?'

Doubt flickered in her eyes.

'No guess, huh?' I said. 'I'll tell you, if you punched him in the nose he wouldn't be taking it as nicely as I am now. He'd probably have a couple of his deputies dig a hole in the woods to plant you in.'

I could see fear in her eyes, because she knew what I was telling her was true. It was more than that, though. If Dan ever found out she knew of his involvement, he'd take care of her just the same. She knew that also.

The fear in her was now palpable. 'You told Dan so he'd send Paul to that motel,' she said.

'No, not me.' I shook my head. 'If I had any idea he was going to do something like that I would've called Phil and warned him.'

'Why do you think it was Dan?'

'I asked him after I heard about the shooting and he admitted it to me. You have to remember, the two of us go way back.'

'How did he find out about Susie?'

'I don't know.' I had her pinned with my forearm, and I used my free hand to gingerly touch my nose. I winced as I did. I could feel the blood dripping from my nostrils.

'Look,' I said. 'If I let go of you, you're not going to punch me again?'

She shook her head. I let go, and sat on the bench and held my head back. I pinched my nostrils to try to stop the bleeding.

'If I had to guess,' I said, talking slowly and deliberately because I was breathing in through my mouth, 'he probably found out the same way I did. When you do coke, Toni, you get a little too free with your words. It's something you should watch.'

'You're lying.'

'Why would I lie? You think I care at all what you think?'

There was a long silence and then she started to cry. It wasn't real loud, but loud enough for me to hear it. I lifted my head and could see her bawling away, her small face screwed up in pain, her shoulders rising and lowering rhythmically. I tilted my head back and closed my eyes. All I could think was, fine, let her feel half as lousy as I do. As I sat there I realized I was still craving cocaine. Even with a bloody and broken nose, if I had a few lines, I would have snorted them up without a second's thought. I guess at that point I had hit rock bottom. I just started laughing thinking about it. It hurt like hell to laugh, but I couldn't help myself.

My nose had stopped bleeding. I got to my feet.

Toni, still crying, asked, 'You won't tell Dan?'

I didn't bother answering her.

When I pushed past the curtains and into the main club, I could feel eyes turning towards me. I imagined what I looked like with my face and shirt smeared in blood. The blonde who I had given a twenty to must've seen me from behind, because I could see her out of the corner of my eye coming towards me, a plastic smile set on her face. When she caught up to me her jaw dropped. And then she backed away.

I stopped in the rest room to clean up the best I could, and then got out of there. When I got to my car, I went through my duffel bag and found my last clean shirt.

Chapter 17

I drove towards Stowe and found a ski lodge that was open off season. I could tell the desk clerk didn't like the look of me, and I couldn't blame him. I must've looked like I'd been in a street fight. It was amazing how much damage a little thing like Toni could do. But I paid cash and he gave me a room.

When I got to my room, I checked myself over in the mirror and saw that my upper lip was as swollen as it felt and that my nose was indeed broken. I left the room to fill up an ice bucket, and when I returned I wrapped ice in two hand towels, lay down on the bed, and placed one towel against my nose and the other against my mouth. As I lay there I tried to think about what I could do, but I guess I was too tired and too wiped out, and at some point I drifted off.

Right before waking, I dreamed that I was back with Elaine and my two daughters, and it was like we were a family again. We were in our old house, but it still seemed like the present. Melissa and Courtney looked like they did in the photographs, both blonde and pretty, both in their teens. Elaine was like she was the other day when I saw her in Albany, except instead of a cold and indifferent attitude towards me, she was warm and relaxed.

We were all sitting at the kitchen table eating dinner. My two girls acted like typical teenagers, rolling their eyes when I asked them questions about how their day went and stuff like that, but at times someone would make a joke and everyone would get a laugh out of it. It felt nice. Near the end, Elaine got up and moved behind me so she could massage my neck and shoulders. My girls giggled at that.

The phone started ringing. Elaine very sweetly asked whether I would answer it.

'Not now,' I said.

'But it might be important.'

'Why don't we ignore it?'

'You should answer it, Joe.'

'I really don't want to.'

'Joe—'

'Okay, okay.'

Then my eyes opened wide and the dream was gone. It took me a moment to realize where I was. The ringing was real, though. I looked over at the phone next to my bed and watched as a red light flashed with each ring.

I didn't want to lose my dream. I wanted to somehow get back into it. I wanted more than anything to be back with Elaine and my two girls. But I was wide awake and they were gone.

I watched the phone and waited for the ringing to stop. Nobody should've known where I was. With each ring I felt my heart turning more into an icy slush. Nobody should've been calling. All I could think was that it had to be a wrong number. But I didn't answer it. Finally, after what seemed like minutes, the ringing stopped.

I waited a long time after that before sitting up. I held my breath and concentrated, trying to listen for anything out of place. The only noise I could hear was my heart skipping to a sick irregular beat.

I was about to get out of bed when there was a hard knock on the door. I almost jumped out of my skin. There was another knock, and then a voice yelling, 'Denton, Joe Denton. This is the Stowe police. Open the door.'

I moved as quietly as I could to the door, looked through the peephole, and saw two uniformed officers standing out in the hallway. I didn't recognize either of them.

I had the chain on. I opened the door a crack, keeping my shoulder against it so they couldn't force it open.

'What do you want?' I asked.

'We have a warrant for your arrest.'

'Can I see it?'

He handed me a paper through the crack. I read it over quickly. It was for missing a meeting with my parole officer. The warrant was signed by Sheriff Dan Pleasant. I couldn't believe that Craig had reported me.

'Let me call my lawyer,' I said.

'You can call him from the station.'

'You're taking me to Stowe?'

'Yes. Now open the door.'

'Can I get dressed first?'

'Go ahead. Make it fast.'

I made it fast. When I opened the door, the officer I had talked to turned me around and cuffed me. He and his partner led me out of the room and through the lodge. We probably didn't pass more than ten people, but each of them stopped to stare as we went by. When we got to the parking lot I saw Hal Wheely and Stan Black leaning against a Bradley County sheriff's vehicle.

'You said you were taking me to Stowe,' I said.

Neither of them said anything. They were on either side of me, dragging me faster as they held me by my elbows.

I started to yell for help and something hard whacked me on the back of my head. Next thing I knew I was in the back seat of the cruiser, with Hal behind the wheel and Stan taking up the passenger seat. The back of my head throbbed, and I sat frozen from the pain for a minute before asking how they knew where to find me.

Hal asked, 'How do you think?'

'Come on, at least tell me that.'

I could see Hal through the rearview mirror smirking. 'I followed you last night.'

'From where, Kelley's? You spotted me there?'

His smirk widened. 'I followed you all night last night. I saw you when you crawled out of your car and curled up like a baby sucking your thumb.'

'You did a lousy job early on,' I said.

'Yeah, well, fooled you later, didn't I?'

He was still smirking, but it seemed to tighten, almost like it was etched on his face. I didn't like the glazed look in his eyes. I also didn't like the fact that Stan was being so withdrawn and quiet.

I said, 'I kept my mouth shut all these years. I could've sent both of you away for a long time.'

'I appreciate it,' Hal said.

'Look, what you're doing now is nuts.'

'Doesn't sound nuts to me.'

'Did Dan ever tell you about my safety deposit box?'

'Why don't you shut up?'

'Stan, what about you, you don't want this, do you?'

'What I don't want is to go to prison because of you,' Stan said.

'Look, I told you to shut up,' Hal said.

I could see his ears turning red. Something about his tone told me that I'd better listen to him. I sat back and watched the road. As we entered Bradley County, Hal turned down a dirt path and headed towards an old quarry that was once used for swimming but had dried up years ago.

As we got closer to the quarry, I could see Dan and one of

his deputies, Josh Stone, leaning against Dan's car. Hal pulled up next to them, and before I knew it, Josh and Stan were pulling me out of the back seat and dragging me onto the ground. Hal joined them as they dragged me to the edge of the quarry and then flipped me on my stomach. Knees pushed into my neck and the small of my back, pinning me to the ground. I tried to lift my head, and for a second could see Dan standing off to the side watching. Then a hand shoved my head back into the dirt. As I was pushed down, I could feel my broken nose being smeared to the side.

The handcuffs were taken off me. While I was pinned to the ground, my right arm was forced out and then bent so my hand was against the side of my face. A gun was shoved into my hand, and my hand held in place with the barrel pushed hard against my temple. Other fingers were on my trigger finger, applying pressure. I had to fight like hell to keep from pulling the trigger.

Dan said, 'Manny's still around. You promised me he'd be gone by morning. I'm getting sick of you breaking your promises.'

I was losing the fight. I could feel the trigger being pulled in. I had only seconds left.

'So long, Joe,' Dan said. 'Believe it or not, I am sorry about this.'

My mouth was being pushed into the dirt, but somehow I spat out that Manny was being taken care of.

The pressure on my finger was relaxed. Someone grabbed my hair and yanked my head up. I started gagging, spitting out the dirt I'd been forced to swallow. After I could breathe, I opened my eyes and saw that Dan had moved over to me. He was squatting, sort of sitting on his heels as he considered me.

'How is Manny being taken care of?' he asked.

'He's going to be overdosed with morphine.'

'And how is that going to happen?'

'His nurse—'

'Joe, you're lying to me again—'

'Dan, it's true. I've been seeing her. It's all set.'

'And why would a nurse do this for you?'

'She has no choice.'

'Why would that be?'

'Look, can you get them off me? My neck and shoulders are killing me.'

'Not yet. Answer my question, Joe. Why does this nurse friend of yours have no choice?'

'She's done it before where she used to work.'

'How do you know this?'

'I played out a hunch and spoke to the Chief of Surgery at her old hospital. He suspects her of killing four of her patients.'

'Sounds unbelievable, Joe.'

'It's true.'

'How come she's not in prison?'

'It's hard to prove. The patient ends up dying of respiratory failure, and nothing specific to a morphine overdose will show up in the autopsy.'

His eyes shifted, and I could tell he was starting to take me seriously. 'How come she hasn't gotten rid of Manny yet?' he asked.

'She needs some time,' I said. I was grunting now because of the pain. It felt like nails were being hammered into my shoulder blades. 'She has to siphon off enough morphine from other patients to do the job. This way she doesn't have to tamper with the machines and there's no evidence of anything.'

'I don't get it. How does she overdose him without leaving a needle mark?'

'She injects the morphine into the IV tubing.'

That brought a smile to his face. 'What's her name?'

'You don't need to know.'

A shadow fell over his eyes as he nodded to his boys. All at once my trigger finger was being pulled back.

'Charlotte Boyd,' I forced out.

I struggled for another few seconds and the pressure stopped.

'I might be giving you a reprieve, Joe,' Dan said. 'I'm not promising anything, but we'll see.'

He stood up and then my head was forced back into the dirt. I could hear one of his deputies breathing hard as I was held down. Not only was he breathing hard, he was beginning to perspire, his sweat dripping on me. I had no idea which of the three it was, but whoever, I hoped to hell he'd drop dead of a heart attack.

Dan must've gotten on his cell phone. He started yelling, 'Goddam it, Harold, I'm sheriff of this county, I have a right to be at that meeting... Well, I at least have the right to know when it is... Fuck you, after all the favors I've done for you over the years?... All right, then.'

I could hear his boots kicking up gravel as he walked back to me. My head was yanked up again, and I saw Dan sitting on his heels, smiling pleasantly.

'So, Joe, when is dear Charlotte going to do the deed?'

'Maybe tonight, maybe tomorrow morning. It depends how long it takes to siphon off enough morphine to fill up a syringe.'

'Why should that take any time?'

'If the other patients have too much morphine taken out of their IV bags, it will raise suspicion.'

Dan sat on his heels for a good minute as he thought it over. Then he nodded at me. 'Okay, Joe,' he said. 'You got your reprieve.'

He stood up and told his boys to let me go.

The gun was taken out of my hand, and they removed their knees from my neck and back. It took me a while before I could push myself up onto my hands and knees. My neck and shoulders still hurt like hell, but I no longer felt as if nails were being driven into my joints. I got myself flipped around so I was sitting on the ground.

'You have any aspirin?' I asked.

Dan shook his head, his eyes amused. 'Sorry, Joe. I don't carry any around with me.' He turned to his deputies. 'You boys have any?' None of them bothered to move.

Dan turned back to me. 'Sorry, Joe, doesn't look like anyone's got any.' He let loose a long, disappointed sigh. 'I had it all worked out for today, Joe. I wrote such a nice suicide note for you. Do you want to hear it?'

I shook my head.

'Too bad. I'm pretty damn proud of it. I had you sending Frechotte to the Green Valley Motor Lodge hoping he'd kill Coakley. I also had you taking responsibility for Billy Ferguson's murder and a couple of others. But in the end, you couldn't live with what you'd done.'

'Who else was I supposed to have killed?'

'It doesn't matter.'

'So that's what Manny has on you.'

He ignored that. 'Let's get back to the business on hand. You heard me on the cell phone, right? You know who I was talking to?'

'Yeah, I know.'

'Grayson's been putting me off,' he said, somewhat bitterly. 'I've been calling him all morning. The prick finally let me know that Vassey's deal is being pushed back to Friday. I guess with the shooting yesterday, our DA friend's tied up until then.

'So here's where we stand,' he continued. 'I want to see Manny gone by tomorrow morning. That's your final deadline. No more reprieves. Understood?'

I nodded. I was rubbing my arms, trying to get some feeling back into them. I asked him how he had planned to explain all my bruises and cuts with a suicide.

'Look behind you, Joe,' he said, smiling as pleasantly as ever.

I turned and saw an eighty-foot drop to the bottom of the quarry.

'We'd toss you over after putting a bullet in your skull. No one would care too much about any bruises or scratches after that. But you know, Joe, even if we didn't toss you down there, I don't think anyone would really care.'

'How about those two cops in Stowe? They were going to go along with a suicide?'

'You should know me well enough to answer that one. Joe, let's hope I don't have to see you tomorrow, okay?'

He hesitated for a second, a glint of humor in his eyes. 'Just out of curiosity,' he asked, 'what happened to your face? One of my boys do that?'

I shook my head. 'I got sucker-punched.'

'Anyone I know?'

'I don't think so.'

His eyes narrowed as he studied at me. 'You should see a doctor and have your nose set properly before it's too late.'

'Thanks for your concern.'

He laughed at that. All of them turned then and started off towards their cars. I struggled to my feet and hobbled a couple of steps forward.

'Can you have one of your boys drive me back to my motel?' I yelled out to Dan.

Without looking back, he answered that I only had a fifteen-mile walk and that it would do me some good to have some time alone to reflect on my situation. I watched as they got in their cars and drove off.

The first mile was the worst, but after that I started to loosen up. I had a bunch of scrapes and cuts, and my shirt – my last clean one – was ripped and pretty much a mess. No real damage was done, though. Once my muscles had a chance to loosen up I was okay.

I spent almost four hours walking back to the ski lodge. A few dozen cars passed me along the way. I tried thumbing for a ride, but no one bothered to stop. That was okay. It gave me a chance to think. And I have to give Dan credit. He was right, I needed that time alone to reflect on things. During the walk back I came up with a plan. It wasn't anything new. For the most part it was what I had already come up with to get back at Junior. I wasn't sure my plan would work, but even if it didn't, it would let me go out with a bang.

Chapter 18

The desk clerk seemed surprised to see me. They had already cleared out my room, and he had to get my duffel bag out of a storage closet. As he handed it to me, he was eyeing my cuts and bruises with some curiosity. I answered the question that seemed stuck on his lips.

'Those cops who took me out of here this morning tried to kill me,' I said.

'Really?'

'Damn straight. I'm lucky to be alive.'

'No shit?'

'No shit.'

As I said before, I didn't care anymore. Word would spread about those two cops, and as far as I was concerned, they deserved whatever they ended up getting. I took my duffel bag to my car and headed towards Bradley. Along the way, I stopped off at the Eastfield Mall and bought a shirt and pair of pants. I wore my new clothes out of the store, and cleaned up the best I could in the mall's rest room.

After that I found a diner and had three cheeseburgers and a milkshake. It was like I had this bottomless hole that I couldn't fill. I probably could've had a couple more cheeseburgers, but I stopped after three. Before leaving I called Craig, apologizing for missing my parole meeting with him the other day, and scheduling another meeting for later in the afternoon. I also called an attorney in Bradley, Jim Pierce, and was able to set up an appointment for within the hour. I still had enough time before the appointment to drive down to the old tannery.

The tannery had been shut down for almost sixty years, and it lay empty until Manny bought it fifteen years ago and moved his bookie operations there. In some ways it made sense – the building is as out of the way in Bradley as you can get – but I often wondered what he wanted all that space for.

The roads leading to the tannery were in rough shape. I guess during the past fifteen years only Manny and his employees ever bothered to drive down them. After twenty minutes of bouncing around, I got to the building.

From the outside the old tannery looked pretty dilapidated. There were half a dozen cars parked alongside it – more than I would've expected. I drove around the building until I got to a pair of dumpsters. In no time at all I found what I was looking for – empty boxes and containers of pseudoephedrine, iodine, acetone, methanol, and other ingredients necessary for manufacturing crystal meth. I suspected that that was behind Junior's push to acquire college clubs. Not only was he manufacturing crystal meth, he was acquiring distribution outlets so he could unload his junk without having to deal with a retailer.

Nobody saw me going through the dumpsters; at least, if they did see me no one bothered doing anything about it. When I was done, I got in my car and headed back towards downtown Bradley.

I arrived at Jim Pierce's office a few minutes before our scheduled appointment, and his receptionist had me take a seat and wait. Next to Harold Grayson, Jim's probably the best we've got. When I was a cop I saw him plenty of times arguing ridiculous bald-faced lies in court without missing a beat, and more times than not convincing the juries to buy them.

After fifteen minutes Jim came out to greet me, and led me back to his office. His attitude towards me seemed curious, and when he got behind his desk he leaned back and pursed his lips while he studied me.

'You look like you've been run over by a truck,' he said.

'It's nothing. I tripped and fell, that's all.'

He knew that was a load of crap, but he didn't care enough to pursue it. 'It's been a long time, Joe. What can I help you with?'

'I need to hire a lawyer.'

'Why me? Isn't Harold Grayson your lawyer?'

'He's not available.'

He raised his eyebrows at that. 'The two of you have a falling out?'

'No, nothing like that.' I paused, and then said, 'There's a conflict of interest.'

'If you want to hire me my rates are one hundred and fifty an hour.' He checked his watch. 'You're on the clock now. What's the problem?'

I went straight into it and told him about Manny, the deal he was making with Phil, and what he was going to confess to. During it all, Jim leaned back in his chair bug-eyed as he listened to me.

'So you're saying Manny Vassey, to protect his son, will be alleging you murdered Ferguson?' he asked.

'Yes.'

'How do you know this?'

'He told me.'

'He just came right out and volunteered this to you?'

'Yeah.' I smiled weakly. 'I visited him a couple of days ago at the hospital and he let it leak.'

Jim's eyes widened as he considered what I was saying.

'So what do you think?' I asked. 'How badly will his confession hurt me?'

He rubbed his chin as he thought it over. Matter-of-factly he said, 'As you probably know a deathbed confession is an exclusion to the hearsay rule. If he does confess there's nothing I would be able to do to keep it out of court. Is there any other evidence you know of that could support his allegations?'

'His son, Junior, paid off a friend of mine, Earl Kelley, to write this.'

I had Earl's affidavit with me and I handed it to him. As he read through the document, I realized that there was more. If Dan could make a deal and slice a few years off whatever sentence he was going to end up with, he'd do it in a heartbeat. He'd tell about the thirty thousand dollars' worth of bets a bookie told him I made after Billy Ferguson's murder. Thinking about that made me sick to my stomach.

Jim finished the affidavit and put it down. His expression didn't look too hopeful.

'This Kelley's a friend of yours?' he asked.

'Yeah.'

'Maybe you need to make yourself some new friends.'

'Maybe, but Junior made it well worth his while to write that.'

'If I were to depose Kelley, any chance he'd recant and admit to perjuring himself?'

'I don't think so.'

'Anything you could say to him to help convince him?'

I shook my head. 'How bad is this for me?'

'I could argue that both Vassey's confession and this affidavit are self-serving, but I think I'd only be wasting my breath. Odds are pretty good you'll end up being convicted of first-degree murder.'

'Why would they buy Vassey's confession? He's a goddam criminal.'

'It doesn't matter. Deathbed confessions carry more weight with a jury than you could imagine. It's the psychology of it. Why would a dying person lie and risk purgatory? I know it's silly, but that's the way juries think.'

'What about the deal he's making to protect Junior from prosecution?'

'I don't think that would matter much. To be honest, the biggest problem we'll have is you. Face it, Joe, people here think you got off too easy for what you did to Phil Coakley. Now Phil wouldn't be trying the case against you, I'm sure one of his assistants would handle it, but he'd be sitting at the prosecutor's table each day reminding the jury what you did to him. They'll be looking for any excuse they can to send you back to prison. It's not fair, but that's the way it is.'

'What if you moved the trial to another state?'

He shrugged. 'I could try for a change of venue, but I don't think I'd be successful with that.'

'Why not?'

He gave a half-hearted shrug. 'I know the judges who'd be hearing this. They've all been having to live with Phil's scars these past years. I don't think there's a chance they'd give you any kind of break, let alone a change of venue.'

Of course, I knew it wouldn't matter where the trial was held. Once Dan told what he thought he knew, I'd be sunk.

Jim showed me an uneasy smile. 'The one thing you have going for you is life without parole is seldom given in Vermont. I know of only half a dozen defendants who've gotten that.'

As I looked at him his smile faded. We both knew that I would be added to that select group.

'So that's it, huh?' I asked.

'I don't know what else to tell you, Joe. If charges are brought against you and you want me to represent you, I'd be happy to do it but I'll need to see eighty thousand dollars in escrow before I can sign on.'

'I don't have that type of money.'

He showed another half-hearted shrug. 'I'm sorry, Joe, I won't be able to help you, then. But I'm sure the court will appoint you a capable public defender.'

As I got up to leave, he checked his watch.

'Joe, we've been talking for twenty minutes. Usually I charge in fifteen minute intervals, but why don't we call it even at fifty dollars? You can pay my receptionist on your way out.'

I took fifty bucks out of wallet and tossed the money on his desk.

It was pretty much what I expected. I don't know why I wasted my time and money with the meeting, but it didn't matter. The only effect it had on me was making me more resolute to carry out the plan I had settled on.

I still had over an hour before I had to meet Craig. I walked over to the Bradley Brewery, got a seat at the bar, and for the hell of it ordered a blueberry wheat ale. As I looked around the place I saw a number of people I knew. Most of them avoided eye contact with me, but there were a few who had been at church when Thayer made his speech on forgiveness, and a couple of them nodded back to me. I guess that was the best I could hope for.

I liked the ale more than I thought I would and ended up ordering a second one. The hour slipped by quickly and before I knew it I had to head over to the courthouse. Craig was waiting for me in the cubbyhole of an office he had there. He was originally from Queens, New York, and had moved to Bradley about the time I had joined the force. I wouldn't say we were ever exactly friends, but back then we used to talk a lot, or more precisely he used to talk a lot to me. For the most part it was a running monologue. He used to seek me out so he could tell me how sick he had gotten of New York and how glad he was to be able to have a quieter and more wholesome life in Vermont.

As I took a chair by his desk, I barely recognized him. He didn't look like he was enjoying the wholesome life he had hoped for. Craig was only a couple of years older than me, but his tight curly hair that used to be a reddish brown had turned gray and had receded to almost the top of his skull. He had also gotten a lot wider and heavier since I'd last seen him. As he sat behind his desk and frowned at me, he looked like a bitter, flabbier version of Larry Fine from the *Three Stooges*.

'What the hell happened to your face?' he demanded.

'You really want me to tell you?'

'What do you mean?'

'You could always ask Dan Pleasant, but if you want I'll be happy to tell you all—'

'Never mind,' Craig said, stopping me. I knew him well enough to know that he wouldn't want to deal with this type of problem.

'But Craig, you sent Dan after me, didn't you?'

'I don't know what you're talking about.'

'Didn't you notify Dan that I missed our meeting the other day?'

'What? I didn't say anything to him about that.'

So Dan was either guessing about me missing my parole meeting or he had one of his boys watching the courthouse. Sonofabitch!

'Really? Well, let me tell you what happened—'

'I said never mind.' There was some panic in his voice. He picked up a folder and flipped through it before putting it down and forcing a stern, almost laughable look onto his face. 'Now about you missing our meeting—'

'I'm sorry about that, Craig. As I said in the message I left you, I had a job interview. By the way, I didn't get the job.'

I could tell he was relieved that I let the other matter drop. He made a loud sucking noise as he breathed in a lungful of air. 'You have to take this seriously, Joe. If you violate your parole I have to send you back to jail. If I do that you'll serve out your complete sentence. That could be another seventeen years.'

I guess I smiled then. It just seemed to be the least of my worries.

'This isn't funny, Joe. I think maybe the problem is you still think of us as colleagues rather than what we are. We're no longer colleagues. We're not even friends. You're a paroled felon and I'm your parole officer. That's our relationship now. You need to accept that.'

'I'm sorry, Craig. And I do accept how things stand.'

'I hope for your sake that's true because you can't be missing our scheduled meetings, understood?'

'Understood.'

He picked the folder back up and frowned at it. 'You moved out of your parents' house without telling me,' he complained, his voice bordering on whining.

'They threw me out.'

'This is what I'm talking about,' Craig said, his cheeks mottling pink and white as he got excited. 'You knew that you were supposed to stay with your parents until you found a permanent residence, and you knew that I was supposed to be kept informed of any address changes. All you had to do was behave yourself. So what did you do to make your parents throw you out?'

'Someone took a shot at me while I was in their house.'

His expression showed that he didn't understand a word I said. 'What do you mean?' he asked. He had a small idiotic smile on his face, as if I were telling a joke he didn't get.

'I was in the house with them. Someone from outside took a shot at me through the window. Whoever it was missed me by inches. If that much.'

The meaning of what I was saying started to seep in.

'I didn't hear anything about that,' he said.

'I'm surprised. I gave a full report to the police. I would've thought somebody would've told you.'

'Nobody told me anything.'

He started to fidget with the folders and pens on his desk. This was more than he had bargained for. Most of his parolees were just ordinary screw-ups. Maybe they served time for drug offenses or borderline petty thefts or an occasional assault and battery because they were shitfaced with alcohol at the time. Usually they were just ordinary folk who were going to toe the line once they got out. He could deal with them. I was different. I brought along troubles that he didn't want to get anywhere near.

'Where are you staying now?' he asked. He realized he was fidgeting, and stopped himself by clasping his hands in front of him. He still couldn't look at me.

'Right now I'm staying in motels. I'd like to permanently move someplace else.'

'What?'

As I looked at him giving his best older bewildered Larry Fine impersonation, I made up my mind about something. Ever since I saw those pictures of my girls I couldn't help thinking that I could move to Albany. I wouldn't force myself into their lives, but I'd be there for them. If I survived this mess, that was what I was going to do.

'I'd like to move to Albany,' I told him. 'That's where my daughters are.'

'I don't know about that—'

'People here are trying to kill me, Craig. If I stay in Bradley, somebody's going to get hurt.'

He looked scared now. This was far more than he ever bargained for, especially the idea that he might have to explain to the parole board why one of his clients ended up being killed under his nose. He cleared his throat and asked what I would do in Albany. I told him that I was planning to go to a trade school and become a plumber.

'I'll see what I can do,' he said.

'The sooner I leave the better. I was hoping to move to Albany by the end of the week.'

'I'll work on it. I'm not making any promises.'

He still couldn't look at me. His eyes were frozen on his clasped hands. As I sat and watched him, he seemed to get more uncomfortable. After a while he was just about squirming in his seat.

'Anything else you need from me?' I asked.

He started to shake his head, but stopped himself. 'You haven't used cocaine since you've been out?'

'No.'

'If I had you take a drug test—'

'Nothing would show up. What's going on, Craig? Phil come by and try to convince you I'm doing coke?'

He shook his head, but he was always a lousy poker player.

'Did you hear how Phil jumped me after church? I had eaten some powdered doughnuts and he thought the sugar residue on me was cocaine.'

'I didn't hear anything about that.' Again he was lying.

'If you want me to take a drug test, give me a cup.'

It was my turn to bluff, because I knew the cocaine I ingested Saturday night would show up in a test. He wavered for a moment and then waved away the idea of the test. Again, he wouldn't want to have to deal with the consequences.

'Forget it. Just get out of here. I'll work on relocating you to Albany.'

As I left his office, he sat frozen, still unable to face me.

It was only four in the afternoon. I was beat. Thanks to Dan's boys my face now felt like raw hamburger, and my nose throbbed as if it had a life of its own. I ran my fingers along its outline. It was more swollen than before and felt as if it were pushed out of place. I walked over to the drugstore and bought some aspirin. I avoided the mirrors inside the store. I didn't want to see how bad my face looked.

When I got to my car, I headed off towards Burlington. This time I was careful about being followed. I pulled over several times and used every trick I knew to make sure no one was behind me. I stopped off once to buy some fast food and then found a roadside motel. I made sure to park in the back so my car couldn't be seen from the road.

When I got in my room I closed the shades. I didn't bother with any ice this time. I knew it wouldn't do any good.

After I looked up what I had to in the phonebook, I ate the food I bought, took some more aspirin, and set the alarm clock for five in the morning. Then I settled back and watched TV. At some point after all the late-night talk shows had finished I must've blacked out.

Chapter 19

A police siren blasted in my ear. As I jerked awake, I found myself in freefall. I flung my arms out and grabbed whatever I could for dear life. Slowly, I got my sense of equilibrium back and realized I wasn't falling. It was pitch black, my heart beating a mile a minute, and all I knew was I was flat on my back. Then I remembered. The police siren droning away was only the alarm clock next to me. It all came back then and I remembered my plan, what I was going to do. I lay in bed long enough for the pounding in my chest to slow down. Then I forced myself out of bed. I took a quick shower, dressed in the same clothes I wore the day before, and left the motel.

It wasn't yet five thirty by the time I pulled onto the road. I felt calm as I drove. One way or another it was all going to be over soon. If it worked as I hoped, I'd be heading to Albany by the weekend.

If it didn't, well, if it didn't...

I forced the thought out of my mind. No matter what, after today they'd at least remember me for something other than what I did to Phil.

I got to the TV station by six. I decided that for what I was going to be doing it would be better to have a TV cameraman with me.

When I got to the lobby a security guard stopped me. I gave him my name and told him I wanted the news director. He got on the phone and I sat and waited. I knew they aired an early six thirty news broadcast and someone would be there.

I didn't wait long before a young kid came down to the lobby to see me. He couldn't have been much older than twenty-five. While it was only a few minutes past six in the morning, he already looked disheveled. His shirt sleeves were haphazardly rolled up and his tie was crooked and uneven. He squinted as he moved slowly towards me. At about three feet away he stopped and held out his hand in a quick, jerky motion.

'You're Joe Denton, right?' he asked.

I ignored his hand and nodded. I was tired of the pretense that anyone actually gave a crap. He stood awkwardly for a moment and then pulled his hand back.

'I'm Steven Wolcott,' he said. 'I'm an assistant news director here. I have to admit, I was surprised to get your call. What can I do for you?'

'I have a proposition I'd like to make.'

'Sure.'

'Can we go to your office and talk about it?'

'I'm sorry, yes, of course. Let's go upstairs.'

I followed him to the elevator. After we got in it, he let out a nervous laugh. He told me there'd been some talk about trying to get me in for an interview.

'You know,' he added, 'ask you questions about what's it like to be out of jail, how people are treating you, whether you have any remorse, stuff like that. You know, give you a chance to get your side of the story out.'

I didn't bother answering him. Once he realized I wasn't going to say anything he gave another short nervous laugh. He tried some more small talk and then stood awkwardly the rest of the way up. When the elevator door opened, he stepped out quickly.

I followed him through the office to a small conference room. After I took a seat, he asked whether I'd like some coffee. I told him I would and asked if he had anything to eat. When he came back, he brought me a cup of coffee and three doughnuts on a paper plate.

He took a seat across from me and clasped his hands behind his head, trying to look calm and in charge, but I could see a mix of eagerness and nervousness in his eyes.

'Tell me about your proposition,' he said.

I took a long sip of coffee and then asked him if he ever heard of Manny Vassey.

He thought for a moment and shook his head. 'Sorry, I've never heard of him.'

'You should've.'

'Why's that?'

'Manny's been running a number of criminal enterprises out of Bradley County for years. Bookmaking, loan sharking, extortion, drugs, prostitution – you name it, he's got his hands in it. And though he operates out of Bradley, his businesses go across the state.'

'Really? Jeez, I wonder why I've never heard of him before.'

I shrugged. 'He's a smart man. He pays off the right people and keeps things quiet. Manny's in the hospital now dying of cancer. His psychotic son, Junior, has taken over and is expanding the business. Junior is now manufacturing crystal meth and distributing it through college clubs that he's forcing owners to sell to him.'

He blinked several times, making a face. 'How much of this can you prove?'

'All of it.'

'Do the police know about this?'

'I don't know about the crystal meth part, but yeah, you got guys on the Bradley police force and in the sheriff's office who know what Manny's been up to. Too many of them are on his payroll to do anything about it.'

I couldn't read from his expression whether he believed me. He could've either been dumbfounded by the whole thing or thought I was nuts, or maybe that I was trying to use them for some private vendetta.

'So what's your proposition?' he asked. 'Do you want to be interviewed on the air about this?'

I shook my head. 'I want to take a cameraman and reporter out with me and show them Vassey's operations in the works. Where his bookmaking and loan sharking operations are headquartered, his crystal meth lab, show his clubs in the act of distributing it, all of it. And I want it shown tonight on your ten o'clock news.'

'Wow. I don't know if we could do something like that—'

'I want a decision now. Otherwise I'm taking this to one of the Boston stations.'

He looked rattled. 'I can't make this type of decision,' he said. 'The news director will have to agree to this.'

'Let's talk to him, then.'

'Her. Eileen Bracket. And she doesn't get in until eleven.'

'Call her up.'

'I can't do that. I'd be waking her up. Eileen doesn't leave here until midnight every night.'

I started to stand. He held his hand out to stop me.

'Wait, okay?' he asked. He bit on his lip as he tried to make a decision. 'I'll call her from my office. Just wait here, okay?'

He left the room in a hurry. While waiting, I ate one of the doughnuts and finished my coffee. Then I closed my eyes and tried to clear my mind. The next few hours were going to be critical. I had to break Junior's operations wide open for what I had in mind to work.

It didn't take long for the kid, Wolcott, to come back. As

he took a seat across from me, he looked more harried than disheveled. He tossed a pad of paper in front of him and tapped his pen nervously against the edge of the table.

'Eileen's on her way,' he said. 'It's probably going to take her forty-five minutes to get here. In the meantime, I need some background information.'

'Go ahead.'

'How long have you known about this?'

'A long time.'

'Can you please be more specific.'

'Maybe fifteen years.'

'And you said that other police and sheriff's officers are being paid to ignore Mr Vassey's illegal businesses?'

'Yes.'

'Could you give me their names?'

'No.' I shook my head. 'You can investigate this yourself later and figure out who's on Manny's payroll.'

'You can't give us any names?'

'No. I'm going to help you expose Junior's operation, but that's all. There is police corruption involved, but you're going to have to discover that yourself.'

'What about the sheriff of Bradley County?'

I hesitated for a second as I tried to decide whether that was a lucky guess or if it was common knowledge that Dan was crooked. I shook my head. 'I'm not ratting any police officers. At least not directly.'

He made a face as if he wanted to argue with me, but it passed. 'Okay,' he said. 'Let's move on. Where are you going to be taking our people today?'

'What do you mean?'

'I need the location of this crystal meth lab, you know, and the other places.'

'If I give you that you won't need me.'

224   Dave Zeltserman

'That's not why I'm asking for it. We want to do our own checking on these locations. We're going to need to do this if we're going to put a story out by ten tonight.'

'Sorry. You'll know the locations when I take your people to them.'

He swallowed back what he wanted to say and then gave kind of a whimsical smile. 'There's not much point to this, is there?' he asked.

'Doesn't seem to be.'

'Why don't I leave you alone, then, until Eileen comes.'

'Sure. I could also use another cup of coffee.'

He was shaking his head when he left the room, but he brought me back a fresh cup. I didn't wait alone for too long before Eileen Bracket showed up, probably no more than twenty minutes. She was about fifty, thin, with a hawk nose and sharp angles all around. She must've rushed over – her hair was still damp from a shower and she had no makeup on, making her thin angular face appear drab and bloodless. As I looked at her, I couldn't help noticing that she had the palest blue eyes I'd ever seen.

Wolcott introduced her to me. Shaking her hand was like holding a cold piece of bone. She took a seat across from me and Wolcott pulled up a chair next to her.

'Steven filled me in on your proposal,' she said. 'I have one question, Mr Denton – why?'

'What do you mean?'

'Why do you want to do this?'

'Because I was a lousy cop,' I said. 'I want to make amends for all the years I let people down.'

'That's bullshit.'

'Not completely,' I said. 'Maybe that's not the whole reason, but it's a good part of it.'

Her lips almost disappeared as they pulled into a thin smile.

She asked, 'What are you really after – hurting Vassey or some of your fellow cops?'

'Neither. And I don't have any fellow cops anymore. I haven't had any for almost eight years.'

'Does this have anything to with the fact that you've obviously been beaten up recently?'

I shook my head. 'Absolutely nothing at all to do with that. And I wasn't beaten up. All that happened was I walked into a tree. At least, that's my story.'

That made her lips pull up a little higher. As she smiled, I couldn't help noticing how pointy her canines were.

'Can I call you Joe?' she asked.

'Sure.'

'What's the urgency, Joe? Why does this have to be broadcast tonight?'

'Does it matter? I'm handing you the story of the year for your station. And you'll end up having dozens more breaking from this one.'

'It matters. I don't like being used,' she said.

'Everything I've said about Vassey and his son is true. So do you want this or not?'

For a moment I thought she was going to tell me to go screw myself, and I think she surprised herself even more that she didn't. Instead, her smile faded from her face, and she nodded slowly. I guess she wanted the story more than the satisfaction of telling me what I could do with myself.

'If you're lying about any of this, I'm going to make your life a living hell,' she said.

All I could think was, you and everyone else. Instead I simply shrugged. 'I'm not lying about any of this.'

She turned to Wolcott. 'Steven,' she told him, 'go tell Tina and Eric we have an assignment for them.'

Wolcott nodded, got up and left the room. As she turned back to me, she showed me her thin smile again. The skin across her cheeks stretched tight against her face.

'The DA in your county, Phil Coakley, the person you maimed. Tell me about that shooting two days ago.'

'I had nothing to do with that.'

Her smile stretched tighter. 'That's not what I asked.'

'I also have nothing to say about that,' I said.

She sat silently, her thin smile pulling tighter as her pale blue eyes stared at me. I couldn't imagine her skin stretched any tighter without it ripping. I met her stare for a while and then got tired of the whole thing.

'Look,' I said. 'I'm going to need some paperwork guaranteeing that if what I tell you pans out you're going to air the story tonight.'

'You'll get the paperwork before you leave.'

The door opened and Wolcott walked in, bringing with him a pretty blonde and a tall skinny kid with a scraggly goatee and a matching ponytail. I recognized the blonde from their newscasts. She looked younger in person, probably no older than early twenties. Eileen Bracket addressed the two of them, telling them who I was and what they'd be doing with me. The blonde was named Tina Hodges and she forced a smile as she held out a hand to me. The skinny kid with the ponytail, Eric, was going to be our cameraman. He kept his distance from me.

It took an hour before I was able to get the paperwork that I wanted, and another forty minutes after that before we got underway. We drove in one of the news vans with Eric behind the wheel and me next to him giving directions. Other than my pointing out where to drive nobody said a word during most of the trip. At one point near the end, Eric asked how I broke my nose. When I didn't answer him he shut up for good. Tina Hodges didn't make a peep from the back seat during the ride.

We arrived at the old tannery a little after ten thirty. This time there were five cars parked alongside it. I directed Eric towards the two dumpsters on the other side of the building. When we got there, we pulled up next to them and parked. I opened both dumpsters and read off the labels of some of the containers.

'All the ingredients for crystal meth,' I said.

Eric took his camera out and started shooting video of what was inside the dumpsters.

'This is so unbelievably brazen,' he muttered. 'Just throwing the stuff out where anyone can get to it.'

I said, 'After fifteen years of doing whatever you want without any fear of the police, you get sloppy. Ready for what's next?'

'We're just going to walk right in there?'

'That's right.'

'And you don't think this is dangerous?' Tina asked, speaking for the first time. Her face paler than before and not quite as pretty as when I had first seen her.

'I don't think so, but we'll see.'

I was pretty sure Junior wasn't going to have any muscle around. Why would he? After over fifteen years of being left alone, why bother? Of course, anything was possible, but I didn't expect to see any of his goons. We got back in the van and drove to the front. I got out first and checked the main door and almost broke out laughing when I found it unlocked. I signaled for the other two to join me.

I opened the door and led the way. I'd been in there before and knew where the gambling operations were. I turned and could see Eric sweating as he carried his camera. Tina looked more distant and scared with each step.

The hallway we were in was lit by a single bulb. I took us down it to the outside of the room where the operations used to be run from. I put my ear against the door and listened. After less than a minute I heard a phone ringing, and then someone talking. I checked the door. It was unlocked. I nodded to Tina and Eric and then opened the door and walked in.

I knew with football season underway things would be in full swing. In the middle of the room were several chalkboards with spreads written on them. To the right, sitting behind a long table, were three guys. They all had computers and phones in front of them. Each of them was staring at us with total bewilderment. One of them was on the phone and I could see his mouth drop as he gawked at us.

'What the hell's this!' one of them yelled. I recognized him from years ago. I couldn't place his name but I knew he'd worked for Manny from almost the beginning. He had always been this fat greasy slob with badly pockmarked skin. Now he was fatter, greasier, and with worse skin. He got up and started towards us. The other two were trying to hide from the camera.

'What the hell all of you doing here?' he demanded. He was moving quickly, heading towards Tina with a clenched fist. I intercepted him, spinning him around and pushing him to the floor. He made kind of an oomph sound as he hit the deck.

'You assholes are in trouble,' he hissed as he lay on the floor. 'Big trouble! Just wait 'til I tell—'

I stepped down on the back of his neck. He let out a high-pitched yelp and then shut up.

Eric took video of the chalkboards and moved to the two guys who were now trying to hide behind their chairs. Tina stood frozen as she stared at me while I pressed my foot down on the slob's neck. He squirmed red-faced on the floor as I put more pressure on him.

'Are you going to just stand there,' I asked, 'or are you going to do your job?'

'What are you doing to that man?' she asked, horrified.

'Don't worry, he'll be fine. Come on, we don't have all day.'

She shook herself out of whatever stupor she had fallen into and moved so she was standing next to the chalkboards. She was still shaking, but Eric took video of her as she pointed out the football spreads and the computers and phones on the long table. He followed her as she moved over to the two jokers who were still trying to hide themselves.

'Are you under the employ of Manny Vassey Jr?' she asked both of them.

Neither of them said a word. They just looked like idiots as they tried to squeeze themselves behind their chairs and out of sight of the camera.

'Are you taking gambling bets?' she asked.

'Get the hell out of here and leave us alone,' one of them moaned.

We had taken enough time. I wanted to get to the crystal meth lab while we still could. From where the dumpsters were located I had a pretty good idea where it was. I went across the room and checked a door there and found it unlocked also. It was so damn careless of them. I swung the door open, and sure enough the lab was right there in plain sight. Two kids were working in it. My guess was they were both probably chemistry majors in college. They looked annoyed when I walked in, and then both went wide-eyed when Eric trailed behind with his camera. Tina squeezed past Eric. She had more color in her face now.

'Who are you guys?' one of the kids muttered.

'We're with WVRT news,' Tina announced as she held out her microphone in their direction. She moved towards them so Eric could take video of her sticking her microphone inches from their faces. 'Are you manufacturing crystal meth here?'

'Yeah,' one of the kids answered. He looked shell-shocked. I guess it hadn't quite dawned on him what was happening until it was too late. When it did hit him, I could see the color bleed out of his face. He turned his back to the camera, trying to shield himself from view. His friend was already covering his face with his shirt.

'Are you working for Manny Vassey Jr?' Tina asked.

'Leave me alone,' he begged.

'Can you please answer my question?'

He didn't move or say a word.

I looked out the door and could see one of the guys talking frantically on the phone. I grabbed Tina by the arm.

'Let's get out of here,' I said.

'I'd like to ask them more questions.'

'We better get out now.'

She was going to argue with me, but I swung her towards the door and something about the look on my face told her she'd better listen. Eric followed, muttering to himself how unbelievable the whole thing was.

The slob had picked himself off the floor and was standing off to the side, glowering at us as we passed by. I should've paid him more attention. All of a sudden I heard Eric yell out. I turned and saw the slob trying to wrestle the camera away from him. I moved fast, got behind the slob, and pushed my foot hard into the back of his knee, and at the same time dug my forearm into his throat and twisted my body. His face turned purple and he let go of the camera so he could claw frantically at my arm. I let go of him and he tumbled to the floor, gasping for air.

All three of us got out of there then, with me trailing behind to make sure none of the jokers we were leaving tried any more tricks. By the time we got outside both Tina and Eric were giggling, more from nerves than anything else.

I got behind the wheel this time and told Eric I'd drive. He didn't seem to mind. He was still shaking from the adrenalin rush of the last few minutes.

'That was, what can I say, fucking unbelievable,' he said, his body still shaking. 'It sure beats shooting video of foliage or a moose wandering around downtown Burlington. Damn, I felt like a real newsman in there.'

'I thought I was going to puke,' Tina volunteered.

'So, chief,' Eric asked, 'where next?'

I checked the clock on the dashboard. Kelley's would be just opening, but I wanted to wait until after their lunch crowd. I also didn't want to hang around Bradley any more than I had to. I had a feeling that Junior and his goons would be looking for us.

'Why don't we head back to your station? We can drop off the video, grab some lunch, and then head out again.'

I could see he was disappointed. He was still caught up in the rush of the moment, but he saw the sense in what I was saying and didn't argue. The ride back to Burlington seemed shorter. I guess we were all caught up in our own thoughts. I kept playing back in my mind Tina announcing the station call letters when we busted in on the crystal meth lab. It made me a little sick thinking about it. Even though the call letters were in big bold print on the camera, most likely none of them had the presence of mind to notice it. I couldn't see any good coming from giving Junior that information. The more I thought about it, the sicker I felt. All I could hope for was that he was in the middle of eating something like a sausage sub when he heard the news, and that it made him choke on it.

When we got back to the station Eileen was waiting for us. She looked tense when she asked Eric how things went. He smiled and put a hand on my shoulder.

'This guy was unbelievable,' he said. 'You should've seen him in action. God damn, it was something.'

'His information panned out?' she asked, her eyebrows rising in both relief and surprise.

'Oh yeah, I'd say so. Let me show you what I got.'

I took a seat while the three of them crowded around a video monitor. A few other people in the office joined them. When they were done, Eileen walked over to me.

'So far so good,' she said.

I shrugged. 'Have you heard from anyone about this?'

'No. Will I?'

'I don't know. Your reporter yelled out your station's call letters while we were there. I wish she hadn't done that.'

'You think Vassey will come here guns a-blazin'?' she asked, her lips curving into another thin smile. I didn't bother saying anything.

'I heard things got rough in there,' she said.

'Not really.'

'Not really? I understand you almost choked a man to death.'

I made a face while I shook my head. 'I think your people got a little too excited. All I did was disable one of Vassey's boys while he was trying to wrestle the video camera away from your cameraman. He was fine when I left him.'

'I'm thinking we have enough for tonight's story.'

She was smiling, staring at me with her pale, almost translucent blue eyes, but she flinched as I stared back. Her smile weakened as she looked away.

'The story's only half done,' I said.

'I think we have enough.'

'We did the hard part. The rest is easy.'

She didn't say anything.

'I know this is Vermont. I know you're comfortable doing mostly stories about leaves changing color, but you are a news station, right?'

She met my stare again, smiling just enough to show her canines. 'That's right. I remember eight years ago doing dozens of stories about a dirty cop who tried to stab a district attorney to death.'

'Then why not finish this story?'

Indecision weakened her. 'We should get the police involved,' she said.

'We won't have a story if we do that.'

'I don't want to put my people in danger.'

'You won't. There'll be plenty of bystanders where we're going next. Nothing's going to happen there. I promise you that. We'll be in and out in five minutes.'

Eric and Tina had wandered over. Eric, grinning widely, asked, 'Are we ready to rock and roll?'

Eileen halfheartedly nodded. Thin lines of worry creased her brow. She turned towards the two of them. 'Be careful, okay?' she asked.

'Don't worry about us,' Eric said, laughing. 'We got a killer here to protect us.'

When we left, I suggested we use one of their cars instead of the van, and Eric volunteered his Honda. First thing we did was drive a couple of blocks to a sandwich shop and have lunch with the station picking up the bill. Then we headed back towards Bradley.

I was a little worried about running into Junior. I had no idea what he'd do if he saw us. The only thing I knew for sure was I wouldn't put anything past him. I felt some relief knowing he'd be looking for either my Mustang or the van. I also knew he'd never expect us to head to Kelley's. Still, my nerves were on edge. I tried to keep it to myself. I joked around and tried to appear at ease. The last thing I needed were for the two kids with me to start panicking.

It was forty minutes past one by the time we pulled into the parking lot at Kelley's. A skinhead type with tattoos all along his neck and the side of his face covered the front door. He did kind of a double-take when he saw us, not quite believing what he was seeing.

As I got closer he moved to block me. I turned him aside with some effort and whispered in his ear, 'This isn't worth getting your skull cracked open for, is it?'

He looked at the camera and then back at me, and I guess he decided it wasn't. He stepped aside and let us pass.

The place had maybe a dozen customers in it. Earl was behind the bar, and when he spotted me he pulled out a cell phone and made a call. His eyes were focused on me as he talked on the phone. I don't think he noticed Tina or Eric until they were well into the club. His head tilted to the side as he tried to comprehend what they were doing there.

I moved quickly through the room, leading Tina and Eric towards the back area. With some luck one of the private rooms would be in use. I nudged Eric and pointed out the dancer on stage. She was completely naked and was staring at us. She seemed disoriented, not quite sure whether to keep dancing or to get off the stage.

'Get a shot of her,' I told him. 'Vermont's a topless-only state. That's one violation so far.'

Eric stopped to shoot some video and then we kept moving.

When we got past the curtains, I started trying the doors. The third one I tried was locked. The doors were flimsy and were meant only for privacy. I doubted Earl ever expected anyone to try breaking one down. I used my shoulder and the door flew open on the first try. A middle-aged man was sitting on the carpeted bench with his pants down to his ankles while a thin dark brunette straddled him as she bounced up and down. I had seen her dancing Saturday night. I remembered her name was Cindy. She started to yell at us and then froze in mid-bounce when she saw the camera and realized what was going on.

Tina moved quickly, sticking a microphone in the brunette's face as Eric shot video of it. She asked, 'You're performing sex acts for money here, is that right?'

The brunette slid off the guy and tried to cover herself. The guy on the bench looked like he was going to have a heart attack. I pointed out to Tina a small container and a cocaine spoon next to him on the bench.

'What's that?' she asked me.

'Cocaine.'

Then, to the brunette, she said, 'Where did you get the cocaine from?'

'I'm not saying anything,' the brunette muttered as she scrambled to get back into a pair of hot pants.

Tina turned to the guy lying prone in front of us. 'How much did you pay for these sex acts? And how much for the cocaine?'

He rolled over on his side and tried to hide his face. 'Leave me out of this, please. I have a wife, for God's sake.'

I heard some noise from behind. I grabbed Tina. She tried to shake me off, but I got her turned around and heading towards the curtains. Eric followed behind us.

'I had more questions,' she started to complain, and then she saw Earl moving towards us with a baseball bat.

'I don't know what you thought you were going to do here, Joe, but you're fucking nuts,' he said.

'We're leaving,' I said. 'Just get out of our way.'

'No, I don't think so.' I could see that vein on his neck beating like crazy and his eyes shining with murder. 'Your two friends here ain't going anywhere with that camera, and you're not going anywhere period.'

'We don't want any trouble, Earl.'

He laughed at that. 'You got a sense of humor, Joe, I'll give you that.' Then he brought the bat back so he could knock the camera – and maybe Eric's head along with it – across the room. I dove for his knees trying to tackle him. Hitting him was like hitting a concrete block, but I knocked him back a few feet. He was able to stay on his feet but he swung off balance and missed Eric by a foot.

'Fucking asshole,' he swore. I was scrambling to get to my feet when he whacked me across the shoulders with the bat. I could see out of the corner of my eye that he swung with one hand and was off balance, but it still hurt like hell and dropped me back to my knees. He stepped forward and kicked me hard in the ribs, knocking me back on the floor. He brought his foot back for another kick, but before he could deliver it there was a dull thud and then a glass crashing next to me.

I looked up and saw that Earl had his hand up to his eye as blood seeped through his fingers. His face was beet red when he turned towards Tina, an open gash along the side of his eye. He glared at her for only a second before turning back to me, but it was all the time I needed. I grabbed a piece of the broken glass and drove upward with it, driving it between his legs. He screamed and reached down, but I knocked his hand away and kept pushing upward. Blood was getting all over my hand. I wasn't sure whether it was his or mine, but I kept shoving the broken glass into him. He fell over. I let go then and watched as he writhed on the floor, moaning and grabbing at his wound. Then I got to my feet.

I looked around. The girl who had been dancing onstage was standing naked, looking on in horror. All at once she put her hands to her face and started screaming. Milling around were all the club patrons, staring at us, trying to decide what to do. Tina looked like she was in shock. Eric was next to her, shaking his head as he muttered to himself how unbelievably incredible the whole thing was. I grabbed Tina by the arm. 'Let's get out of here,' I told her. She didn't seem capable of anything, but once I started dragging her, her legs moved on their own. One of the patrons, a heavyset bearded guy in a flannel shirt and overalls, tried to stop me. I shoved an open palm into his chin and he staggered back. After that no one else tried anything. My side hurt like hell. I figured Earl cracked one of my ribs, but

I kept moving and dragging Tina with me. By the time Tina and I reached the exit Eric came to life and sprinted after us. As we got out of there I could still hear the dancer screaming her head off.

'We better get moving,' I told Eric. He fumbled for his car keys and dropped them a couple of times before he got the door opened. He was shaking like a leaf.

'Holy shit,' he said. 'Damn. I wish I had taken video of that.'

My hand stung. I looked down and realized I had more than just Earl's blood on me. My hand had been sliced open by the broken glass. I took my shirt off and wrapped it around the wound.

'Are you okay?' Eric asked.

'I sliced my hand with the glass. I'm going to need stitches.'

'There's a hospital in Bradley,' he said. 'Let me take you to the emergency room.'

'No thanks, just get out of here. You can take me to a hospital in Burlington.'

Tina seemed to wake up from the back seat. 'We should call the police.'

'Uh-uh. Not here we shouldn't,' I said.

We were still on one of the back roads when I spotted a black Range Rover speeding towards us. I lowered myself and saw Junior's two goons in it. Duane was driving and Jamie was next to him with his head bandaged up. They looked over at us, but neither of them saw me as they passed by. I turned and watched them through the back window. I knew they were racing towards Kelley's. I pretty much guessed Earl had called them when he first saw me.

'Are we in danger?' Tina asked. She sounded scared. As I looked at her I noticed how close she was to crying.

'I don't think so,' I said. 'Once this story airs, Junior's history. Don't worry about him.'

When we got to Burlington, we stopped off at the Chapel

Memorial Hospital's emergency room. I got a tetanus shot and sixteen stitches for my hand, which they also bandaged up. I also had my chest X-rayed and found that I had a couple of bruised ribs, nothing broken. After that we stopped off at a department store and Eric ran in and bought me a new polo shirt and a pair of pants. I needed a new pair of pants because I had bled over the pair I was wearing. We then drove back to the station and I changed in the men's room. When I got out, Eileen was waiting for me. Her edges seemed even sharper than before.

'You promised me nothing was going to happen there,' she said in a voice that could cut glass.

'Either of those two get hurt?' I asked.

'Tina's in shock.'

'She's a gutsy kid. She'll be okay. If she hadn't nailed Earl Kelley with that glass I'd probably be dead now.'

'Damn you, you promised me!'

'Yeah? Why should you've believed anything I said? Look at me. I'm a dirty ex-cop and a paroled felon. If you're going to believe me that's your problem.'

She was livid. 'You sonofabitch.'

'What are you complaining about? You have your story. And it's a good one. I'm the one with the bruised ribs and a sliced hand.'

'You almost killed a man in that club.'

I made a face. 'It was self-defense. He was going to take Eric's head off with that baseball bat if I didn't do anything. And he was going to do a lot worse to me. Anyway, he'll live.'

'You just about castrated him!'

'Look, he was trying to kill me.' I was starting to get annoyed. It was bad enough that my hand throbbed like crazy and that I could barely breathe without a searing pain sucking my breath away, but now I had to listen to this?

'Eileen,' I continued, trying to keep my voice under control, 'just be happy, okay? You got a great story. There was no other way of getting it. If you had gotten the cops in Bradley involved you would've been shut down from the start. Let's just finish this up and show that college club distributing crystal meth.'

'We're done. I'm not sending you out with any of my people again.'

It was pretty much what I had expected. It didn't matter, though. I had thought the matter out when were driving back from Bradley.

'You don't need me for this last part,' I said. 'The club is the Blue Horn in Eastfield. Get the state police involved if you want. Have one of your interns or someone young go there tonight and buy crystal meth, and then send the police and Eric in. It will work fine.'

She wanted to argue with me. I could see it in her eyes, but there was nothing to argue about.

'You're still going to interview me on the air tonight, right?' I asked.

'I'm going to have to. I can't find any other link between Manny Vassey, his son, and that old tannery you broke into.'

'What do you mean?'

'I checked at the Registry of Deeds and that property is owned by a June Hathaway.'

'I never heard of her.'

'You wouldn't have. She died in seventy-two.'

'So Vassey has a bogus owner on the deed. So what? Someone's been paying the water and power bills there. And buying supplies. And paying for the rubbish removal. You'll find a link if you dig around.'

'I hope so.'

'You'll find one,' I said. 'Anyway, someone's going to talk. If not one of the guys we caught on video then one of the cops on Manny's payroll. Someone's going to roll over on him to protect themselves. You'll tie Manny and Junior up in this.'

'We'll see. But we will need you to talk about what you know on the air tonight. In the meantime, the Registry of Deeds is open for another half-hour. It's probably a waste of time, but I'll send one of my people over to find out what name is on the Blue Horn's deed.'

She wavered a moment before leaving. I could see the uncertainty creeping into her eyes and then spreading and dulling her hard edges. I could almost hear the thoughts running through her. What if I was lying about Manny and Junior's involvement? All she had at the moment was my word on it.

I should've been expecting something like that. It shouldn't have come as any surprise. I don't know. Maybe I was too distracted by the pain ripping into my side and the raw throbbing in my hand, and maybe that was keeping me from thinking clearly, but I couldn't help worrying. My plan was to bust Junior's gambling and drug operations wide open and make it political suicide for Phil to strike any deal protecting him. I knew that given enough time Manny and Junior would be tied to what was going on in that tannery and their other businesses. For now it would have to be my word against theirs.

I hung around the station. Around six Eileen found me and told me what I was expecting – that according to the deed the Blue Horn had been sold three months ago to June Hathaway. She had the name of the previous owner and she was going to try to track him down and see whether he was willing to make a statement. At a quarter past seven Tina found me and asked whether I wanted to join her for dinner. My stomach felt as if it were in knots, but I needed something to kill the time so I went with her.

We ended up going to a steakhouse about a mile from the station. Tina ordered a sirloin and I stuck with a salad and cream of mushroom soup. It was about all I felt I could handle.

She was trying to smile at me, but concern was wrecking it.

'How are you feeling?' she asked.

'I'll be okay,' I said. 'No serious damage done at least.'

'That was really amazing in there,' she said. 'I thought that bartender was going to kill all of us.'

'He gave it his best shot. I guess it just wasn't good enough.' I paused for a moment to take a bite of my salad and to look at Tina. She was very pretty, there was no arguing about that, but it was the way she was looking at me that got to me. Maybe years ago when I was quarterbacking my high school football team, Elaine might have looked at me like that, but probably not even then. I don't think any woman, or really anyone, had ever looked at me with the admiration with which Tina did at that moment. It choked me up a bit.

'You were really amazing in there, Joe.'

'You were pretty damn good yourself.' There was something contagious about her smile, and I couldn't help smiling back. 'That was quick thinking on your part. If you hadn't nailed Earl with that glass, I would've been taken out of there in a body bag.'

'I can't believe I did that,' she said, laughing. 'It just happened. I guess it was reflex.'

We ate quietly after that, but it was comfortable quiet. I even realized I had stopped worrying at one point. Near the end, Tina showed me an uneasy smile.

'Joe, I don't know if you've been watching our broadcasts, but for the last couple of weeks we've been hitting you pretty hard.'

'That's okay. I deserve it.'

'I don't know if that's true anymore. What I saw today was incredible. For those things to be going on shows that the whole Bradley police force has to be dirty. It's no wonder you ended up the way you did. But what you did today was amazing. You're going to be single-handedly responsible for cleaning up this whole area.'

'I appreciate that,' I said. 'Not every cop on the Bradley force is dirty. Some are, but not all. I ended up the way I did because of my own mistakes. I have no one to blame.'

The way she looked at me right then almost stopped my heart.

'Why don't we find someplace we can be alone, Joe?'

I wanted to. God did I want to. But she was almost twenty years younger than me. There was more to it than that. I didn't even know if I had a future past the next few hours. But there was still more. There was Charlotte. I know it's crazy, but I started feeling guilty. As nuts as Charlotte was, I knew that in some bizarre way we were meant for each other. That at some level we understood each other and that we could help each other. As beautiful and sane as Tina was, she didn't have a clue what was inside me.

'Tina,' I said. 'It's eight thirty and we got that news broadcast at ten.'

'We have enough time.'

'I've got to be honest,' I said. 'I want to more than you could ever imagine, but I'm feeling pretty beat up right now.'

'I'll be gentle.'

'Why don't we give it a few days and see how we're feeling then?'

That just heated her up more. The desire flushing her face was almost too much for me. I almost weakened. But Jesus, I couldn't do that to her. Instead, I just sat back and looked into her eyes. She showed me a little smile, took a business card from her pocketbook, wrote on the back of it, and handed it to me.

'Don't wait too long, Joe,' she said, showing me probably the nicest smile I'd ever seen. I looked on the back of the card and saw that she had written her home number on it and had drawn a big heart next to it. I put the card away in my wallet.

We finished our dinner and headed back to the station. When we got there, I found out that things had gone as planned at the Blue Horn. One of the interns bought several hits of crystal meth and then the state police raided the place. They got almost forty thousand dollars' worth of drugs in the raid and the station shot video of it all. Eileen had one of her reporters over at the state police headquarters, but it sounded like none of the Blue Horn employees that were rounded up were willing to say who they worked for.

The station was able to condense the video they shot into a ninety-second clip. They opened with Tina reporting the story. After that I was brought on and interviewed live for about three minutes. It went better than I could've expected. Tina acted as if everything I was saying was a proven fact, even though there was nothing yet tying Manny and Junior to any of it.

After the broadcast Eileen came over and offered me her hand.

'I have to admit you did some good work here, Joe,' she said.

I thanked her. As I was getting ready to leave, Tina came over and kissed me on the cheek. When I turned to say something to her, she grabbed me around the neck and kissed me long and hard on the mouth. When we separated her eyes were sparkling.

'Don't wait too long to call me,' she said. I felt a lump in my throat as I watched her walk away.

My head was buzzing as I made my way to my car. I couldn't help thinking of Tina, of the way it felt when she kissed me, of how badly I realized I wanted her. I guess I was too caught up in my thoughts to notice them, at least until it was too late. At the last second I caught sight of Jamie's bandaged head out of the corner of my eye. Then I felt the blow to my damaged ribs. He must've used brass knuckles. The pain from the blow dropped me to my knees and brought hot tears to my eyes. It froze me. I couldn't breathe, I couldn't move.

'We've been looking for you all day,' Jamie whispered in my ear. Then I took another shot to the ribs. The pain exploded in me. And then everything went black. I felt a sensation of being picked up and thrown. And then nothing.

Chapter 20

I couldn't have been out for more than a couple of minutes. At least, I don't think so. When I came to I was in the back seat. Duane was next to me, a hard smirk on his face as he stuck a nine-millimeter automatic into my side. Jamie was up front driving.

'Look who just woke up,' Duane said, his voice just above a whisper.

'Have a nice nap?' Jamie asked, chuckling to himself.

Duane shoved the gun harder into my side. 'It's not polite to ignore a civil question,' he said, his smirk tightening on his face.

Softly, because of the pain, I said, 'Yeah, I had a nice peaceful nap. Thanks. How's your head?'

'A lot better than your ribs,' Jamie said. 'By the way, we're not here for any collections, but you probably know that.'

'You want to guess what we're here for?' Duane said, his mouth inches from my ear. His breath smelled like raw sewage.

'Did you watch the news tonight?' I asked.

'It don't matter,' Duane said in a soft whisper. 'It's not going to change what's going to happen tonight.'

Jamie chuckled to himself over some private joke. Then he said, 'Mr Vassey's waiting for you. He bought himself a new butcher's apron for the occasion.'

I closed my eyes and tried to think. I knew Junior's order was to bring me back alive, and I knew Duane would be slow pulling the trigger. The gun was mostly for show, he'd use it only if he had to. I had nothing to lose so I took my chance.

I doubled over and grabbed my side. 'I think you broke my ribs,' I moaned.

'Ain't that a shame,' Jamie said, chuckling harder. Duane joined in, his body convulsing lightly with amusement. I had my elbow drawn in as I was clutching my side. I whipped it around as hard as I could and caught Duane under his chin. His head snapped back and I pushed the gun away with my bandaged hand while I punched him with my good one. The problem was because of my ribs I couldn't get a hard enough blow in, otherwise I would've knocked him out and had his gun. Instead he was able to fight back.

'Goddam it!' Jamie swore. Tires squealed and the car swerved to a stop. From the corner of my eye I saw Jamie's gun swinging towards my head. I moved, but not fast enough to avoid it. It ended up being more of a glancing blow. It didn't knock me out, but it slowed me down enough for Duane to pull his gun away from me. He hit me hard across the side of my face with its barrel, opening a gash under my cheek. He was breathing hard, his eyes blind with rage as he brought his gun back up again. But the orders were to bring me back alive. Reluctantly he got himself under control.

'You okay, Duane?' Jamie asked.

'Yeah, I'm okay. This goddam piece of shit.' Then to me, 'I'll be with you all night tonight, watching. I promise you that.'

I only had that one shot. That was all. There was nothing else left in me. My abdominal muscles were spasming so bad I couldn't breathe. For a moment I thought I was going to suffocate because of it. It seemed to take minutes before my muscles relaxed enough so I could gasp in air again. Then I fell back into my seat and closed my eyes. There was nothing else I could do. As I sat there I could feel blood dripping down the side of my face. Duane leaned over, his sour breath almost making me gag. During the rest of the trip he whispered in my ear, telling me in great detail everything they were going to do to me.

When the car stopped, I opened my eyes and saw we were at the side entrance to Junior's house. He must've been waiting for us because he barreled out of the side door and came at us at a jog.

'Hey, Joe, glad you could make it!' he yelled.

Duane pulled me out of the back seat, and before I knew it Jamie was on the other side of me. The two of them were dragging me towards the house, and I just hobbled along, unable to do anything about it.

Junior had caught up to us and was standing in front of me. 'You think you can pull that shit on me and get away with it?' he asked, breathing hard from his jog. An ugly grin broke across his face. 'Whatsa matta, nothing to say anymore?'

He brought his fist back and punched me in the stomach. It doubled me over. At that split second I both heard a rifle shot and saw half of Jamie's bandaged head fly away. He toppled over like timber that had been cut. Junior stared at him wide eyed and then dove to the ground. I fell over and twisted myself around so I could look behind me. In the moonlight I could see a rifle barrel coming out of the bushes about forty yards away. Duane had his nine-millimeter out and was firing towards it. An orange flame shot out of the rifle barrel, cutting Duane just about in half, but he kept firing as he fell. He must've hit something because a dull moan escaped from the bushes and the rifle fell.

Junior was lying just a few feet from me, his ugly face frozen in fear. I scrambled on top of him and started punching him flush in the face with my good hand. If I hadn't been weakened by my ribs I would've killed him. Instead I only knocked him out. I gave him a few more shots and then crawled off him.

It took me a while to get to my feet. Both Duane and Jamie were about as dead as you could be. I hobbled over to the bushes and got down on my hands and knees to see who it was. I was surprised to find Scott Ferguson lying there. He had taken a bullet to the chest. He was still alive, but just barely.

I asked him who he was trying to kill, me or Junior.

His breathing was labored, coming out in short violent gasps. His index finger signaled for me to come closer. It took some effort because of my ribs, but I leaned forward and put my ear against his mouth.

'Fuck you,' he said.

I think he died then. I looked around and saw a shell casing on the ground. I picked it up and saw that it was a seven-millimeter.

He must've been there for Junior. Maybe when he saw me he decided to kill both of us. Maybe he decided Junior and I were in on Billy's death together. It was probably something like that, but the only thing I knew for sure was if I hadn't doubled over my head would been blown apart instead of Jamie's.

I wiped off the shell casing with my shirt and dropped it back on the ground.

Nobody had bothered coming out of Junior's house. Most likely he had sent his wife and kids away for the night. His nearest neighbor was at least a quarter-mile away, but there was a good chance somebody heard the gunshots and called the police. I wanted to get out of there before they showed up.

I started towards Jamie's car, moving as fast as I could, which wasn't very fast. I was still twenty yards away when I saw the lights flashing. I stood frozen, watching as a sheriff's car pulled up to me. Hal Wheely got out of it. His eyes narrowed as he looked around him.

'Get down on your knees and put your hands on your head,' he ordered.

'Hal, I can explain this.'

He had his gun out, pointing it at me. 'I'm not telling you again,' he said.

I did as he told me. He pulled my arms behind me and slapped cuffs on my wrists. Then he yanked me to my feet.

I hobbled along as he dragged me to his car. When I tried stopping at the rear door, he shook his head. I didn't catch on until he opened his trunk.

'You're kidding,' I said.

But I knew he wasn't, and I knew I had no other choice, so I got in.

Chapter 21

I must've been in that trunk for hours. At first it was unbearable. Every bounce felt like a knife ripping into my side. Then my arms and legs started cramping. At some point I must've gotten used to the pain. I had to've because I dozed off. Or maybe I blacked out. In either case, I was gone. Next thing I knew Hal was slapping me in the face and dragging me out of the trunk.

We were in the middle of the woods somewhere. As Wheely dragged me to the front of the car I could make out a cabin to the left of us. He pushed me onto a dirt path that led to the cabin.

'Hal,' I said, my voice coming out as barely a whisper, 'this doesn't make any sense anymore. It's over.'

'Will you just shut up,' he snapped.

'Did you see the news tonight?'

'Just shut your face!'

He shoved me hard from behind, sending me flopping to the ground. I almost ended up being dragged the rest of the way to the cabin. When we got inside he pushed me over to a wood stove and then used another pair of handcuffs to cuff my right ankle to the stove.

'Unless you can gnaw through bone you're not getting out of there,' he said, showing me a dead smile.

'Will you listen to me, Hal?'

He shook his head and left the cabin.

I was alone for maybe twenty minutes when the door opened and Dan Pleasant and Wheely walked in.

'Jesus, Dan,' I croaked out. 'This is all over now. You don't have to do this.'

'How is this all over?' he asked.

'Did you watch the news tonight?'

'Yeah, I watched it. I have to give you credit, Joe, you did a good job screwing us over royally.'

I tried talking, but started coughing instead. My throat was so damn dry. I tried again. 'That's not why I did it. Phil can't make a deal with Manny now.'

'He can't, huh? Why not?'

'It would be political suicide.'

His thin smile disappeared as he stared at me. 'That's your problem, Joe. You have to make things so damn complicated. You didn't do shit tonight. Phil was politically dead when he was caught in that motel room with that hooker. Nothing you did is going to stop him from making a deal with Manny.'

'Dan, you're wrong,' I said, but as I thought about it I realized he wasn't.

'You don't look so sure of yourself anymore, Joe,' he said. He turned to Wheely. 'Does he Hal?' I watched as Wheely slowly shook his head. Then to me, 'Damn it, Joe, I gave you so many chances and you just kept screwing me and lying to me about it. And after everything I did for you? Goddam it!'

He handed Wheely a flashlight. 'Shine this on him, okay, Hal?' As Wheely shined the light on me, Dan took my picture with a digital camera. He seemed satisfied with the results and put the camera back in its case.

'What are you going to do with that picture?' I asked, my voice now a bare whisper.

'Maybe I'll tell you later,' he said. His pleasant smile came back as he looked at me. 'I can't promise you anything, Joe. The only thing I can tell you now is that I'm going to keep you alive until morning. What happens then, we'll see. Now why don't you tell me what happened at Junior's house?'

'Why don't we trade?'

'Sorry, it's not going to work that way. Now Joe, I'll tell you, I'd like nothing more right now than to kick the living hell out of you. But I'm going to restrain myself, at least as long as you're cooperating with me. So what happened at Junior's?'

I tried to answer him but I couldn't, my voice was gone. I tried to croak out that I needed water. He looked annoyed. 'Hal, can you get him some water?'

Wheely left the cabin. I heard a car door open and close, and then he came back with a water bottle. He let me have a few sips, just enough so I could talk.

'Two of his boys picked me up outside of WVRT. They were going to torture me in Junior's playroom. I guess Scott Ferguson had gotten it in his head that Junior and I were responsible for his brother Billy's murder.'

My voice cracked on me and Wheely gave me a couple more sips. I cleared my throat and tried again.

'He was hiding in the bushes,' I continued, my voice now a hoarse whisper. 'He must've been lying in wait for Junior. I could tell from the way he smelled that he'd been drinking, but I guess he was sober enough to blow Jamie's head off and cut Duane in half. He tried shooting me a few days ago through my parents' bedroom window.'

'Who shot Ferguson?'

'Duane did.'

'And you worked Junior over?'

I nodded. 'How badly did I hurt him?'

'Not bad enough. He checked into Bradley Memorial, but he'll probably be released by morning. I'll tell you, Joe, that's a nasty cut you got on your cheek.'

'I'll live.'

'Maybe. We'll see.'

He was laughing to himself over that. As he turned to leave, I asked whether he could at least cuff my hands in front of me.

'Sorry, Joe, I can't do that.'

'How about giving me some more water?'

'Not now. We'll see in the morning. Joe, some advice. We're fifty miles away from anyone. Don't bother yelling for help.'

Both of them got a chuckle over that and then they left.

I had a long night after that. The physical pain was bad enough, but then I start thinking about everything I had done to end up where I was and it made me sick inside. I kept playing it over and over in my mind and feeling sicker as I did. Then I started thinking of my daughters. I kept seeing them the way they were in those pictures, and I kept hearing Courtney's voice as it sounded over the phone the other day. I was overcome with such a sense of loss that I started crying. I didn't want to – Jesus, the last thing I wanted was for Dan or any of his boys to walk in on me like that – but I couldn't help myself. It seemed a long time before I was able to stop. Then I started praying. Praying that I could somehow have another chance with my girls. I kept it up until daylight. At some point I went numb, unable to think or feel anything.

It must've been daylight for hours before Dan came back. He was alone and was carrying a small paper bag. He showed me a little smile as he stared at me.

'You haven't been crying, now, have you, Joe?'

'Why don't you just get it over with.'

'Get what over with?' He was smiling his pleasant smile. 'I've got good news. Manny died this morning of respiratory failure. You're going to be walking out of here alive.'

I almost burst out crying then. I had to bite my lip to hold it back.

'Don't you have anything to say, Joe?'

'Get these cuffs off me,' I said.

'I can't do that. It's not over yet. But I'll cuff you in front. Just don't try anything stupid.'

He placed the paper bag next to me, and then got on his knees so he could uncuff me. I couldn't have tried anything even if I wanted to, my arms were too stiff. It took some effort but I moved my hands in front of me so he could cuff me.

'Goddam it, you smell ripe, Joe. There's a sandwich in that bag. Also a bottle of water. It's all you're going to get today so you might want to save some for later.'

'Awfully considerate of you.'

He chuckled and gave me a thoughtful look. 'Not really. After everything I've been through, I don't want you dying on me now.'

'Why isn't it over yet?'

'Be patient.'

I reached into the bag and got out the water. I fumbled a bit before I was able to get the top off. After taking a long drink, I put the water down. Dan watched with amusement sparkling in his eyes.

'Anyone looking for me over what happened at Junior's?'

He shook his head. 'Junior didn't mention you.'

'How about Earl? Did he file a complaint against me?'

He shook his head again. 'No. I wouldn't worry about that either. From what I understand he'd be sending himself to prison if he did.'

I picked up the water again and drank almost half of it. When I put the bottle down, I forced myself to meet Dan's eyes.

'You forced Charlotte to kill Manny,' I said.

He just smiled at me.

'Damn it, why isn't it over?'

'Bye, Joe.'

He left then.

The day dragged on. My mind kept racing over what must've happened. Dan must've approached Charlotte, showed her the picture he took, and gave her a choice – have me die and her exposed, or get rid of Manny. It must've been something like that. But why wasn't it over? I racked my brains trying to think of why, but I couldn't come up with anything.

It had been dark for hours when I heard a car drive up. It seemed to take forever for the footsteps to approach the door and for Dan to walk in. He was carrying some clothes and he gave me a grim look as he nodded towards me.

'It's over now, Joe.'

I didn't say anything. I just sat still as he took the cuffs off me. I sat for a while trying to rub the aching out of my joints.

'Why don't you put those clothes on, Joe,' he said.

'I need some help standing up.' He gave me his hand. It took some effort but I got to my feet. I had to move like an old cripple as I got out of my shirt and pants and put on the clothes Dan had brought me.

'How is it over now?' I asked.

'You're going to hear about it anyway,' Dan said, shrugging. 'Somehow Junior figured out that your nurse friend was responsible for Manny's death. Early this afternoon he abducted her. My office got a tip on it. I got a search warrant and me and my boys raided his playroom. He was there with a couple of his boys. We ended up shooting it out. It was really something, Joe. Bottom line, Junior's dead.'

'What about Charlotte?'

He shrugged uneasily. 'She was half chopped up when we got there. There was no way of saving her.'

'You killed her.'

'Be careful, Joe. This is over now.'

'You tipped Junior off to her,' I said, my words sounding distant and hollow. 'You followed her and watched Junior take her. You waited until you knew she'd be dead before you raided that room.'

'Look, it's over, okay? And don't start playing all high and mighty with me!' A hot anger flushed his face. He clenched his fist and took a step towards me. With his other hand he grabbed my shirt collar and pulled me forward so my face was inches from his. 'You could have done what you kept promising, but shit, no, you left it up to me.'

He let go of me and took a step away. The anger had drained from him, leaving his face sickly pale. 'What was I going to do? That woman was a loon. You could see it in her eyes. I wasn't going to let her hang around and hope she'd keep her mouth shut. And I needed Junior dead. But Christ, Joe, you've got no one to blame but yourself for any of this.'

'You killed her.'

'Shut up, Joe. It's over now. Just shut up. Anyway, what's the big deal? You told me she murdered four people. It was only justice catching up to her.'

It wasn't justice. Not to die like that. I tried to think what it must've been like for Charlotte, but I was too numb to think. Too numb to really feel anything.

'I talked to Simpson this afternoon,' Dan said. 'Your relocation to Albany is all set. Call him next week and he'll give you a name and number of a parole officer there to contact. I had your car towed to Bradley. I'll drive you over and that will be it. You'll get in your car, drive to Albany, be with your daughters, and I'll never see or hear from you again, right?'

I nodded. I followed him to his car. During the ride back he tried some small talk, but after a while it was like listening to the wind.

Chapter 22

After Dan dropped me off at my car, I got out the bottle of aspirin that I kept in my glove compartment and chewed on a handful of them. I then found a twenty-four-hour convenience store, bought some food, a six-pack of beer, bandages, and antiseptic ointment. I headed off to Eastfield after that and stopped off at the first motel I came across. The desk clerk didn't look like he wanted to give me a room. I couldn't blame him, but I paid him cash and he handed me a key.

I spent some time trying to clean out the gash under my cheek and my other cuts and scrapes. It stung like hell when I put the antiseptic ointment on. After bandaging up my wounds up as best I could, I filled up the tub with hot water. When I took off my shirt and looked at myself in the mirror, I saw my side was one big purple bruise. I had no doubt that I had some cracked ribs. It didn't matter, though. Over time they'd heal.

I ate the food and then gingerly lowered myself into the tub. As I lay in it, I had two of the beers. For the most part they were tasteless, or at least they seemed that way. After I got out, I dried myself off, and lowered myself onto the bed. I tried to picture Charlotte, tried to imagine how she looked when her eyes were calm and not jumping around like ping-pong balls. I tried to concentrate, but I couldn't picture her. She was gone. As much as

I wanted to mourn her there was nothing left for me to mourn. My memory of her had faded away. After a while I gave up trying. Then I closed my eyes.

Next thing I knew it was two thirty in the afternoon. I had been asleep over fourteen hours. I felt groggy, disoriented. It was as if the world had shifted somehow. I lay there for another half-hour. I felt this sense of disquiet that I couldn't shake. I just felt so damn alone.

I got up and found Tina's business card in my wallet. I was able to get her at her desk.

'Hi,' I said, 'I think I've waited long enough.'

'Really?'

'Can I stop by later, maybe at seven, and we could have dinner?'

'I'd like that, Joe. I can't wait to see you.'

I felt better then. Her voice had sounded so sweet. I just hoped I'd be able to talk her into moving to Albany with me.

I checked the clock and saw that it was a quarter past two. With a forty-five-minute drive to Burlington that left me four hours to do what I needed to do. I took a shower, dressed, grabbed my duffel bag and got out of there.

I still had the paperwork for the police pension on me. I hadn't thrown it away yet. I looked it over, signed it, and took it over to the post office. I figured I'd collect the thirty-four sixty a month while training for a job, but once I got settled I'd drop it.

My stomach was feeling empty. I didn't think I could wait until seven – also, I had that blueberry wheat ale on my mind, so I stopped off at the Bradley Brewery and ordered a cheeseburger and an ale. As I was eating my food I saw Phil Coakley walk in. He noticed me, hesitated, and then walked over and sat on the stool next to me. I could see his arm was still in a sling.

'You've been busy the last few days,' he said.

'Yeah. You caught the news broadcast Wednesday night?'

'That's not what I'm talking about.'

'What're you talking about, then?'

'All the deaths and shootings we've had. Let's see, Scott Ferguson, Jamie Hubbard, Duane Wilcox, Manny Vassey Jr – oh yeah, and a young nurse, Charlotte Boyd, who was hacked to death. And of course Susie Baker, and my own self being shot.'

'I had nothing to do with any of that, Phil.'

I could feel him staring at me.

'From what I understand,' I said, 'Sheriff Dan Pleasant and his boys shot Junior after he had murdered—'

'Hacked to pieces.'

'Okay, hacked to pieces that nurse.'

'Charlotte Boyd. You should at least call her by her name, Joe. I know you dated her.'

'Okay, so I dated her.'

'Funny, though, she didn't seem your type.'

'I had just gotten out of jail,' I murmured. 'I was lonely.'

'I still can't see it. The only thing I can see is that in some way you were responsible for her death. My guess, you're responsible for all of them.'

I turned to him. 'What do you want, Phil?'

'I want to see you punished for what you've done.' He sighed. 'But I guess that's not going to happen, at least not in this lifetime. But Joe, I hope you end up rotting in hell.'

He got up and walked to one of the empty tables.

I finished my burger and ale. I didn't bother looking at him when I left the bar. It wasn't worth letting him get to me. It was over. I squinted against the sunlight as I walked outside. It was a new day. What was past was past.

I drove over to my parents' house. I didn't really care about saying any goodbyes, but there were things of mine that I wanted to give my girls. Some football trophies, the game ball for a division championship, some books – just some small things.

The door was unlocked. I yelled out, nobody answered, so I went straight to my old bedroom. As I was collecting my things, my dad walked in.

'What are you doing here?' he asked.

'I'm leaving for Albany tonight. I'm getting some of my things together for my girls. I'll be out of here in ten minutes.'

He stood silently and watched me, his face growing more haggard every second. I guess he reached a point where he couldn't help himself.

'Look at you,' he cried out. 'You're all beat up. God knows what you've been doing. And you're going to go to your daughters for what? To screw them up the way you screwed yourself up?'

I wanted to ignore him, but he got to me. I turned to him. 'Look,' I said, 'I was hoping we could have some sort of amicable goodbye, but I couldn't care less anymore. Go to hell, okay?'

I turned my back on him. I could hear him leave the room. I was a little surprised to hear him come back less than a minute later.

'Joey,' he said, his voice not quite right, 'I can't let you do this.'

I turned around and saw that he was holding a Colt .45, pointing it at my stomach.

'Jesus, where did you get that?'

He was shaking as he held it. He started crying. 'I'm sorry, Joey, I can't let you do this.'

'Dad, you look ridiculous holding that gun. Just give it to me.'

I reached for the gun. The last thing I expected was for him to use it.

He shot me in the stomach.

I slid down the wall and sat on the floor and watched as the red circle in my stomach grew outward. At first all I could think was *Damn, another shirt ruined*. Then, as I looked up at my dad and saw him weeping, I had a clarity of thought that I hadn't had before. I knew I couldn't blame him. He was only trying to protect my daughters – his granddaughters. How could I blame him for that? How could I after everything I'd done?

As I lay there I thought about all the people who had died recently. Maybe most of them deserved what happened to them, but not all of them. I might not have pulled the trigger, but I caused all of it. I could have gone to Phil and confessed my crimes. I could have sought real atonement for what I had done. Instead I tried to hide and cheat the system, and because of that, and because of what I was, all those people died.

I had to be honest with myself about what happened and about other things, things that I didn't really want to admit to myself. What happened to Charlotte was really no great surprise. When I told Dan about Charlotte, I knew I was trading her life for mine, but I didn't care. Just as I knew when I told him about Phil and Susie that he wouldn't try busting Phil on a morals charge. I knew him well enough to know what he'd do. I might have been kidding myself at the time, but I knew all along what I was doing. That promise I made about living in a way my daughters could be proud of – fuck, I did a lot since then that they could be proud of, didn't I? It was as worthless as any I had ever made.

I should also admit I killed Billy Ferguson. The story I gave Manny afterwards was the obvious one – the guy wouldn't pay up and things got out of hand. The truth, though, I needed that thirty grand. My luck had to change. I had to win a few bets so I could grow that thirty grand and pay off Manny and be free of him. That was the plan anyway. But of course the bets I made were losers and a week later I was no better off than before. Whatever bookie gave Dan his story was on the level.

So there you had it. The multitude of crime I'd committed. How could I blame my dad for what he did? He knew what I was and it was about time I admitted it to myself.

As I watched him weep, I had my first real unselfish thought in my life. He shouldn't have to go to jail for protecting my girls and I didn't want them to have to lose their grandfather.

There wasn't much left of me. I knew I was going fast. Even if he had a change of heart and called for an ambulance, I knew I'd be gone before they got to me. I could barely speak, but I whispered for him to get me a pen and paper. He just stood in front of me, his face one big crease as he wept.

It hurt like hell to talk, but I tried again. 'Pen, paper.'

He probably had no idea what I wanted them for, but he got them for me. It took almost everything I had left, but I scribbled as neatly as I could, 'Sorry – Joe' on it. I made sure not to get any blood on the paper. It wasn't much of a suicide note, but it would do. Besides, those two words probably made as much sense as anything I could've written.

I pointed to his gun. I mouthed the word 'gun' to him.

Maybe he thought I was going to shoot him. If he did, he didn't care because he gave his gun to me. He stood in front of me for a moment, and then staggered back, collapsing into a chair. Through his weeping, he told me over and over again that he loved me, but that he couldn't let me hurt my daughters. At that moment I wanted to love him also. More than anything I wanted to truly love my two daughters.

I put the barrel of the gun against my bullet wound. It would probably look funny committing suicide by shooting yourself twice in the stomach, but hell, let them prove otherwise.

It was a struggle holding the gun up, and an even bigger struggle trying to pull the trigger back. That's the problem with a Colt .45; it takes some strength to fire it. As I strained to pull the trigger, I started thinking of Dan, of how he'd react when he heard I'd committed suicide. It was really kind of funny if you thought about it. After everything he had done only to end up having to go to prison when my safety deposit box was opened. As I thought about it I started laughing. I guess with the little strength that I had my laugh came out more as a wheeze. My dad probably thought I was suffering through my final convulsions. He started weeping even harder. I would've liked to have told him not to worry about me, but I didn't have the strength to say anything.

So there I was. Wheezing and straining, straining and wheezing, trying to get that damn trigger pulled back. For a second I thought I wasn't going to make it. Then I felt the trigger release. My whole body seemed to explode with the shot that followed. But I just kept thinking of Dan, and maybe of other things, and wheezing my little laugh with whatever I had left. It got so cold, but I just kept laughing. Then I didn't feel anything. I was still laughing. It seemed to grow louder, echoing throughout me. At first there was nothing but blackness. Then I could see the flames. They were far away, but I was flying downwards towards them. I was getting closer every second. And through it all I kept laughing.

What can I say?

I laughed all the way to hell.